The oncoming car accelerated, its roar filling her ears.

Adrenaline screamed through her body, and she put on a burst of speed born of pure terror. There it was. She had reached the Mini. Throwing herself on it, she scrambled up onto the roof and held on as the careening car whizzed past her, missing the Mini by centimeters.

Alex began to shake violently. Who but a criminally negligent idiot would drive like that through here? Easing herself off the roof, she found her legs unsteady. What she wanted was a chair. But first she had to get out of the alley.

Before she had gone far, however, she heard another squeal and was suddenly blinded by a pair of headlights approaching her from the opposite end of the alley. She froze. Could it be the same car? She must think. Think! But her mind wouldn't work. She stood staring, mesmerized by the headlights.

Of Deadly
Descent

Of Deadly Descent

A Mystery

G. G. Vandagriff

Deseret Book Company
Salt Lake City, Utah

Library of Congress Cataloging-in-Publication Data

Vandagriff, G. G.
    Of deadly descent : a mystery / G. G. Vandagriff.
        p.   cm.
    ISBN 1-57345-167-3 (pbk.)
    I. Title.
    PS3572.A427M97   1996
    813'.54—dc20   96-17151
                                                                          CIP

Printed in the United States of America
10   9   8   7   6   5   4   3   2   1

In loving memory of my mother,
Maxine Catherine Henkle Gibson

The ruling passion, be it what it will,
The ruling passion conquers reason still.
—ALEXANDER POPE

ONE

Alex had long loved Oxford. When she and Stewart had first come down from Scotland by train eleven years ago, they had arrived in the early hours of a June morning. Leaving everything except Stewart's cameras to be called for, they had immediately set out on foot to explore. Eventually crossing St. Aldates Street and venturing through the massive gates of Christ Church College, they had met an eerie vapor seeping up from the river, drifting across the meadows and flower gardens, threading its way around the high college walls. Seen in this aspect, everything had appeared hushed, otherworldly, almost haunted.

Feet crunching the gravel in the quiet, they had made their way among college buildings to the High Street, awed by the slumbering mass of honey-stoned architecture that housed the ghosts of so many great minds. Even from her viewpoint on the ground, Alex had been able to see many of the hundreds of spires which crowned it all. Some were elaborate in gothic profusion, others classically simple and straight, but all were nobly correct in their reach toward heaven.

Suddenly bells had begun tolling, chiming, ringing, from dozens of towers, churches, and chapels all over Oxford. Then the sun had broken dramatically through the mist, striking the golden Cotswold stone, burning away their idle fancies and revealing a robust Oxford bursting with life and ideas. In what had seemed like minutes, cars were careening down the High Street, fearless students on bicycles were weaving in and out of the traffic, and pedestrians of every race were jostling one another along the pavement.

Despite his photographer's eye for the spectacular, Stewart had been characteristically down-to-earth. "The monks were a canny lot, weren't they, Alex? Nothing self-effacing about medieval architecture. Good propaganda. Buy our brand, don't make trouble, and you, too, can live in a setup like this when you meet your Maker."

Remembering this observation, Alex smiled grimly to herself. "Well, Stewart, what do you think?" she asked aloud. "Is heaven as magnificent as Oxford?"

Of course there was no one beside her in the bus but Briggie. Clutching her duffle with unusual ferocity, Alex's white-haired friend looked at her in some reproach: "In heaven they drive on the right side of the road."

The picture of comic terror, her white, wiry hair on end from a night passed on a train, Briggie suddenly relaxed her hold on her bag to pat Alex's knee. "When I picture Stewart in the spirit world, I see him pacing."

Alex turned her face back to the window. Her words had been spoken in jest, but there was real wonder behind them. Many things had changed in eleven years. Not only had Stewart died, but she had evolved from the person she had been as his wife into a woman who was quickened by an entirely different set of values, a new perception of reality. Given the chance, would her husband have accepted the gospel she had embraced? Could he ever have abandoned his deep-seated cynicism about organized religion? At one time she wouldn't have questioned that the bond between them was strong enough to forge an eternal union, but lately she had found herself wondering.

With an effort, Alex shook off the dilemma. This was to be a watershed trip. She was going to jump-start her emotions, make a new beginning, embrace what was left of her life. It was time, and she hoped that time would also bring the answers she needed.

"Look around you, Briggs! Have you ever seen any place like it?"

Gold flags glinted from the four corners of Magdalene Tower. Though the November trees were bare, the landscape was far from stark with the college walls glowing their warm honey color in the morning light.

The bus swerved to avoid a bicyclist.

"No." Briggie answered shortly, renewing a death grip on her belongings.

Alex became lost in her memories again—visiting the Victorian Covered Market with its smell of espresso and fish, croissants and fruit, wandering into the Town Hall to see the upstairs exhibits of armor and royal robes, ducking into a coffee house for the morning papers. No matter how long they had stayed, it was never long enough.

Stewart wasn't going to leave her in peace at Oxford. This was like some sort of disjointed time warp—the Alex she was today being carried back by every sight, sound, and smell to another life, another Alex, a person to whom Stewart had been the center of existence. But painful as it was, perhaps this was where she needed to be. She needed to be able to touch him, feel him, to know whether they were still connected.

First things first, however. She gripped her briefcase purposefully in her lap. She was here on business. RootSearch, Inc., in the persons of Alexandra Campbell and Brighamina Poulson, had been hired to find the legal heirs to an American meat-packing fortune. The situation was made somewhat piquant by the fact that the fortune had been amassed by Alex's father and grandfather and that any cousins she might find would quite possibly disinherit her.

It was her own fault, of course. It was she who had exposed the skeleton in the family closet. But be that as it may, inquiries in France had led them here, and now Alex must put away her memories of Stewart and try to absorb the astounding possibility that she might actually have cousins in Oxford.

"I can't believe it," she told Briggie as they alighted from their cab at the Randolph Hotel.

"What?" her friend asked, surveying the large stone building with its elegant canopied entrance.

"That we're really staying at the Randolph. It was far too grand for Stewart and me. I wonder what it'll be like?"

It was lovely, straight out of early Dorothy L. Sayers—cream-colored walls, hardwood floors covered in Persian rugs, stone columns, and an immense stone fireplace. Alex could almost see Lord Peter Wimsey registering at the desk while Bunter followed the bell captain up the stairs.

"Richard insisted," Briggie reminded them both. From behind the desk, a very correct young man with a toothbrush mustache was eyeing their sweatsuits with disfavor.

"Your father wouldn't expect you to hole up in some two-bit bed and breakfast," the lawyer had told them last night on the telephone. "I'm sure he'd insist on the Randolph. Depending on how the chips fall, what you spend on this trip may be the only part of his estate you'll ever get. Enjoy it."

But she doubted whether she or Briggie looked much like Randolph material. Setting her duffle on the floor, Alex took a moment to finger-comb her black ringlets before making her way to the desk.

"Campbell," she told the clerk firmly. "My attorney made the reservations for us."

The little man's face cleared. "Oh, yes, Mrs. Campbell. He rang this morning. We've booked a suite for you. If you'll just sign here?"

Bathing in the enormous footed tub, Alex began to shed her travel grime. Now that she was so warm and comfortable, her thoughts turned guiltily towards her mother, who was not. Here she was, living it up at the Randolph, basking in the mellow English atmosphere she loved—and there was her mother, alone in the Winnetka house, fresh out of the hospital, wrestling with the devastating new knowledge that she had a deadly disease. Being suddenly widowed had been hard enough. At that moment of crisis, Amelia Borden had bravely entered the psych hospital and fought to overcome her twenty-year-old drinking problem. Alex had been there those three months. She had seen the battles her mother waged when it would have been so much easier to drown her grief, to get past feeling, thinking, remembering. But Mother had made it through to the other side, winning Alex's admiration after their many years of estrangement. The day had finally come when Amelia Borden was ready to reenter the real world and come home.

That's when the weird things had started. First, while knitting, her fingers had suddenly ceased to function for a short while. Then, she'd simply lost control over her legs and fallen. This had alarmed Alex so much, she had taken her unwilling mother to a doctor, who had diagnosed multiple sclerosis.

How could Mother possibly handle this heartbreak sober when she had lived for so long in that fuzzy nether world where there was no pain or unpleasantness? Alex had wanted to stay with her, at least another month, but Daniel and Briggie managed to convince her that she needed to begin living her own life again. This job needed doing so her father's estate could be settled. Her mother was obviously going to need the money.

Still, she felt guilty. She vowed she would call her mother before the day was over.

After a shampoo and a change of clothes, Alex was ready for Oxford. Mr. Toothbrush Mustache probably wouldn't think her clean jeans and cableknit turtleneck much better than her sweats, but she'd packed for a French cemetery excursion, not a trip to Oxford.

Seizing the telephone directory, Alex looked for Philippa Cuendet. There was no Philippa, but there were a number of other Cuendets. A Philip lived on the Woodstock Road, an Edward lived in an outlying area, and a Dr. John Cuendet lived on Crane's Walk. Copying down the addresses in her palm-sized spiral notebook, she called through the bathroom door to Briggie, "I'm going for a walk. Why don't you take a nap?"

There was no answer. Easing the door open a crack, she saw her friend surrounded by carnation-scented foam, head lying on the rim of the tub, fast asleep.

Smiling, Alex closed the door and crossed to the desk to

leave a note. Poor Briggie. She really didn't like travel. She would be glad to get back to her cat, her Bronco, and her big white house in Independence, Missouri.

Outside on the pavement, Alex paused to orient herself. Where would she go? Should she pop into the Eagle and Child, have some soup and bread, and commune with the ghosts of Stewart and C. S. Lewis? Or would it be a better idea to take the Oxford Nipper up the street to Woodstock Road and begin her inquiries? She wasn't at all certain how she should proceed.

Trying to make up her mind, she reached St. Giles' Street, a main thoroughfare, and watched for her chance to cross. There, next to the Martyr's Memorial, wasn't that Etienne? His dark handsomeness stood out clearly, flanked as he was by two short blonde women in white.

"Etienne!" she called, raising a hand, trying to make herself heard above the roar of the traffic.

A double-decker bus whooshed between them. When it had passed, Etienne began to cross the road and then halted. Even from where she stood, Alex could see him stiffen. Following his glance, she saw a woman lying completely inert in the road while the bus screeched to an abrupt halt.

How odd. Then, as her brain interpreted the scene before her, Alex's hands flew to her throat. She felt suddenly nauseated.

Only an instant ago, the woman in white had been standing on the curb, fragile and alive. Now her broken body lay dead in the road.

TWO

A crowd had moved into the street, surrounding the body, but Etienne was not among them. While Alex had struggled with her nausea, he had apparently vanished. Or had he been there at all? What would Etienne be doing in an Oxford street anyway?

A bobby was running towards the scene now, waving his arms and blowing his whistle at the traffic in an effort to divert it. Soon, several men in business suits were helping him to block off the area, and Alex walked numbly back inside the Randolph to find someplace to sit down.

"There's been a horrible accident," she told the man at the desk. "Maybe you had better telephone for an ambulance. A woman was run over by a bus."

The desk clerk reached for the telephone. "Perhaps you should take a chair, Mrs. Campbell. You look as white as a sheet."

Following his suggestion, she seated herself in an enormous wing chair. Her knees were quaking. Sudden death affected her this way. The world was tilting, wildly off balance. Fear tore through her consciousness like wildfire: there was no one in charge of the universe. Chaos and confusion reigned unchecked. There was nothing to stop them.

Balling her hands into fists, she scarcely felt the bite of her fingernails. Did the woman in the road have a family? Of course she would have someone. And they would feel just as she had when Stewart died—blind, deaf, and dumb with shock. Unbelieving. And then the pain would start . . .

Slow down. Breathe, she told herself. *You've grown past this. Death is part of life. There is a God.*

If she didn't start moving, she was going to have a panic attack, and she certainly couldn't do that in the lobby of the Randolph. Forcing herself out of the chair, she climbed the stairs to her room.

Stretching out on the bed with the huge, carved headboard, she took deep breaths and felt the fear and anger ebb away. This was now. The accident in the road was not about Stewart. This had nothing to do with her. People died in accidents every day.

She would get past this. She must. Plenty of women lost their husbands. It happened every day. And they went on.

Drawing a deep breath, she propped herself on her pillows and frantically searched her mind for some other image to focus on. Etienne. She would make herself think about Etienne. Could she have been mistaken? Had she imagined him?

What on earth could have brought him to Oxford this morning? It had only been twenty-four hours since they had said good-bye in the little French village where he had been born. Closing her eyes, she willed herself to reconstruct that scene. They had been eating lunch . . .

"So you go to Oxford, Alexandra?" Etienne's hazel eyes looked into hers, their expression unreadable.

"Yes. We leave for Paris on the evening train." Alex drank the last of her mineral water in an effort to avoid those eyes.

The tiny restaurant with its white tablecloths and little sprays of purple chrysanthemums was bustling. It was only the size of an average American living room, with whitewashed walls and floors of uneven flagstone, but it contrived to have that essential, intimate atmosphere in which the French celebrated their meals. Everything from the baguettes to the chicken *en casserole* was succulent and freshly prepared with obvious pride and dedication. A microwave oven would be a desecration.

Etienne signaled for the waiter and gave an order for two *creme brulles*. "They do them extremely well here," he told her. "In fact, this little cafe has *un chef merveilleux*. He is my uncle. The brother of my father. I can tell you that you will not find a chef so good, even in Nancy. But I make a digression." He smiled at her lazily. "I, too, am going to England. You see, I am London liaison for my firm in Strasbourg. My little holiday is over."

"I'm sorry it wasn't a happier one," she told him, toying with a teaspoon. She had met Etienne two days before in a churchyard where his grandfather was being laid to rest.

"But it was not all bad," he said softly. She could hear the smile in his voice and looked up. He was so one-hundred-percent-Hollywood that she wouldn't have believed he was a bona fide Frenchman had she met him under any other circumstances. Twinkling hazel eyes that crinkled at the corners, chiseled features, a cleft chin, and slightly crooked teeth all gave him a dashing air that made it very difficult to believe he was real. He even wore a cravat in the open neck of his shirt.

"Perhaps I could see you in England?" he was asking. "Oxford is only an hour from London, you realize."

"I'm going to be pretty busy, Etienne. This is a business trip for me."

"Ah, yes!" He leaned back and regarded her steadily. "Your business. It is from something that Genevieve told you that you go tearing to Oxford."

She smiled at his idiom. "Do you always call your grand-mother Genevieve?"

His eyes sparked with amusement. "We all do, you know. And she is not my grandmother, but my great-grandmother. It was her son, my grandfather, that we buried yesterday, not her husband, as you might have thought." He chuckled lightly. "My father tells me she was very distressed when I was born. Fifty-eight is too young for a great-grandmother. She is almost ninety now, but she is not yet used to it. But think! By now she might have been a great-great-grandmother."

Fifty-eight to ninety. That made him thirty-two, Alex calculated swiftly—far too young for a mature American widow of
thirty-five. Besides, there was bound to be a narcissistic personality beneath that exterior. "Yes," she said aloud. "She was just
sixteen at the end of the First World War, wasn't she? It is
extremely lucky for me that she has such a good memory."

"She remembered your soldier," Etienne prompted.

"You want to hear the story?"

"Of course. If only because Genevieve forbade it."

Alex laughed. That part *had* been rather comic.

Two days before, she and Briggie had been examining
lichen-covered headstones in a churchyard blanketed with
fallen leaves when suddenly a funeral party had emerged from
the little gray stone church. Quietly, Alex and Briggie had left
the cemetery by the tiny wrought-iron gate, intending to wait
until the burial was accomplished. Sitting across the street at a
cafe with orange and white awnings, they had drunk fizzy
lemonade and watched through the window until the mourn-
ers departed. The man she now knew as Etienne had been
among them, an elderly woman in black on his arm.

Briggie had remarked dreamily, "He looks exactly like Cary
Grant."

Oddly enough, the two had entered the cafe and taken the
table next to them. The old lady was an interesting sight. Her
jet-black hair was obviously dyed, worn in an elaborate
chignon, her face was heavily powdered, and her lips were
painted carmine red with fingernails lacquered to match. Even
in her great age, her carriage was erect, and she exuded the air
of one who is accustomed to domination.

Etienne had fired rapid orders to the waiter in French, and
soon the pair of them were drinking cognac at three o'clock in
the afternoon.

After a moment or two more of conversation, Alex and
Briggie had asked for their check and then risen, intending to
return to their investigations.

"*Un moment!*" the old woman had cried with surprising
eagerness. "*Sont vous Americaines?*"

Alex had turned, and the handsome man rose gallantly to perform introductions. "My grandmother, Madame Guison." He bowed slightly. "I am Etienne Guison."

Briggie had stepped forward, her hand outstretched to the older woman. "Brighamina Poulson, from Independence, Missouri," she informed them, shaking hands firmly with both. "This is Alexandra Campbell." She indicated Alex, who was watching the proceedings with amusement. Briggie was clearly taken with the Guisons. At fifty-nine, she considered herself in the prime of life and always registered appreciation for a handsome physique.

"Perhaps you could help us," Briggie had addressed them. "We are looking for the grave of an American soldier. He was billeted here in World War I."

The old lady tilted her head to one side, her eyes bright. "The war? The Great War? What is his name, this one?"

"Well," Alex began haltingly. "His name was Joseph Borden, but we don't know if he knew that." The Frenchman's look was merely polite, but the older woman had widened her eyes, her interest clearly deepening.

"And why?"

"He was wounded." Alex indicated her temple. "He may have lost his memory."

To her surprise, Genevieve Guison had nodded a short, stiff nod. "You are looking for him. Like the Englishwoman. Why?"

Someone else was inquiring after a man with no memory? Before Alex could ask about the Englishwoman, Briggie intervened, "We have been hired by his family to find him. No one knows what happened to him."

Etienne had smiled then, his sudden charm almost blinding. "Ah, the American root diggers! One hears of you. But why do you look for him in the village? He will be in the American cemetery."

"He's not," Briggie had said firmly.

The old lady agreed. "No. He is not. He did not die in the Argonne," she informed them, her small eyes glistening.

"You knew him?" Briggie and Alex chorused.

"Of course. I will tell you. Etienne, you must go."

He had tried to change her mind to no avail. She waited stubbornly until he climbed into his large black Citroen and drove away.

So this morning Etienne had sought Alex out, presumably with the intention of learning the story from her. And she could see no reason on earth why he shouldn't have it.

"She remembered a young American soldier they called Joe," Alex told him. "He didn't know his name. They just called him Joe because he was an American. It seems that your family, or rather your great-grandmother's family, the Moreaus, actually took him in and nursed him back to health. He had lost his papers somewhere, and all the Americans were being sent home. He had nowhere to go. Apparently, the Moreaus were very fond of Americans. Somewhere along the line it became obvious that Joe was used to money and had a good education. His French was good."

Etienne nodded for her to continue.

"Well, your great-grandmother isn't quite clear how it happened—I definitely detected some jealousy—but somehow he met Marcelle Cuendet."

Her listener appeared to consider a moment. "That would be the sister of Roland Cuendet, the old man at the chateau?"

"Yes. She was his older sister. According to Gene—your great-grandmother—"

"Call her Genevieve, if you wish. She would be flattered, and it makes conversation so much easier."

Alex grinned. "She really doesn't seem like anyone's great-grandmother, does she? Anyway, Genevieve said that Joe and Marcelle fell in love, but Marcelle's parents were opposed to the match. I gather the young man she had been engaged to was killed in the war, along with most of the rest of their generation. Marcelle didn't have a wide range of suitors, but there was an elderly aristocrat they wanted her to marry. She and Joe ran away to England."

"Have you visited old Roland in the chateau?"

"No. He is in Italy. But we spoke to his granddaughter,

Simone. She thought it was all terribly romantic. Her parents were in Paris, so I didn't meet them, either. But Simone told me her father had given Marcelle's letters that the family still had to an Englishwoman named Philippa Cuendet, who came inquiring here a couple of months ago. She was from Oxford and said she was Joe's granddaughter. She was trying to trace his identity. Here," Alex paused, pulling an old envelope out of her denim bag. "This is the setup." Drawing a quick descendancy chart of the Cuendet family as she knew it, she passed it along to him.

She went on. "This woman in Oxford might be just what I'm looking for."

"So. This Joseph Borden, he is certainly the mysterious Joe

Maurice Raoul Cuendet m. Madeleine Beaulieu

Marcelle m. Joe Cuendet (Borden?)

?

Philippa Cuendet

Roland m. Louise du Bois?

Maurice m. Henriette Limoges

Simone Cuendet

who lost his memory, then? He went to Oxford, I assume? This is why you go there now?"

"We don't know if Joe is Joseph Borden, but it looks promising. Simone said that according to Philippa, he got some sort of job at a preparatory school, teaching French. He never recovered his memory, so he went by his wife's name, Cuendet."

"And Marcelle's family? They never made inquiries about his identity?"

"No. Apparently, they washed their hands of Marcelle. It was amazing to me that they kept her letters. I was touched by Simone's excitement. She's obviously romanticized the family mystery. If it hadn't been for Genevieve, of course, we never would have put all the pieces together. She has a remarkable memory."

"It was the happiest time of her life, the Great War."

Alex shuddered. "But it must have been horrible! The barbed wire, the trenches, all those acres and acres of wasted land. And the dead. There were so many dead."

"I think one of them was the man she loved. He was an American, anyway. That is why she wanted to speak to you. She is mad about Americans."

"But surely she married? Guison is a French name."

"Oh yes. But my great-grandfather, he was an old man when she married him. All the young ones, they were killed in the war. He could not compare with this American."

"How sad."

"Yes, well. We are all a little tired of hearing it."

"That's why she wouldn't let you stay and listen."

"Yes." Etienne crossed his long legs and fixed her with laughing eyes. "It seems an odd profession, yours."

"It's fun," she told him with a grin. "Besides, I suppose there's no harm in telling you: Joseph Borden is my first cousin, twice removed. I'm doubly interested."

"Ah, so you are doing this to satisfy the curiosity? It is not merely business?" His eyes would not leave hers.

"That, too." Alex looked away. "But actually we have been hired by the estate. There's a considerable inheritance involved."

Etienne lit a cigarette. "And what does your husband think about your leaving him?" he asked negligently.

"My husband is dead."

A lazy smile spread on the Frenchman's face. "Then you will have time for the theater. You cannot work all the time. And Englishmen are so tepid."

"I find Englishmen charming, actually," she responded.

———————

Well, if that had really been Etienne in St. Giles' Street, he had certainly lost no time in seeking her out in England. But where had he disappeared to?

THREE

A n ambulance shrieked in the street outside, but Alex did not look out the window. Instead, she rolled over onto her stomach. Suddenly, she was extremely tired.

She was awakened by the telephone.

"Hello?"

"Alex?"

Struggling to full consciousness, she realized it was Daniel Grinnell calling from Kansas City. "Hello," she said warmly. His voice was surprisingly welcome.

"Dad tells me you're hot on the trail. How's Oxford?"

"Wonderful, thanks partly to him. He's footing the bill for us to stay in the most wonderful old hotel." Alex gave a great yawn and checked her watch. It was three o'clock in the afternoon here—nine in the morning, K.C. time.

"You know he's not paying. Your father's estate is. So you're staying at the Randolph."

"How did you guess?"

"In another life, I was a Rhodes scholar. I envy you, but England can be cold in November. Are you and Briggie going to bundle up and go punting on the Cherwell?"

She laughed. "Somehow I can't see either of us handling a punt very well. We'll have to leave that to Etienne."

"Who is . . . ?"

"The mysterious Frenchman in the case. He's followed me to Oxford, and already there's been a suspicious death."

"Alex. Not again!"

"Just kidding. It was an accident. Some poor woman fell under a bus."

"And this Etienne?"

"Disappeared. There's nothing remotely sinister about it, really."

"Where were you?"

"Across the street."

"It doesn't sound like much fun."

"I don't expect it was much fun for the woman who fell under the bus, either. It was bad at first, but I'm fine now. I've just had a nap. I think Briggie and I will go to Brown's for dinner and then start work tomorrow."

"Have a steak and kidney pie for me."

"Sorry. I can't stomach the idea of eating kidneys."

"They're wonderful. Sort of like mushrooms."

"Ugh. How are Marigny and Maxie doing?" Maxie was Briggie's tiger-striped cat who customarily boarded with Daniel's daughter, Marigny, when business demanded out-of-town investigations.

"Both fine. Marigny has a gymnastics meet in the morning. She's practicing on her balance beam, and the cat is enthralled."

There was a silence, and suddenly Alex felt awkward, remembering the scene at the airport. It was the first time she had allowed anyone to do more than give her a chaste peck since Stewart's death. Unlike Stewart's casual, confident caress, Daniel's kiss had been tentative, questioning. And she hadn't known the answer to the question. For some time they had been standing at the beginning of a road which Alex had not yet decided to take. Allowing herself to be loved by a psychotherapist would be like allowing someone else into her soul. He saw far too much as it was. Basic instinct had compelled her to keep him at bay. But it hadn't been easy.

"Daniel?" she asked quietly.

"Yes?"

"I miss you."

"I miss you, too."

Alex was sitting at the vanity table, which was skirted in a rose-hued Liberty print, poking at her hair with a pick when Briggie entered the suite.

"Daniel called," she told her. "Maxie is fine. Where have you been?"

"Etienne and I were just having afternoon tea. They had a good herbal peppermint, as a matter of fact."

"Etienne? He came here?"

"Yes. I told him you were sleeping. Actually, he was on his way here earlier, but he told me he saw an accident. It sounded really gruesome."

"It was. I saw it, too. What did he tell you?"

"He had just been around to the police to make a statement. I guess they have identified the poor woman. He wants to talk to you about it. I have a hunch he likes drama. He refused to tell me any more."

"Did he say why he disappeared?"

"Disappeared?"

"Well, left the scene of the accident. I was standing across the street and it seemed like he just vanished."

"No. He didn't mention it. Are you sure?"

Alex shrugged and looked at herself critically in the mirror. She saw a fine-boned face with a square jaw and winged brows over dark blue eyes. What she failed to see was anything remarkable enough to stir Etienne to such obvious pursuit. Perhaps he had inherited Genevieve's passion for Americans.

"He's waiting downstairs, Alex. He wants to see you." Briggie was looking at her curiously.

"What's the matter, Briggs?"

"Do you like him?"

"He's attractive. Obviously. A little too attractive."

"What's that mean?"

"Too handsome to be real, don't you think?"

"Handsome enough to be dangerous. And I noticed something else. He was married until recently. Maybe he still is. There's a white line where his wedding band was."

"Briggie, the detective."

Her friend stood up and began to unpack her duffle. "How was Daniel?"

Alex laughed. "Don't worry. I won't fall for Etienne. I don't go for obvious types. I like my men convoluted and interesting-looking."

"Stewart was handsome," Briggie objected.

"Only when you got to know him. His face was a little too thin without the beard. It was his eyes I fell for."

Her friend sighed, "You must have had a clear conscience is all I can say. He could see right through people. It was spooky."

Laughing, Alex asked, "Did he detect some deep, dark secret, Briggs?"

"Several," her friend chuckled. "He would have had Etienne figured out in two seconds flat. On the other hand, it doesn't take a seer to figure out that Etienne's definitely interested in you."

"Why, do you suppose?"

Alex's mentor looked up, a tart expression on her homely, lined face. "Coy doesn't suit you, Alex."

"I'm not being coy! I mean, I meet this man three days ago in France. We talk for two minutes. I have lunch with him two days afterwards. Now, twenty-four hours later he's on my doorstep in Oxford. Don't you think it's a little excessive?"

"Would you have thought it excessive if Stewart had behaved that way?"

Alex was taken aback. "No. But we were young."

"You're no old lady now, honey. And Etienne certainly isn't an old man. He's spent the last hour trying to find out everything he could about you."

"What did you tell him?"

"I told him about Stewart dying and how you came home to live with me. I didn't think you'd want to talk about it, but I thought he ought to know that you've had a bad time. I didn't mention your father's death or anything about the case we're working on."

"Did he ask?"

"No. I'm telling you, Alex, it was you he was interested in, not Joseph Borden."

For some reason, it still didn't sit right, Alex thought as she descended the stairs. Etienne had seemed lazy to her, self-indulgent. His life in London must be replete with attractive young women. Why would he go to these lengths to pursue her? Whatever Briggie said, it was out of character. Etienne had seemed only idly interested in her, as though he felt obliged to make a pass at anyone who was reasonably attractive. He had to live up to his billing as a seductive Frenchman, after all.

She found him in the lobby seated in the chair she had occupied that morning. He looked less French in a coat and tie. Contrary to her expectations, he didn't kiss her hand but merely stood and smiled in a friendly manner.

"Hello, Alexandra."

"Hello. I saw you earlier. Just before the accident."

His brow wrinkled. "Yes, I thought I saw you. The woman near me became hysterical, and I was obliged to lead her away."

"Oh. I wondered where you went."

"Yes. I'm sorry I disappeared." His eyes were solemn. "You must think it is very strange that I have followed you here so quickly. But you see, I remembered something."

"You couldn't have telephoned?"

His face broke into a happy grin. "Of course. But I am in no hurry to get back to my desk. A trip to Oxford—it sounded pleasant. And, of course, it is pleasant to see you again."

Alex dragged out her armor with difficulty, straightening her back and biting her lower lip. "What have you remembered?"

"There was a man who came to Bar-le-Duc once. He was an Englishman, but his name was Cuendet. Would you like to go for a walk while we talk?"

Nodding wordlessly, Alex led the way out of the hotel. They stepped onto the tree-lined St. Giles' Street and automatically headed south towards the bustling shops of Cornmarket. Etienne held her elbow, steering her between the pedestrians.

"You have been to Oxford before? There is a quiet walk where we can talk?"

"We could walk along the river," she said, "but it's pretty far from here. I know you just had tea, but I haven't had anything since breakfast. Would you mind if we went to the Eagle and Child?"

"The Eagle and Child?"

"It's an old pub. They serve soup and homemade bread. It's just down the street."

Alex's favorite pub was a puzzle of inglenooks, fireplaces and old school photographs. Tradition had it that once upon a time, C. S. Lewis and J. R. R. Tolkien made a regular Sunday habit of sitting by the fire here and playing chess. She could just picture them. Even today there was a white-bearded professor-type in his tweed jacket, smoking a pipe and reading an antique volume of some sort. Stewart would have whispered in her ear, "Undoubtedly a salesman from Birmingham," and gone to order her a pint.

Etienne, however, seemed an exotic in the plain English surroundings. Seating her with exquisite politeness in an empty inglenook, he asked her if she would like him to order her soup.

"Please," she responded. As she watched him walk to the back of the pub, she thought to herself how impossibly suave he was. What was he really doing here?

When he returned, Etienne brought with him two glasses of wine. "Your soup will come," he told her. "I hope you like this burgundy. It is a good year, and I thought it might go well with the day."

Alex sighed. "I'm sorry. As I told you in Bar-le-Duc, I don't drink wine."

"But I still cannot understand it. You don't like it?" He was clearly incredulous.

"It's not that. It's just that I'm a Latter-day Saint. We don't drink wine."

"What is a Latter-day Saint?" he demanded. His eyebrows were practically at his hairline. She might have been confessing she was a Tibetan monk.

"A member of The Church of Jesus Christ of Latter-day Saints. *Eglisé de Jésus-Christ des saints des derniers jours.* I'm sure there must be a branch in Strasbourg or Nancy. We don't drink alcohol."

"But wine! One doesn't drink wine because of the alcohol! One drinks wine because . . ."

Alex grinned at his ferocity. At that moment, Etienne seemed very much like Stewart. He would have reacted in exactly the same way. "Etienne, I'm sorry," she repeated. "You'll have to drink both glasses, I'm afraid."

"For you, that is a pity, for this is a good wine." He smiled his Hollywood smile as though he might still convince her.

Alex decided suddenly that she had better keep her wits about her. Wine or no wine, Etienne's charisma was heady stuff. His self-assurance, the underlying assumption that he could have whatever he wanted—all these things reminded her a little too much of Stewart. But then maybe it was partly because she was in Europe again. She had fallen in love with Stewart in Paris. In Kansas City, she seemed to have far more control over her susceptibilities. "You were going to tell me about this Cuendet who visited Bar-le-Duc."

"Yes." He settled himself in the shabby comfort of his chair and took out his cigarettes. "There is not a lot to tell, but it may be a clue. I remembered it because of Genevieve."

"She reminded you?"

"No, no. I was on the plane from Strasbourg when I remembered. I was thinking about Genevieve and her passion for Americans, when I remembered this Brit, Cuendet, who said he had an American grandfather. He came one summer a long time ago. I think it was near my eighteenth year. He was asking in the village, just like you, and it was my day to help Genevieve with her marketing. We met him in the bakery. He was buying a baguette."

"What a good memory you have."

"He made an impression, that one. He had on his bicycle gear, you see."

"You mean the little black shorts?"

He grinned. "Yes. And a T-shirt that said . . . Let me think. It was the name of a college. Also, he had the helmet and the . . . " Etienne made rings around his eyes with his fingers.

"Goggles," she laughed.

"Goggles?"

"Right. They keep the bugs out."

"You are a bicyclist?"

"Not in that class. But at one time or another, I bicycled my way around a lot of Scotland. Go on."

"Well, this Cuendet noted Genevieve's age, obviously. He thought she might know about his people, I suppose. He was very polite. He introduced himself, but I am afraid I have forgotten his first name."

"Umm. Too bad."

"He was looking for his ancestral home, he said."

"And?"

"Genevieve directed him to the chateau, of course."

"And?"

"That's all. I think he stayed some time at the chateau. I have the idea he was on his summer holiday."

"And you came all the way to Oxford to tell me that?" she challenged.

Etienne leaned back in his chair and let his eyes travel leisurely over her face. "Of course."

Alex found herself staring mesmerized at the smoke wreathing around his head. Sitting up straighter, she tossed her head to get an errant ringlet out of her eyes. "It's too bad you got mixed up in that accident," she said.

"Yes," Etienne drew on his cigarette. "That was another queer thing I wanted to tell you."

"What was?"

"The victim. You won't believe this, Alexandra, but her name was Cuendet. Philippa Cuendet."

FOUR

"Philippa Cuendet!" Alex exclaimed.

"Yes. The woman you say was making the inquiries in Bar-le-Duc. Was she coming to see you, do you know?"

"How could she be? I didn't even know where to find her! No one in the family could possibly have known I was here!"

A young man with a shaved head and a jewel in his nose placed a plate of lentil soup and whole wheat bread in front of her. Etienne watched her unnervingly as she buttered the bread.

"It must be a coincidence, then," he said.

"Did you mention anything to the police about my connection with the Cuendets?"

"No," Etienne shrugged. "I decided it was not for me to tell them this. If you would like, you may tell them yourself."

"I would like," Alex said firmly. "If it is the right Philippa Cuendet—and I think it highly unlikely that there are two people of that name in Oxford—then I think the police will want to hear my story."

"Yes. And I imagine the family will gather for the funeral. It will be your second funeral in three days."

"Are you trying to make me think I'm Typhoid Mary or something?"

"Who is Typhoid Mary?"

"It's an expression. Implying cause and effect."

Etienne took a moment to work this out. "I was only making the observation. Funerals are not my favorite pastime."

"Nor mine," she said wearily. "I buried my father three months ago."

Etienne smoked silently for a few moments. "I am sorry," he said finally. "I did not know." Then, "This estate. It is the estate of your father?"

"Yes. It's a long story. Suffice it to say now that Briggie and I have found out that Joseph Borden might have not only survived the war but also had heirs. If so, then my father's money might not legally belong to my mother. It was probably never legally my grandfather's. If this Cuendet family are Joseph Borden's heirs, it really belonged to them. It's my job to find out."

"And disinherit yourself?"

"I never counted on the money," she insisted. "I never even had any idea how much there was!"

Etienne waited for her to elaborate. When she didn't, he smiled and leaned confidingly across the table, whispering, "And how much is that?"

The too-interested look in his eyes annoyed her. It was the first time he had stepped out of character. "The company's assets are huge," she equivocated. "At least they seem so to me. And there is a considerable personal fortune."

"You must be very honest, Alexandra Campbell, for the executors to trust you with such a task. You will get none of the money?"

"That is for the courts to decide. There is a good chance my mother and I might still inherit something."

Etienne smiled his lazy smile. "And then you will not need to do this root digging anymore."

"I'll go on with my work, regardless," she told him. "It's my passion."

Her companion raised his eyebrows quizzically. "Surely there is room for another passion or two?"

Briggie was right. There was a white stripe on his left ring finger. She laid her napkin carefully on the table. "Have you been divorced recently?" she queried.

Her companion stiffened, a hostile look flashing into his eyes. "Why do you ask?"

"Your left hand. There was a wedding ring there once."

Clenching the hand in question, Etienne asked, "Are you always so careless?"

"Careless?"

"Perhaps that is not the word." He became red as he searched for the right phrase. Alex suspected it was not often he was thrown off his stride. "Uncaring," he said finally. "You do not hesitate to introduce the awkward subject."

"I'm sorry if you thought it was uncaring. Your conversation led me to believe you were interested in my company. I don't go around with married men."

His brow cleared. "I understand. How American. I should have expected it."

"Well, Monsieur Guison, are you married or not?"

"No longer," he said, his voice suddenly brusque. "We can dispose of that topic of conversation. Would you like me to take you to the police station?"

The constable on duty was a heavy man with a florid complexion and oversized hands and feet. Alex grinned absently. A greater contrast to her last policeman, Lieutenant O'Neill of the Winnetka Police, could not be imagined. The police station was a modern building, however, not all that different from home.

"My name is Mrs. Alexandra Campbell. I'm here from America on business and believe I might be related to the woman who was struck by the bus in St. Giles' Street this morning."

Blinking, the constable appeared to review her statement in his mind.

"Related?" he said finally. "How would that be?"

Alex gave a brief account of her purpose in coming to Oxford. "But," she concluded, "it can only be the most amazing coincidence that she was killed outside my hotel. You see, I haven't even begun my inquiries."

The constable nodded slowly. "I think you had better talk

to our CID man, Mrs. Campbell." Pulling the telephone towards him, he dialed a number that he read from the blotter in front of him. "Constable Coleman here, Sergeant Higgins. Is the Chief Inspector about?"

Pause.

"I have a young woman here. An American. Possible relation of the deceased. Just arrived in Oxford this morning. I think he'll want to interview her."

Pause.

"Yes. Well. I'll tell her then."

Hanging up the instrument, the policeman turned to Alex. "Sergeant Higgins would like you to go along to the victim's house, if you'd be so kind, ma'am. He's sending a car for you. He'll only be a moment. It's not far."

Etienne touched her elbow lightly. "Alexandra? You would like me to accompany you?"

The question managed to convey a tone of intimacy that annoyed her. "No, thank you."

"I understand," he murmured. "Perhaps when all this is over, you and Madame Poulson will be my guests for dinner." After squeezing her arm, he was gone.

"Another relative?" the constable asked as the door closed behind Etienne.

"No. An acquaintance. He witnessed the accident as well."

"As well?" the constable echoed.

"Yes. Didn't I tell you? I was standing on the other side of the road when it happened."

Her story interested Chief Inspector Hubbard very much indeed. Their interview took place in a small yellow sitting room, which Alex imagined to have belonged to the dead Philippa. The policeman was practically cadaverous, he was so lean. His eyes resided in deep hollows, and their gaze was extremely intent. She would have felt very guilty had she done anything remotely against the law.

The house was attractive, a large honey-colored Regency

structure on the Woodstock Road. She remembered the address from the telephone book but couldn't think whose name had gone with it.

"And you arrived in Oxford only this morning? There is no way any of these Cuendets could have known you were coming?"

"I don't think so. As far as I know, they didn't know of my existence. And none of them had the least reason to expect that they might be heirs to an American fortune. You see, this Joe Cuendet, who might actually have been Joseph Borden, never regained his memory."

Hubbard looked her over and sighed. "A nice, juicy motive gone west. It seems a pity."

"You don't think it was an accident?"

"Intelligent people don't generally fall conveniently under the wheels of a bus. She was standing on the pavement. There is no possibility that she tried to cross the road in front of the bus. I have a witness who says she felt someone lunging through the crowd at Miss Cuendet. It was so sudden, the witness just watched the woman fall. When she figured out what had happened, she turned around to try to find who had pushed her, but it was too late. There was just a crowd looking suitably horrified."

Alex was stunned. Though the coincidence had seemed remarkable, she hadn't seriously considered that the death could have been anything other than an accident.

After a moment, she asked, "Tell me, Chief Inspector, do you have any idea how many of these Cuendets there are?"

"We haven't gone into that yet, but I can tell you this much: the victim was a spinster of about forty-six who lived here and managed the household for her father, Judge Philip Cuendet. He's pretty cut up about the whole thing. Seems he lost her twin brother four years ago in another accident. Fellow was a barrister—riding his bicycle down to the courts when he was hit by a touring bus. The old man's got another son, apparently, but he hasn't shown himself as yet. That's all we know at the moment."

"Would it be possible . . . I mean," Alex fumbled for words, "do you think Judge Cuendet would see me? Do you think it would be all right if I told him about why I'm here?"

Appearing to consider her question, the Chief Inspector studied a watercolor painting of irises that hung over the small white fireplace. "Yes," he said finally. "I think it might be a very good idea. But I think it would be best if we had the whole family together when you do it. That way we can study the effect, if you know what I mean. No one will have any warning if we tell them at the same time. And then, if, by some incredible chance, one of these people already knows what you are up to, he might give himself away."

"My news should make them all quite happy, I expect."

"Yes. But people's reactions to things of this sort can sometimes tell us quite a bit. It depends, of course, on their acting ability."

"What would you like me to do, then?"

"Go quietly away and back to the Randolph. I will gather everyone as quickly as I can and ring you there. It may be quite a formidable undertaking to get them together. We don't even know that they all live in Oxford, though if one of them killed her, he was certainly in Oxford this afternoon. It may be well into the evening before we're ready for you."

"I'll be waiting," Alex told him. " Thank you for seeing me, Chief Inspector."

" Thank you for coming in. Oh, just one more thing," the policeman's brow puckered. "Did Constable Coleman tell me how you learned the victim's name? I've forgotten."

"I don't think so," Alex told him, pausing with her hand on the doorknob. "It was another incredible coincidence. A man I met during my inquiries in France was a witness to the accident. He learned her name when he went down to the station to give a statement."

"You had better sit down again, Mrs. Campbell. Who was this man?"

Alex seated herself again in the daffodil-colored chair. "Etienne Guison. His great-grandmother, Genevieve Guison, was the one who told me about the man named Joe marrying into the Cuendet family." She explained the ins and outs of the Cuendets.

"And this man, this Etienne, he knew your business with the Cuendets?"

Alex wrinkled her forehead. Just how much had she told Etienne in France? She couldn't remember. "I'm not sure. I had lunch with him yesterday in Bar-le-Duc, and I told him the story about searching for descendants of my grandfather's cousin. I believe I might have mentioned that there was an inheritance involved, but I wasn't specific, I don't think." Then, realizing the direction the questioning was taking, she stared at the Chief Inspector. Was it possible Etienne was involved? "But what possible motive could he have?" she asked. "He doesn't even know the Cuendets!"

"You can't be certain of that. Perhaps he is in league with one of them. Perhaps that is how they found out about the inheritance. What is he doing in Oxford?"

"It's not as strange as you might think. He works in London. He was only in France for his grandfather's funeral." Tossing her hair back, Alex looked the detective in the eye. "He says he came to see me."

For the first time, Chief Inspector Hubbard smiled. It was a nice smile, in spite of his teeth being seriously yellowed by tobacco stains. "I don't find that too hard to imagine. But all the same, I think we'll look into the situation."

Alex declined the inspector's offer of a lift back to the Randolph. It was only a moderate distance, and she needed to be alone, to walk and to think.

The world was going crazy again. Plunging her hands into the pockets of her peacoat, she challenged this knowledge firmly by looking defiantly around her. The oaks that lined the road were ancient and had been here for centuries, if not millennia. This road, leading from Oxford into the village of Woodstock, had been traveled by tradesmen, scholars, and soldiers for something close to six hundred years. For that long, at least, knowledge of truths had been evolving here, traditions established whereby ordinary men knew what they could expect from life. Of course, there had always been a darker side to the human condition, but here, at the seat of reason, evil had seemed more distant, perhaps because of the abundance of proof showing the heights humankind could scale. A day didn't pass without at least one concert, one play, one reading of poetry . . .

It was no use. All this was just one vast impermanence, an extension of that corruptible thing called the "arm of flesh." Alex kicked a soda can viciously. But why did she have to be reminded of this in such a gruesome way? Why did evil stalk her so persistently?

Was she responsible for Philippa's death? Had its inevitability accompanied her like some hideous plague as she crossed the channel this morning?

First Stewart. Then Daddy. Now Philippa.

Feeling the anxiety climbing within her, Alex walked faster and tried to reason with herself. She didn't want a repeat of this morning. Not here in the street. Stewart's death in a terrorist plane crash had been a random act of violence. It could have happened to anyone. But it had happened to *him*. And through him to her. Because of its random nature, she had come to realize that she would never feel entirely safe in mortality.

But she *had* found a measure of peace. When Briggie had taught her the gospel, when she had come to believe in the life beyond this one where ties could and would endure throughout eternity, she had felt less violated. She had begun to trust in a God who could evolve such a perfect plan.

Then had come Daddy's death and the awful, searing guilt. Believing her own insensitive probing had led to his murder, she had shouldered the responsibility of finding his murderer. As she had put the puzzle pieces of the mystery together, she and the Lord had succeeded in righting her world again.

But now a third time. It was too much. Walking faster, anger shredding her peace of mind, she demanded, *Will it ever end? Isn't there anyplace I can find peace?*

She had arrived at the Randolph. Sighing, she climbed the stairs, reluctant to face Briggie in this frame of mind.

Her partner was calmly waiting for her, writing a stack of postcards to her myriad offspring.

"You two must have really hit it off," she said.

Alex sank wearily into a deep armchair, realizing that as far as Briggie knew, she had spent all this time tête-á-tête with the Frenchman. "I've been with the police, Briggie. They don't think that death this morning was an accident. They're treating it as murder."

Turning to face her, Briggie searched her face. "You're not kidding, are you?"

"Of course not. I'm afraid it's that rotten money again. The victim was Philippa Cuendet. The Englishwoman who was making enquiries about Joe Cuendet in France. Remember?"

The older woman nodded, speechless for once.

Alex told her everything she knew. "I can't rid myself of the feeling that it's my fault. I mean, it has to be connected to the money somehow, but why would anyone kill her?"

Briggie ran her hands through her hair until it stood on end. "She's the family history nut, obviously."

"It seems that way."

"And she was on her way to see you."

"Presumably."

"What if she knew something that would disprove your theory?"

Alex closed her eyes and sighed. Briggie was capable of lightning leaps of intuition, it was true. But this seemed more insupportable than most. "What theory? That Joe Cuendet and Joseph Borden were the same person?"

"Yes. She's been researching. What if she had hard evidence that he was someone else? There's an inheritance involved. Someone else liked your theory better. They killed Philippa because she wouldn't go along."

"There are about a million things wrong with that idea."

"Like what?"

"Like no one knew about my theory. No one knew I was

coming. No one knew about the inheritance. And killing Philippa isn't going to do any good if Joe Cuendet really wasn't Joseph Borden. We're not going to settle this estate with anything less than hard evidence."

Briggie sat down on the bed across from Alex, her eyes bright with intelligence. "First of all, we don't know that the family in France hasn't been in touch with Philippa. Second, we don't know that Philippa didn't tell them all that you were coming."

"But how would she know where we were staying?"

That gave Briggie pause. But a moment later the light was back in her eyes. "She would have assumed anyone with an inheritance footing the bill would stay at the Randolph. All she would have to do is call to confirm it."

Alex put a hand over her eyes. *Here we go again.*

"It's possible," Briggie persisted. "I think you should at least mention it to the police."

Memories of her friend's last encounter with law and order brought a little smile to Alex's lips. "Briggs, I don't know if Chief Inspector Hubbard is quite ready for you. I'm not sure that I am."

"Meaning?"

"Someone's died. This isn't just an abstract puzzle. Someone died again because of this horrible money. It's a curse. A curse I brought with me."

Going to sit on the arm of her chair, Briggie put an arm across Alex's shoulders. "I'm sorry, honey. I got a little carried away. Of course it's terrible. But we'll get to the bottom of it."

"On your tombstone they're going to write, 'I finally got to the bottom of it,'" Alex told her bitterly.

Her friend chuckled. "Well, we can moan and groan and wring our hands, or we can do something. I'd much rather do something."

Drawing a steadying breath, Alex stood. This, in a nutshell was why she loved Briggie. She knew, deep inside, that Briggie was God's answer to the terrorist. "So would I. Okay, so help me to decide what to wear to meet possible relations in."

"Could you use a little moral support?"

Alex looked at her friend, trying to decide how Chief Inspector Hubbard would view Briggie's inclusion in the night's events.

She grinned. "Sure."

FIVE

As Alex stood at the doorway surveying the elegant powder-blue Regency drawing room with its full assortment of English types, she felt odd, strangely numb, as though she were outside herself. She was glad of Briggie standing next to her, solid and four-square. It gave her a kind of borrowed substance, at least. The scene before her seemed unreal. All seven of these people, possibly Alex's cousins or cousins-in-law, conversing in normal tones, were presumably mourning Philippa. Unless one of them was a murderer. He or she had other things on his mind.

Judge Philip Cuendet, the victim's father and owner of the house, was a large fleshy man with a beaky English nose and thick white hair like her grandfather's. Dressed in a charcoal-gray pin-striped suit with a starched white shirt and navy-and-red-striped tie, he appeared to be in his late sixties or early seventies. Just now, he stood on the hearth, listening to Chief Inspector Hubbard and observing his relatives, a thumb under his chin as he stroked his upper lip with his forefinger. Alex had no trouble imagining him on the bench.

Clearing his throat, the judge faced the assembly. "This is Chief Inspector Hubbard, who requested that you come here tonight. He is investigating Philippa's death and has something to tell us."

Instantly the room became quiet, and the policeman took over smoothly from the judge. "I first want to offer you my sincere condolences on the death of Miss Philippa Cuendet. I am sure it has been a great shock to all of you, and I don't wish to make this time any more distressing than I can help. Judge Cuendet has graciously assisted me in assembling you here because a rather unusual coincidence has surfaced." He turned to Alex, who moved from the doorway into the room. "A woman who could be an American relative of yours is not only here in Oxford but actually witnessed Miss Cuendet's death."

All heads instantly turned her way. She felt the surprised scrutiny of seven pairs of eyes as the chief inspector introduced her. "This is Mrs. Alexandra Campbell and her friend Mrs. Brighamina Poulson from Kansas City, Missouri. You'll want to hear what Mrs. Campbell has to say."

Somewhat nervously, Alex moved in front of the fireplace. After giving a good deal of thought to what she should say, she had finally decided that the more professional she was, the better it would be for all concerned.

"This may not seem to be very relevant at first, but I think you will find it interesting," she began. "In 1918, a man named Joseph Borden was wounded at the front during World War I. We'll never know what happened exactly, but his papers were either lost or stolen. They turned up in the States in the possession of someone else."

Alex paused to wet her lips. She had their attention all right. She began to feel less nervous.

"It is possible that this Joseph Borden we are searching for might have been the man you knew as Joe Cuendet. I am a professional genealogist, and my partner, Mrs. Poulson," Alex paused to indicate Briggie, "and I came over to France a few days ago to try to find out what had become of Joseph Borden, who also happens to be a cousin of mine. There is a probate matter involved, and it has become necessary to find out exactly what became of him." Pausing, Alex drew a steadying breath. "We thought we would find out that he had died a short time after the war, but we had no idea why the War Office had no record of it. All we knew was that he had been discharged with a head wound and never turned up in the States. We combed the area where his company had been billeted, looking for his grave in all the churchyards. Eventually, by

happy coincidence, we happened to meet Madame Genevieve
Moreau Guison, a very old lady, whose family had taken in a
nameless, wounded American known as Joe, who had lost his
memory. She told us of his marriage to Marcelle Cuendet and
of Philippa Cuendet's recent trip to Bar-le-Duc. That of course
led us here."

A long-haired brunette with the otherworldly air of a
Renaissance Madonna, broke in, her dark eyes intensely serious, "Did Philippa know you were coming?"

"That's the funny part," Alex replied. "I'm staying at the
Randolph, and she was killed across the street before she could
cross. I hadn't been in touch with her. If she knew I was coming, it wasn't from me."

A hulking man in a chrome-yellow silk shirt and paint-
spattered jeans put down his whisky glass, looking speculatively
from Alex to the Madonna. Alex was reminded forcibly of Jane
Eyre's Mr. Rochester. His face was long and melancholy, his
black hair unkempt, his hands large and powerful. "How will
you know for certain if your Joseph Borden and our Joe
Cuendet are one and the same?"

"As I said," Alex told him, "I'm a genealogist. I'm trained
in this sort of thing. There will be ways we can prove identity."

The man contemplated his drink in silence for a moment
and then asked, "Why has this only now come to light? If it's a
probate matter and Grandfather was presumed dead, I assume
someone else has been living on his money all these years?"

There was nothing slow about this bunch. Alex hoped the
chief inspector had been watching faces; things were happening too fast for her.

Before she could say anything, Briggie intervened, "I
wouldn't count my chickens before they were hatched, if I were
you. We don't know if Joseph Borden *is* your grandfather."

"Just tell me this: How big an estate are we talking about?"
Mr. Rochester persisted.

Alex flashed a look at the chief inspector, who nodded
briefly. She continued, "There is a business worth approxi-

mately twenty million dollars. There is also a personal estate of several million."

A tall, blond man with a profile reminiscent of a young Olivier raised one eyebrow and whistled. Belying the casual pose were the intensity of his blue eyes and the set of his jaw. This man was tensed like some sleek animal—restrained but ready to spring.

Hearing the amount of the fortune affected Judge Cuendet as well. Clearing his throat, he crossed to a lavender-striped chair where he sat suddenly as though his knees had given way.

Mr. Rochester grinned broadly, his melancholy miraculously gone.

"It's a rotten shame John couldn't be here," a fourth man said. Pencil-thin and with a leathery tanned face, he was taking a pipe from his pocket. "He and Philippa are . . . were . . . the family historians. Been trying to solve the puzzle of Grandfather for years. Of course, we never dreamed of anything quite so spectacular."

The judge nodded sadly, "Philippa would have been thrilled. This is all horribly ironic."

"John's at a conference in Norway," a golden-skinned blonde informed them sadly, "or he wouldn't have missed this for the world." In her dreamy fashion, the woman seemed focused intensely elsewhere. But when her warm brown eyes settled on Alex, she was surprised to see tragedy in their depths.

"My husband's a doctor," the beauty was explaining. There was just the hint of a French accent. "A famous specialist in AIDS research. I am Olivia."

With some uncanny sense, Alex felt she could predict the way Olivia's head would turn or the way she would smooth back her thick, long hair. Déjà vu? Or had she seen her before?

The Madonna had moved over to Judge Cuendet and laid a square, neat hand on his shoulder. "I'm afraid all this has put Philippa's accident out of our minds for a moment."

"It's all right, Hannah," the judge said, patting her hand.

"It's all right. A possible new cousin with tales of a fabulous fortune doesn't turn up every day."

An older, dumpling-shaped woman with a face that reminded Alex of a faded rose spoke up. "I suppose you must be very confused, Mrs. Campbell. There are so many of us. Why don't you introduce us all, Philip?"

"Of course. Our manners seem to be shot to pieces. What are we to call you, my dear?" the judge asked.

"Alex. And yes, I would like to know everyone. I'm just sorry I've come at such a sad time."

"So am I, Alex, but we welcome you all the same. I'm Philip, Joe and Marcelle Cuendet's middle child. This," he indicated the dumpling, "is Antonia Lamb, my elder sister."

Alex fumbled in her denim handbag. "Do you mind if I write all this down? I'll get mixed up if I don't."

"Be our guest. If we'd known you were coming, we could have had my nephew John here with all his charts and whatnot. He and Philippa have traced the Cuendet side back rather a long way. But, of course, you're not interested in that."

By the time everyone had been introduced, Alex had grouped them into three columns headed by the three offspring of Joe Cuendet: Antonia, Philip, and the absent Jean. Jean, it appeared, lived in Wales, wrote thrillers, and was married to a famous cook who had her own television show. Their son John, the AIDS research specialist, was married to Olivia, whom Alex now gathered was the internationally famous actress, Olivia du Bois. That explained her familiarity. John and Olivia apparently had no children.

The dumpling, Antonia, had been widowed for five years. In her column was her elder son Charles, the blond Olivier, who was a theater critic for the *Times* and a tutor at Christ Church College. Her younger son, Frederick, the tanned pencil, turned out to be an archaeologist and was married to Hannah, the Madonna. They had two daughters and a son at school.

The judge himself had only one surviving child, Edward, the man who had reminded Alex of Mr. Rochester. He was the dead Philippa's brother. (Oddly enough, Mr. Rochester's Christian name had been Edward, too.) This Edward, it appeared, was an artist and apparently divorced, as he told her that his two children lived with their mother.

Alex sketched all these facts onto a descendancy chart:

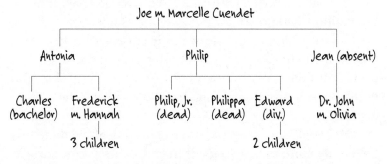

As she took all of this down, the handsome Charles stood silently looking over her shoulder. "Now that you've got us all classified," he said when she finished, "perhaps you'll tell us how you happened to witness Philippa's accident. It seems too coincidental to be true."

There was an undercurrent of bitterness in his voice. Alex wondered if her preoccupation with genealogical details offended him somehow.

"Yes, I can't get over it," Alex told them. "It was like a nightmare. She was standing by the Martyr's Memorial in the middle of St. Giles' Street, and I was on the other side. I had just come out of my hotel when it happened."

"What time was this?" Hannah wanted to know, her ivory Renaissance brow corrugated with intensity.

"I've no idea. Perhaps the chief inspector can tell us."

"It was close to half past ten," Hubbard contributed.

"Did she trip or something?" Olivia queried.

"Not that I saw," Alex replied.

"But why wasn't Philippa at the library?" Hannah demanded. "She starts work at ten o'clock. She shouldn't have been out at that hour."

"It was her day off," Hubbard answered. "She was to have worked Saturday this week, so they gave her the Monday off."

The room absorbed this information in silence. Alex felt an undercurrent of tension stirring. Were they beginning to be aware that the policeman's presence wasn't entirely benign?

"Edward, have you any idea where she was going?" Hannah asked Mr. Rochester, her voice sharper than before.

"We hadn't spoken for weeks. I may have been her brother, but Philippa had no use for me. Everyone knows that."

He sat gazing at the floor, body sprawled in his chair. Something in his pose, a vague diffidence perhaps, made Alex wonder if Edward's attitude might be an artificial skin. But perhaps she was romanticizing. It was a bad habit she was trying to cure.

"Yes. Well," the inspector interjected. "I'm afraid there may be slightly more to this accident than appears on the surface. At any rate, there will be an inquest. It would be just as well if everyone remembers what he can. To be perfectly frank, the police tend not to give an overabundance of credence to coincidence. *Was* it coincidence that Miss Cuendet just happened to be crossing to Mrs. Campbell's hotel? I don't think we can rule out the possibility that someone had told her of Mrs. Campbell's arrival."

Again, there was silence. This time Alex could almost hear them putting two and two together.

"But we didn't even know of Alex's existence, much less that she was in Oxford," Frederick, the tanned archaeologist, objected equably as he drew on his pipe. It took a lot to dent Frederick's equanimity, Alex decided.

The inspector heaved a sigh. "There *is* one other item that could go far towards explaining the circumstances. Mrs. Campbell mentioned a Guison family she met in France, who was in fact responsible for her deciphering her relationship to you. An Etienne Guison is here in Oxford also. He knew what Mrs. Campbell's purpose was here. He heard of it in France yesterday and followed her across the channel last night. Did he contact any of you?"

Alex surveyed the faces in front of her. Each one of them appeared blank, puzzled.

"Why would he?" Olivia asked, her voice still sad and a little dreary. "We don't know him."

"Nevertheless, I think the inspector's right," Hannah pronounced firmly, her dark brows now forming two straight lines in her Madonna face. "There is too much coincidence to swallow here." Examining the countenances of her in-laws, she continued, "It's obvious that somehow Philippa knew Alex was coming today. She's been working with John on the family history. She was just as keen as he was." She turned to Hubbard. "What does this Frenchman have to say for himself?"

"He says he doesn't know any of you," the policeman answered.

Frederick walked to where his wife stood and patted her on the arm. Alex read bemused tolerance in his thin, leathery face. "Coincidences do happen, Hannah. I see them in my work all the time."

"But even in archaeology there always turns out to be some kind of common denominator, Frederick!"

"My dear, look at it this way," he said reasonably. "If anyone knew Alex was here, why wouldn't they say so? News of that sort would have made the rounds of the family in no time."

"Not," his wife said darkly, "if someone intended to push Philippa under a bus."

SIX

Why on earth would anyone want to do that, Hannah?" Frederick asked, his voice seeming unnaturally loud in the hushed room.

"I don't know. Obviously, it must be connected with Alex's visit. What do you think the chief inspector's doing here? Facilitating a family reunion?"

Alex sensed the seven pairs of eyes turn to her again. She felt guilty, as though she had been responsible for bringing a deadly virus into the family. She couldn't think what to say.

"Mrs. Lamb is quite right, I'm afraid," Chief Inspector Hubbard told them soberly. He assumed a new stance, raising his chin and squaring his thin shoulders. Until now he had been content to remain in the background, his cadaverous face impassive as his eyes took in every detail. Now Alex sensed he was ready to make his move.

"I'm not convinced Miss Cuendet's death was an accident. It isn't as easy as you might think to fall under a bus. We have a witness who contends that she was pushed, and I'm afraid I believe it. Mrs. Campbell will also swear that Miss Cuendet hadn't started across the street when the bus came. One moment she was standing on the pavement; the next moment she was falling."

Silence. Judge Cuendet put a hand over his eyes as though to block out the horrible vision. "But surely you must be mistaken. Who on earth would do such a dreadful thing to Philippa?"

Hannah, her pale face a shade paler, hadn't moved from

her post behind his chair. She gave his shoulder a squeeze. This creature was living up to her saintly appearance. Though down-to-earth and realistic, she was definitely the nurturer of the bunch.

"Will you be able to prove this?" Edward wondered, helping himself to more whisky. Though his voice was impassive, Alex noticed his hand was shaking.

"In time, I believe so. With such a motive staring me in the face, I decided to facilitate this family reunion, as Mrs. Lamb put it."

Edward tossed back a dose of his whiskey. "I suppose the motive has something to do with Joseph Borden's money?"

"Think about it," the policeman instructed. "On the very morning a possible cousin turns up to inform the Cuendet heirs that they might inherit a fabulous fortune, a Cuendet meets her death. Presto: fewer heirs."

Olivia shuddered. "What a beastly idea."

"If it's murder, my bet's on this Frenchman," Hannah announced abruptly, leaving her post by the judge and going to sit in a vacant chair next to Olivia du Bois. Her eyes were suddenly fierce. "He must be mixed up in it somehow. Tell me about him, Alex. How much of the story did he actually know?"

Once again, Alex tried to remember her conversation with Etienne the day before. It seemed impossibly long ago. "I believe he knew most of it," she conceded. "But I don't see that that gets us anywhere. How would he know Philippa, and what on earth would he have to gain from murdering her?"

Hannah folded her hands neatly in front of her. "He must be involved, nevertheless. He's from Bar-le-Duc. Perhaps he's some Cuendet connection. Illegitimate or something. It's only logical. Where was he when Philippa was killed?"

"Standing beside her," the chief inspector answered.

"Then why haven't you arrested him?" Edward demanded, looking more than ever like Rochester in a fit of pique. "He's obviously involved in this thing up to his neck."

"Motive?" the inspector asked blandly.

"Hannah's got the nub of it," Frederick said, supporting his wife. "He must be a connection. I mean, we must face it. Who knows what Grandfather's indiscretions might have been? He lived with this man's family, didn't he?" He paused to look around the room brightly. "It only stands to reason when you think of it. I mean, none of *us* would kill Philippa on the off chance that we might inherit something. We were fond of her!"

Briggie went to stand by Alex at the fireplace and folded her arms across her chest in a confrontive fashion. "Suppose Philippa knew something that would prove Joe Cuendet wasn't Joseph Borden?" she postulated.

"Briggie, that's a long shot and you know it," Alex replied shortly.

But the chief inspector was observing Briggie with interest. "That's an intriguing motive, Mrs. Poulson. Do you have anything more concrete than guesswork?"

"Not at this point," she admitted. "But Philippa *was* the family historian. She had been to France recently. If anyone was in a position to disprove the theory, it would have been Philippa."

"But it works the other way, too, Briggie," Alex stated. "She would have been in a position to *prove* it as well."

"Then why would anyone kill her?" Briggie wanted to know. "You'd think they'd *want* her help."

"There's still the motive of reducing the number of heirs," the chief inspector reminded them. Moving over to Alex, he asked, "May I see that descendancy chart, Mrs. Campbell?" She handed it to him. "Let us assume that the Cuendet fortune would be divided equally between the three heirs of Joseph Borden. Roughly, how big is the personal estate of your father, Mrs. Campbell?"

"I'm not sure. It's invested. But I believe his portfolio is worth around ten million dollars. The house is worth half a million at least."

"So," the inspector continued, "together with the business that's roughly thirty million dollars. But let's say the courts award Alex's mother her husband's personal estate. The business is worth close to twenty million. Assuming the courts award it to your family, that's almost seven million dollars for Mrs. Lamb, the judge, and Mr. Jean Cuendet. With Miss Cuendet out of the way, that means an entire seven million would go to Mr. Edward Cuendet upon the death of the judge."

"Just what are you implying?" Edward inquired coldly. "That I murdered my sister?"

"Where were you this morning at around half past ten, Mr. Cuendet?"

"I'm damned if I'll tell you."

"I'm certain he was in his studio," Hannah asserted coolly. "He paints every morning. You can ask anyone."

"Restrain your heroics, Hannah," Mr. Rochester said, his voice hard. "I don't have to listen to this." He stood up and walked out of the room.

Frederick coughed as the front door slammed. The judge cleared his throat. Charles said, "Edward tends to the temperamental, obviously."

"Being suspected of murder is enough to ruin anyone's day," Briggie observed.

"Perhaps the murderer even thought that the fortune would be divided equally among all the living heirs," the inspector reasoned thoughtfully. "There would be a lot less to go around that way. Certainly that thinking gives everyone a motive."

Hannah paused to consider this, her large eyes sad. "I'm afraid you're right."

"My son seems a lot more hard-hearted than he is," Judge Cuendet interjected, shifting in his chair. "He's actually quite cut up about all of this. It makes him unbearably rude."

Olivia gave a gentle laugh. "I'm sorry, Uncle. I know he's your son, but he's always unbearably rude. Being a misunderstood artist gives him the right, you know." Lifting a sheaf of hair off her shoulder, the actress turned to the policeman. "All the same, Chief Inspector, I'm afraid you've got it wrong. The Cuendets aren't the kind of family they would have to be to do something like this. Even Edward. Look at them! Not one of them has chosen the kind of work that would make them wealthy: Frederick is an archaeologist, Charles a tutor and a journalist, Uncle Philip a judge, Edward an artist, and my husband a research doctor . . . "

"Who has access to your pots of money anyhow," Frederick added with a grin. "She has a point, certainly. We're all fond of our creature comforts, but none of us has ever thought much past that."

"We do what we love," his brother Charles added with one eyebrow raised, Olivier-like, "in the naive hope that money will follow."

"If one of us murdered Philippa," Hannah told the policeman earnestly, "it would surely have been a bit premature. There's a long way to go before we ascertain whether the Cuendets do, in fact, come in for this inheritance."

The chief inspector regarded them with a serious expression. "Unfortunately, it's been my experience that where large sums of money are concerned, few people are immune to impulsiveness and greed."

"I agree," the judge replied. "But greed and impulsiveness are one thing; murder is quite another. I can't believe any of us would have murdered Philippa over this."

His sister Antonia stirred herself to add, "I shouldn't pay too much attention to Edward's behavior if I were you, Inspector. He's always been highly strung, but he wouldn't hurt a fly. I feel it would be far more profitable from your point of view if you tried to discover a motive for this Frenchman. He's the unexplained element in all of this. What did you say his name was?"

"Guison. Etienne Guison."

"The name is unfamiliar to me. Does it mean anything to you, Philip?"

The judge shook his head. "Absolutely nothing. Our parents seldom talked about the family in France. However, it is possible that these Guisons are some remote connection. Philippa would have known. She was quite pleased over her findings at Bar-le-Duc. I only wish I'd listened more closely to what she told me."

"Do you mean Philippa might have met Etienne?" Olivia queried. "Then he would have known her!"

"When she was in France?" Alex inquired. "But he didn't say anything . . . "

"Why, it was just a couple of months ago," Olivia continued. "I remember now. She told John about an old Frenchwoman she had met." The actress contorted her face into a fleeting portrayal of a haughty, elderly Frenchwoman. For a moment, she looked amazingly like Genevieve.

"That was Etienne's great-grandmother," Briggie said.

The chief inspector frowned. "This Madame Guison had met Philippa Cuendet?"

"Yes," Briggie assured him. "She told us about it."

"I don't think Etienne was there, though," Alex objected. "He works in London. He was only in Bar-le-Duc for a funeral this last week."

"I'll make a note to check," Hubbard said, taking out his notebook.

Suddenly remembering Etienne's description of the bicycling Englishman, Alex asked, "Did any of you take a bicycle tour in France . . . say . . . around fourteen years ago?"

"A bicycle tour?" Hannah repeated. "What are you referring to, Alex?"

"Something Etienne said. He met an Englishman in the village who claimed to be a Cuendet. He said he had an American grandfather."

Hannah looked at her husband Frederick, who exchanged puzzled looks with Charles. The latter looked amused. "Bicycles aren't exactly Frederick's or my cup of tea. We row."

"What about Mr. Edward Cuendet?" the inspector asked.

Olivia grinned, showing perfect teeth. "Edward on a bicycle? He'd never do anything so strenuous. It may have been my husband John, of course." The actress shrugged. "Fourteen years ago is before my time."

"It sounds the sort of thing John would do, though,"

Hannah said. "He's very keen on the family. He would want to see the chateau. There is a chateau, isn't there?"

"Of course," Antonia told her daughter-in-law. "Samuel and I took the boys when they were young. And Philip, you've been over, haven't you?"

"Yes, during the war. Marched near there when we were chasing Jerry. Grandfather Cuendet died of a heart attack the day France surrendered to the Germans, so I never met him. Uncle Roland was too old to fight, but he was away doing his bit for the Resistance. Can't recall that I ever met anyone named Guison, though."

"What about Uncle Jean? He and Aunt Bit go to France regularly, don't they?" Frederick inquired, pipe between his teeth.

"You can ask them," Olivia said, pulling a minute speck of something from the sleeve of her cashmere sweater. "If you can find them. Myself, I think it's rather pointless. They're in America now. Bit's doing a television special and Jean a book tour. What can they possibly have to do with all this?"

"Have you an address or telephone number where they can be reached?" the inspector wanted to know.

"John probably has."

"When will Mr. John Cuendet be home?"

When the actress smiled this time, it was as though the sun had come out. "Dr. Cuendet," she corrected gently. "I expect him tomorrow afternoon. His conference will be over this evening."

Hannah stirred impatiently in her chair, crossing and then recrossing her long, trousered legs. "I suppose you want our alibis, Chief Inspector? I'm afraid I was working in the garden. No witnesses."

Hubbard wrote briefly in his notebook. Alex thought the Madonna's imperturbability rather jolted the rest of the room. Her manner certainly juxtaposed oddly with the sweet wistfulness of her countenance.

Suddenly she hoped that Hannah was right about the Frenchman. "In case you'd like to interview Etienne Guison, he is waiting at the Randolph," she told the policeman. "We're supposed to go to dinner."

"Your alibi, Mr. Lamb?" the policeman asked Charles.

"I would have been the last person on earth to hurt Philippa." A muscle twitched in Charles' cheek as he ran a hand over his head. Somehow the gesture conveyed tremendous restraint. Alex was reminded again of the dangerous animal held in check. "But for the record, I was probably having morning tea about then. Corner of the High and Queen Anne's Lane. Not much chance that anyone there can tell you exactly when I was in."

Alex knew the tea shop. It was near St. Edmund's Hall where she and Stewart had roomed during one of the photography courses he had taught. It was not an unreasonable walk from there to the Randolph—twenty minutes perhaps, if you walked fast. She shook herself. It seemed fantastic to imagine any of them coolly sallying forth to murder Philippa.

"Frederick?" Hannah prompted.

Her husband looked mildly amused. "Do you suspect me then, Hannah?"

"Certainly not. That's why I want you to tell the inspector where you were. You couldn't possibly have murdered Philippa."

"Yes. Well . . . I was in college somewhere, Inspector. I don't have a tutorial that hour, and I spend it doing odd jobs—collecting my mail, making copies, looking up references, that sort of thing."

"Which is your college?" Inspector Hubbard asked.

"Oh, yes. Well, Balliol, actually. Handy for the scene of the crime, unfortunately. Swear I didn't do it, of course."

"Then you won't object if I ask you what odd jobs you were engaged in this morning."

"Let me see," Frederick appeared to recollect with difficulty.

"Darling," Hannah prompted. "It was only this morning. Surely you can remember."

"Well, just let me think. Right. I finished with Nestleroad

at ten. Spent about a quarter of an hour hunting up my notes
for the lecture I'm giving tomorrow night. Went to the porter's
lodge to collect my mail. Then . . . oh, yes, I popped down to
Blackwell's to see about that new work of Corbet's. It wasn't in
yet, so I went back to college. Read my mail, I think . . . No. I
had a word with Stevens, first, and then read my mail. Was reading it when my students arrived for my eleven o'clock tutorial."

Hannah rolled her large, black eyes and shook her head.
"I don't suppose you remember when it was you left Blackwell's
or if you spoke to anyone there?"

Blackwell's was the largest bookstore in Europe and one of
Alex's favorite haunts. Frederick could hardly have chosen a
fuzzier alibi. The store rambled back to front with nooks and
crannies and floors above and below. It would be next to
impossible to prove how long he had been there. Alex found
herself surprisingly concerned over this. She liked Frederick.
She liked Hannah, too.

"Spoke to the head clerk. Don't suppose he'll remember
me. He was swamped with inquiries. It looked like they were
short-staffed this morning."

While the chief inspector was busy writing, Judge Cuendet
cleared his throat and laid a finger alongside his beaky nose. "I
tried cases all morning. Took a break about quarter past ten.
Spent it in chambers. Was back on the bench sometime before
eleven. My clerk can tell you."

"Well," Hannah said. "That just leaves Antonia and Olivia."

Antonia avoided her daughter-in-law's candid eye, straightening herself in her chair and fussing with the lacy collar of her
jersey print dress. "I was at a coffee at the Women's Institute.
We're planning a Christmas dinner for the homeless, you
know. I'm hopeless about the time, but I know I arrived there
before half past ten, because I was bringing cakes, and they had
to be there by then."

"Good," the inspector told her. "May I just have the
addresses of some of the women who can confirm you were
there?"

While the inspector was noting down those addresses,

Hannah said to Alex, "This isn't exactly the ideal way to make each others' acquaintance, I'm afraid."

"No," Alex agreed. "If I hadn't come, perhaps Philippa would be alive."

"Yes. Well, it's hardly your fault if someone was off balance enough to decide to murder her. I must say, though, I really can't believe it was a member of the family."

Alex thought again of Etienne, his smooth manners and his easy charm. Remembering his behavior that morning, she said, "If Etienne hadn't told me Philippa's name, I wouldn't be here. I never would have had any idea I was connected to the accident outside the hotel."

Hannah appeared to think that over. "You're a good genealogist, I take it?"

"I hope so. What I stumble over, Briggie generally sets me straight on."

"So you would have found us eventually?"

"I'm sure I would have."

"So. Perhaps this Etienne figured it would be less suspicious if he told you rather than let you find out for yourself. Besides, if he's the murderer, it immediately increases the field of suspects."

"Good point, Hannah," Briggie agreed.

"Now, Mrs. Cuendet," the inspector was saying to Olivia, omitting the use of her stage name. "What were your movements this morning?"

"I had a late performance last night, so I was at home in bed," she said. The air of sadness had returned. "My housekeeper will verify that, of course."

"You were there all morning?"

"Yes." Olivia eyed the policeman speculatively, perhaps wondering why he seemed immune to her charm. "Some people don't realize it, but acting is exhausting work."

"That wraps it up then, does it, Chief Inspector?" Charles said, looking at his watch.

"Have you a date, Charles?" Hannah asked.

"As a matter of fact, I was wondering if I could run Alex back to the Randolph."

"Sure," Alex answered, "if you'll take Briggie, too."

"I'm afraid I've only got a sports model," he apologized.

"I'm going to the Randolph," Hubbard told them. "I'll take Mrs. Poulson. Perhaps each of you would be good enough to give me your address and telephone number, and then I'll leave you in peace," the policeman said, turning to a fresh page in his notebook and handing it first to Charles.

When everyone had complied with the chief inspector's request, he raised his eyebrows in Briggie's direction.

"I'm with you, Chief Inspector," she told him, preceding him out the door.

"You're staying on at the Randolph?" Hannah asked Alex.

Nodding, she slipped into the coat the judge was holding for her.

"I'll ring you. Frederick and I will want to see plenty of you while you're here, murder or no murder."

It was perhaps inevitable that the handsome Charles would own a sleek black Jaguar. As Alex climbed in, she smelled leather and Polo cologne. The combination was probably overwhelming to most women, but the whole production struck her as a bit too calculated. Like Etienne, he seemed obvious, and his dismissal of Briggie hadn't gone down well with her.

"So, what do you think of us, Alex?" he asked.

"Well, these aren't exactly ideal circumstances to meet you in, but I hope it turns out we're related. The only other family I have is my mother."

"What about your husband?"

"Stewart's dead," she said shortly.

He blinked and looked at her as though really seeing her for the first time. "I'm sorry."

"It's all right."

Charles started the car, and she studied his profile. He really was amazingly handsome, in a cold marble Greek-god sort of way.

"I can't imagine what that would be like not to have relatives," he remarked. "I've been tripping over cousins and aunts and uncles all my life."

"Do you remember your grandfather?"

"He didn't die until I was nineteen. It's odd, though. When you grow up with a mystery like Grandfather not knowing his real name, you sort of take it for granted. It wasn't really discussed until after he died, when John and Philippa started to get serious about this genealogy business." He cleared his throat as though he were suddenly hoarse. "No. What I wanted to ask you was . . . Philippa. You saw her go down."

Alex looked at him with new sympathy. "It was very quick," she assured him. "I don't think she suffered."

"What a ghastly, horrible way to die!" He thumped the steering wheel and then gripped it fiercely.

After several moments, he asked, "You're absolutely certain you didn't see him push her?"

"Etienne, you mean? No. And I was watching him."

"Fond of him, are you?" His tone lightened suddenly, and Alex felt his contempt whip her smartly.

"I hardly know him," she replied evenly. "But you can judge his character for yourself. He should be waiting in the lobby of the Randolph unless the chief inspector has made off with him."

They were pulling up to the hotel now. "I'd be charmed," he said grimly. "But it'll be a trick to find parking."

After a short hunt, they spied a car just pulling out of the tiny parking strip in the middle of the street. Charles maneuvered the long nose of his car into the spot, shut off the ignition, and went around to help her alight. Surprised by this gallantry, she endeavored to get out of the XKE gracefully. It was a good thing she wasn't wearing a skirt.

Briggie and Etienne were seated on a large couch in the lobby, talking so earnestly that they didn't even see Alex enter.

"This is Charles Lamb," she announced, striding into their midst. "Charles, this is Etienne Guison."

Etienne was on his feet in an instant, shaking hands. "You will join us for dinner, I hope?"

"I'd be happy to. I don't know about Alex, but I'm starved." He seemed suddenly to be all affability.

Glancing at Etienne, she noted with amusement that he was sizing up Charles, each unconsciously smoothing his hair and straightening his tie. They reminded her of rival roosters.

"Where are we going?" Briggie asked, struggling to her feet.

"Brown's all right?" Charles asked.

"Perfect," Alex told him, gratified that they had at least one taste in common.

Brown's was a purely twentieth-century Oxford institution. Large, open, and airy with hanging plants, high tables and stools in blond wood, it was completely counter to the usual womblike pub. Packed to capacity with students, professors, and other Oxford types, its food was delicious, a mixture of solid English fare with an international twist exhibited in its hors d'oeuvres and desserts.

The first difficulty they encountered was, predictably, over the wine.

"Alexandra doesn't drink wine," Etienne explained to Charles as he was about to order a bottle of beaujolais. "I don't think Briggie does either. They are something called saints of later days."

Charles looked at her, again as though he really saw her. "A Mormon? You're a Mormon?"

Alex nodded, amused. "Actually, we're called Latter-day Saints. Our church is The Church of Jesus Christ of Latter-day Saints."

He stared at her and then laughed. "I can't believe we might actually have a Mormon in the family."

"What's wrong with that?" Briggie asked stoutly.

He turned to face his questioner, still amused. "I find Mormons rather exotic—for Oxford, at least."

Etienne nodded. "They don't drink alcohol."

Alex's amusement turned to annoyance. "You make it sound as though we were freaks," she said. "I don't suppose either of you practices any religion at all."

Etienne grinned. "I couldn't take anything seriously that stood between me and my wine."

Charles merely shook his head, returning to the wine list. Alex imagined that the idea of sharing a bottle with Etienne was galling to him.

Looking at Charles over the tops of the half glasses she was using to read the menu, Briggie said, "We really don't have horns, you know."

"I never believed for a moment that you did. It's just . . ."

"Yes?" Alex took him up.

"How can any thinking person belong to such a dictatorial, reactionary organization in this day and age?"

Briggie bristled.

Alex smiled. "Do those labels make you feel like an avenging angel or something?" Since her conversion to the Church, Alex had become weary of the tags her "intellectual" friends tried to stick on her.

"What do you mean by that?" Charles asked.

"You don't need to save me from myself. I can think, believe it or not."

He was looking at her with interest but said nothing.

"I don't suppose you've ever met a Mormon?"

"Well, no." He raised an eyebrow.

"Or seriously studied what we believe?"

"We do get the occasional newspaper over here, you know."

"Have you read the Book of Mormon?"

"I've never seen a copy."

"I'll see that you get one. I think you will find it interesting. Long before your Celts and Druids were squatting in their huts, we had a real civilization going in America. If your Oxford education taught you how to study something in depth before offering a criticism, you should find it fascinating."

"I'll look forward to reading it," he replied, grinning widely for the first time in their acquaintance. The effect was blinding.

SEVEN

Etienne has been telling me about his family," Briggie volunteered over the oysters.

The Frenchman drew his eyebrows together in annoyance.

"Yes?" Charles prompted. "Any American named Joe in his family tree?"

"I do not understand," Etienne replied, a crease between his brows. "You surely can tell that I am French!"

Alex asked Etienne to tell Charles about the English bicyclist.

"What did he look like?" the Englishman queried when Etienne had finished his account.

"I could not really tell. He had on the helmet over his hair. I remember only that he had fair skin. He was sunburned. Oh yes, and his legs. They were hairy."

"It might have been John, or perhaps my cousin Philip, who was killed last year. He went up to the chateau, you say?"

"Yes. I remember he stayed in the vicinity for a few weeks. They gave a party for him, but my family was not invited."

Alex saw that this was a slight that rankled even at this distance. Was there a rift between the Cuendets and the Guisons, or was it simply that they existed on different social planes?

"Fourteen years ago," Charles was calculating. "I was in Paris myself that summer. I wonder why John or Philip didn't look me up?"

"Well, you can ask John at least," Alex told him.

Briggie put her fingertips to her temples. "Hand me that descendancy chart you drew, Alex."

Reaching into her denim bag, Alex pulled it out. Briggie studied it.

She tapped Philippa's name. "It's pretty awful down there in black and white. Poor Judge Cuendet! Only one surviving child. How sad."

"Yes. And Edward seems to be the chief inspector's number one murder suspect," Charles said.

"Ah!" Etienne interjected. "They are calling it murder, then?"

"Yes," Charles told him. "We are all suspects. Except Briggie and Alex, of course."

The Frenchman refilled his glass. "Why do the police think it was murder?"

Not wasting any words, Charles laid out the chief inspector's reasoning.

"*Mon dieu!* The inheritance is so large? I had no idea, Alexandra." He looked at her in reproach.

Briggie had been studying the descendancy chart. "I still like my theory better," she mused. Then she added, "Not everyone on here is a suspect. Jean is in the U. S. John's in Norway . . ."

"So his wife thinks," Charles said with a wry grin. "Actually the fellow's only in London."

"Ah!" Etienne looked wise. "*La femme?*"

Charles raised an eyebrow at the Frenchman and then turned to Alex. "No. The poor fellow just wasn't all that keen on speaking at this conference. It was useless for him to tell Olivia that, of course. She thinks he walks on water and was thrilled that he'd finally been recognized by the AIDS research community. What she doesn't understand and never will is that he doesn't care about all that. He can't bear to be separated from his research." Charles paused to sample an oyster. "He told me he arranged with a colleague to use a lab in London for a couple of days. If you knew John, you'd understand. He simply didn't want to go the rounds with Olivia. And he's an absolute fanatic about all this." Charles shifted his gaze from Alex to his plate. "Their daughter died of AIDS, you see."

"Died of AIDS? But there's no daughter listed here," Briggie objected.

"Yes. Well, we don't like to bring up Victoria if it can be avoided. Olivia's been through enough. The poor child only died last year."

"Did she have a blood transfusion or something?" Alex asked.

"Yes. She had a bad heart and had to have surgery five or six years ago. They weren't screening the blood supply as well then as they are now, and she was infected with HIV. They didn't know it for some time, of course."

"That's why she looks so sad."

"Yes. She can't have any more children, you see. Victoria was her world. She was a prodigy at the piano and a sweet child besides. We all miss her, of course, but I'm afraid Livy had a complete breakdown. She's only just gone back to the stage."

Looking instinctively at her friend, Alex noted that Briggie was studying Charles with unabashed frankness. His public school manner had altered completely while talking about his niece. There was real grief there. As when he had spoken of Philippa. The oyster plates were taken away, and the main course was served. Alex sliced into the six inches of puff pastry that made up the crust of her steak-and-kidney pie. Though doubtful about the kidneys, she had decided to try the dish for Daniel's sake. Sitting between two such overpoweringly handsome men, she had a sudden, uncomplicated desire for her American friend, with his square wrestler's frame, freckles, and ginger-colored hair. She found herself missing his easy understanding.

"So. What will you do with this great inheritance, Charles?" Etienne was asking.

"Of what possible interest can that be to you?" the other man responded.

"Tell me about your mother, Charles," Briggie intervened quickly. "We must be about the same age. What does she like to do?"

For several restful minutes, Charles reverted to type and

amusingly discussed the charitable functions of the Church of England in Oxford. Then Briggie began a description of her own work with battered women.

Etienne spoke to Alex in a low voice. "It does not bother you to see all these strangers and know that they will have your father's money?"

She shrugged. "I grew up with lots of money around, Etienne. I know it's a cliché, but it doesn't always bring happiness. Look what happened today."

"The police, they really do think it is murder then. Charles was not trying to shock me?"

"No, he wasn't. They do suspect murder."

"And these Cuendets, they are all suspects?"

At this point, Charles and Briggie's discussion petered out. Overhearing Etienne's question, the Englishman broke in, "So are you."

"I?" The Frenchman stared. "Why?"

"I should think it was obvious. Alex told you why she was coming. You followed her here. You were standing next to my cousin when she was pushed. I can't think why the devil you're not in custody this minute."

Laying down his knife and fork, Etienne faced Charles, an angry flush deepening the color of his neck and face. "What are you saying?"

"Just what exactly is your game, Guison?" Charles demanded. "Did you meet Philippa in France?" In spite of his outward composure, Alex sensed his inner tension.

Etienne removed the napkin from his lap, placing it carefully on the table. "You are accusing me? You think I did this thing? I?"

"The thought had crossed my mind. You must have some stake in this."

Standing, Etienne removed his wallet and tossed fifteen pounds in notes onto the table. "I do not know this Philippa Cuendet. I had nothing to gain! It seems to me you are merely searching for the scapegoat. I do not intend to offer myself. Good evening, ladies. I am desolated that I cannot remain, but

I will not talk any further with this madman." He turned and shouldered his way through the crowded restaurant.

No one said anything. The waiter came in the silence to clear their plates and take orders for dessert. They waved him away.

Charles was attempting to get a grip on himself. "I apologize, ladies, for ruining your dinner." He, too, removed his wallet, placed two twenty-pound notes on the table, and stood. "I was very fond of my cousin Philippa," he said tightly. "Very fond. Perhaps you will excuse me."

He too left them.

"Whew!" Briggie breathed.

Staring after him, Alex struggled with conflicting emotions. "I'm not doing too well today, Briggs. I thought Charles was British public school through and through, but either I was wrong or the facade has broken clean off."

Her friend patted her hand. "Well, I don't know what you mean by 'public school', but I have a feeling he's not himself. Etienne's obviously your typical temperamental Frenchman."

"I don't know," Alex said, hunching forward on her elbows and idly surveying the crowd of turtlenecked professors and students in tattered blue jeans through the restaurant's haze of cigarette smoke. "The more I think about them, the more contradictory I find them. Charles isn't as cold as he appears, and Etienne's not as hot. He's calculating, Briggie. He's let the mask slip a couple of times. Any idea why the chief inspector didn't stay to question him tonight?"

"He got an emergency call on his car radio while we were going back to the hotel. He and Etienne arranged to meet early tomorrow morning."

Briggie took a bite of brown bread. "So, Alex. Do you believe Hannah is right about Etienne?"

"I don't know. It would certainly explain a lot if he had a stake in all of this. He *could* have let John know I was coming."

"Genevieve could have had a child by Joe Cuendet, I suppose. We could probably check to see if there's any funny business with her marriage to Guison."

"I thought you had it all figured out that one of the Cuendets had done it to prevent Philippa from queering their pitch?"

"I think at this point it's best to keep an open mind."

Alex couldn't help a grin. "And to you that means suspect everyone."

"Well, someone did it, Alex."

She sobered. "It would account for a lot of things, if that someone was Etienne."

"I think he's arrogant enough to think he could pull it off."

Their waiter came with the bill. Alex placed the men's money on top of it and handed it back. Both she and Briggie were silent for a moment as they considered the other candidates for suspicion.

"I hope Hannah didn't do it," she said. "I like her, don't you? For someone who looks so fragile and otherworldly, she's incredibly forthright."

"Yes. She has a good head on her shoulders. For my money, she and the judge seemed the only ones who did."

"Not Frederick?"

"He seemed to have trouble with the basics. My guess is, he's hopeless with day-to-day things."

"Well, I'm not taking anything for granted. He could have been acting a part, for all we know. And there was certainly nothing slow about Edward."

"No. This family seems to run to intense types, doesn't it? He'll be glad of the money, obviously. I bet he has a drinking problem."

After the waiter returned with their change, Alex left a suitable tip, and they shrugged on their jackets, made their way through the close-packed crowd, and exited into the night.

It was amazingly balmy for November, which was fortunate because they had to walk the few blocks back to the Randolph. The moon was full, and it was just possible to make out the spires silhouetted against the brightened night sky. Bells pealed from St. Giles' Church, and though it was ten o'clock, people still filled the streets, spilling out of concerts, coffeehouses, and pubs. Talking with their hands, they paused to laugh or expostulate, sometimes in the middle of the street. The charm of her surroundings overcame Alex once again. In the air, in the way the Oxonians walked and talked, she felt the intense vitality of a place where creativity abounded. For seven hundred years, the best and the brightest had flocked here, and their ghosts lingered in the architecture, the gardens, and the ancient traditions.

"It's an affront to know that something really horrible could happen here. It seems all wrong. This is the seat of reason."

Briggie tucked a hand through Alex's arm. "Horrible things can happen anywhere. You know that."

"I know that rationally. But emotionally this place has always been a sort of Camelot for me. It makes me want to find some obscure little subject no one else cares about and devote the rest of my life to researching it right here. It's been doing that to people forever. Did you ever read *Gaudy Night?*"

"Uh-huh. I thought it was the worst of all the Lord Peter Wimsey books. I felt like Sayers preached too much and didn't pay enough attention to the mystery. It was like she was trying to defend the fact that she wrote mysteries for a living."

"Hmm. I didn't see it that way. I thought she was showing the charms and the pitfalls of the feminine scholar's life. What I liked was their single-minded pursuit of truth."

"Daniel would say it was about obsessions. Those women had a pretty cockeyed view of the world."

"I don't suppose you have any obsessions, Briggie?"

Her friend grinned suddenly. "Only baseball and fishing. They're not likely to do anyone any harm."

"So how can an obsession with truth harm someone?"

Her friend pondered. "This is getting a little out of my league. All I can tell you is that all those women in that book had a kind of niche. None of them even wanted the whole picture. They just concentrated on one little area. Abstract, I think you call it. They lived in the abstract. That can be pretty dangerous, seems to me."

They had reached the Randolph. Walking through the quiet lobby, they ascended the stairs to their room.

"My point is," Briggie continued as she got out of her parka, "Camelot wasn't real. It's just a myth people get all excited about. Like those women in *Gaudy Night*. Real life isn't abstract; it's real. People bleed."

"I guess I just can't give up hope that there's some place safe and secure on this earth," Alex sighed. "You have no idea how scary I find it that acts of violence can happen anywhere, anytime."

"Well, if there were a place like that, it wouldn't be in a place like this."

"I think you're off base, Briggie. There's a lot of truth here. People have been striving to find it for hundreds of years. That striving's brought about a lot of good."

Briggie held up a hand in surrender. "Okay, Alex. Maybe I'm just feeling like a fish out of water. Leave it at that. Don't you think it's time we called Richard and gave him a report?"

The lawyer was astounded by their news. "You've located them already? You've only been there a day."

Alex explained about Philippa. The attorney was silent during her recital and for a few moments afterwards.

"Now let me get this straight, Alex. You witnessed a murder?"

"The police think so."

"You realize, of course, that this might be dangerous for you."

"Not really. I didn't see anything. I didn't even know who she was."

"And the police think one of the Cuendets did it?"

"Either that or Etienne Guison, the Frenchman I told you about last time I called. He was standing on the curb near Philippa."

"Until I met you, Alex, I never would have believed how hazardous it could be to be a genealogist."

"Most genealogists only encounter people who have been dead a long time. That's certainly the way I prefer it," she said ruefully.

"Well, I'll need to come over and meet these people and get all the evidence I can. How difficult do you think it's going to be to establish proof?"

"Philippa was the family genealogist. If the judge will let us, I think we should start with her research. I know she had letters and things of her grandmother's. And I didn't think of it at the time, but I'm sure they must have a picture of Joe somewhere. We ought to see a resemblance."

"It'll take more than a smile to satisfy the probate court. I'll need to go to France and take a sworn statement from that Guison woman, too. A lot of the Cuendet claim will rest on her testimony." He was quiet for a moment. "How is Brighamina?"

"Here. I'll let you talk to her."

While Briggie and Richard talked, Alex went into the bathroom to brush her teeth. She was amused. Until recently, Richard would never have intentionally sought Briggie's company. They were as unalike as two people could possibly be and had had a running feud during the entire year they had known each other. Then, in trying to track down the murderer of Alex's father, they had proclaimed a truce of sorts. Throughout the investigation, they'd made a particularly lawless combination and, in the three months since had maintained a cordial relationship. Though they were still wary of one another, there seemed to be a growing respect on both sides.

When Alex emerged from the bathroom, Briggie had hung up. "The Royals are trying to trade for a new shortstop. Richard's going to leave word with the night clerk downstairs about his plane reservations. I told him we were going to bed."

In spite of being extremely tired, Alex lay awake, trying to absorb her myriad impressions of the day. Her reunion with Oxford had begun so differently from the way it had turned out—the rush of memories brought on by the town, the bittersweet battles with Stewart's ghost, and then suddenly

Philippa lying dead in the road. Reality had challenged her eleven-year-old ivory-tower fantasy. People bleed. Briggie was right. Pure thought couldn't answer the hard questions. It only managed to phrase them more elegantly.

But she didn't want Briggie to be right. She wanted to believe that this was still an extraordinary place where extraordinary people did extraordinary and important things. This was the point at which her mind touched Stewart's, C. S. Lewis's, and J. R. R. Tolkien's. Or did being a Latter-day Saint put her in some kind of separate category? Was there any longer a connection between Stewart's world view and hers?

Turning away from that painful question, she forced her thoughts back to her original query. How did the Savior she had come to believe in answer the hard questions? Getting out of bed, she went over to the window. There were the spires towering against the night sky, serene as ever, as though they had not that day presided over a murder. As though four centuries ago they had not seen Archbishop Cranmer burned as a heretic at the front gate of Balliol College less than half a mile away.

There was no Camelot. Briggie was right about that. Alex leaned her forehead against the glass, against the view and all that it meant to her. The world *was* a dark place. In spite of all his reason and talent, man could always destroy—he could murder, torture, abuse, abandon.

Just then a lone bell began to chime the quarter hour. Its tone was pure and sweet, calling to mind Easter lilies, stained glass, and the fan-vaulted ceilings of vast stone churches. The warm, sweet peace of the Spirit knocked softly at the door to her consciousness. Why did she hesitate so long to take comfort from her beliefs? She hadn't yet let the light in all the way. The old *Weltschmerz,* that heavy weight of worldly pain, still lurked in the dark crevices of her mind.

Lifting her head once more, she took in the scene before her. It was just Oxford, and there was nothing magical about it, really. There *was* hope, but she had been looking for it in the wrong places, in all the old temporary strongholds she had conceived before she had found the whole truth. She must make a conscious effort now to root out the old, scary thought patterns that had become so ingrained over the years.

Shutting her eyes, she summoned a vision of the Garden of Gethsemane as she had come to picture it. She had never actually been able to visualize her Savior in prayer, but she sensed him kneeling, his heart twisted, almost breaking under the burden of the same tragedies that beset her mind. Taking a deep breath, she consciously let go of Philippa's murder and all the chaos it represented, seeing the blackness in her mind as a thing of spirit, drifting from her until it rested on the shoulders of Him who had borne all things. Swallowed up in the larger cosmic pain that her Savior was enduring, her individual horrors acquired a different perspective. Beside those bowed, trembling shoulders and that innocent, exhausted psyche whose human tabernacle bled at every pore, her sufferings seemed minuscule.

But it was impossible to linger in that Garden of earthly despair for long. The intensity of pain was beyond her comprehension. She must go on, finish the story.

Now she imagined him beside the Garden Tomb on the morning of the Resurrection—whole, triumphant, victorious. One punctured hand gently stretched towards her. On the palm was a jagged, clean scar. They were past the blood now. She felt the words, "Alex, you can't bear these things alone. You were never meant to. I am the only one who could, and I have done it already. Do what you can, and leave the rest to me."

Reaching out in her mind's eye, she took the proffered hand. Then an odd thing happened. Warmth flamed inside her so purely that the pain was burnt away, leaving only a calm sweetness in its place.

EIGHT

The following morning, Alex awoke to find Briggie in her Kansas City Royals' nightie doing sit-ups in the doorway between their rooms.

"What time is it?"

"Nine o'clock."

"My gosh, why did you let me sleep so late? Have you already eaten?"

"I slept until eight-thirty myself. We were worn out, I guess."

Tossing aside her goosedown comforter, Alex went to the wardrobe and pulled out her jeans and magenta pullover. In ten minutes she had dressed, washed her face, brushed her teeth, put on mascara and lip gloss, and was ready to go.

"We're going to get this cleared up, Briggie!"

"Of course we are," her partner agreed, pulling a sweatshirt over her white hair. "We've done it once. We'll do it again."

"We've got to focus on an action plan."

"We'll do it at breakfast."

Alex paused midstride and looked at her watch. "Oh, no. It's the middle of the night in Chicago. I forgot to call Mother last night."

Briggie patted her arm. "She's going to be okay, Alex. Her AA sponsor is keeping an eye on her, isn't she?"

"Yes, but . . . "

"You can call her later. I'll remind you."

As they descended into the lobby, a tall, distinguished-looking man in a navy blue suit arose from a Queen Anne arm-chair where he had been reading a newspaper. Etienne.

"Good morning, Alexandra, Briggie. May I join you for breakfast?"

Alex wanted to decline. She had serious business in mind, but on closer inspection, she saw that the Frenchman's eyes had bluish shadows underneath and that the lines from his nostrils to the corners of his mouth were more deeply etched than she remembered. In spite of herself, she was concerned.

"Are you staying here, Etienne?"

"Yes. We will talk about it at breakfast, if you permit?"

She nodded, and they walked together into the restaurant. Alex had a craving for a full English breakfast this morning. Briggie ordered the same. Shuddering at their hearty appetites, Etienne ordered coffee and a croissant.

"So," Alex said. "You decided to stay in Oxford. What about your job?"

"I have told my employer that I am called away on a serious personal matter."

Alex raised an eyebrow. There was definitely a difference in Etienne this morning. Gone was the lazy charmer. The look in his eyes was all business.

"Being suspected of murder is a serious matter, wouldn't you say?" he queried. "I have been with the inspector of the police since seven o'clock this morning."

Briggie turned over her coffee cup and set it back in the saucer. "I think it's time you told us why you followed us to Oxford, Etienne."

Spreading the linen napkin on his lap, he replied, "Whatever Charles may say, it had nothing to do with the Cuendets. I have absolutely no connection with them whatever, and so I told the inspector. Surely you must believe me."

"We'd like to believe you," Alex told him. "But how did Philippa find out about my arrival, if it wasn't from you?"

"I have no idea. It is not my responsibility to account for that family, whatever they may say."

The waiter brought Alex and Briggie steaming plates of

fried toast and tomatoes, mushrooms, eggs, and bacon. Before Etienne he set a solitary croissant.

Briggie said, "I could get used to this. Umm."

"So you don't intend to tell us why you came?" Alex asked after her first savory bite of bacon.

He grinned, but his eyes remained cool. "I shouldn't need to tell *you*, Alexandra."

"If you mean you came to see me, Etienne, I'm flattered. But I'm afraid I just don't believe you."

"Are you always so difficult?" he wondered. "Perhaps you have not yet recovered from the death of your husband."

"Stewart has nothing to do with it."

"Hasn't he? Then you do not find me sympathetic, attractive?" His tone was teasing now, and some of the amusement reached his eyes.

"You know very well how attractive you are."

Shrugging, he settled back in his chair and looked at her levelly. "You know, it is in your interests to help me."

"What do you mean?"

"Hasn't it occurred to you that you could be in danger?"

"It's occurred to *me,*" Briggie interjected. "Alex attracts danger like honey attracts bees."

"Why would I be in danger?"

"You witnessed a murder," Etienne said.

"But I didn't see anything! Just you standing there on the pavement, and then the bus. Whoosh! Suddenly there's Philippa in the street."

"The murderer cannot know that you didn't see anything. So. While he is free, you are not safe. As for me, I am not going to let that family or the English inspector of the police cast me as the scapegoat. I am going to find the murderer myself. I want you to help me."

Alex was impressed. She hadn't thought Etienne capable of such exertion. "We want to find the murderer, too. What do you need?"

"Whoever killed your cousin must have been standing near me on the pavement. It was obviously one of the Cuendets.

Perhaps I would recognize whoever it was, if you were to arrange for us to meet."

"What a good idea!" Briggie beamed.

Sampling her fried toast, Alex pondered. "I don't exactly know how we're going to go about it. You're not number one on their popularity list, you know."

"I have thought about this. Perhaps you could invite your family here. A little dinner tomorrow. I could be conveniently placed at another table."

Alex nodded. "What do you think, Briggs? Richard will be here by then, and I could say I'd like the family to meet him."

"I think it's a great idea."

"*Bon.* Then, with any luck, tomorrow night we will know the identity of the murderer." Etienne raised his coffee cup in a salute. "I will trust to you to arrange it with the family. I will speak to the inspector of the police. Now, what do you do today?"

"I was thinking," Alex mused, "that we might go take a look at Philippa's research and then see Charles's mother, Antonia Lamb. I have an idea that she would be the one most likely to have a picture of her father. I think that when we solve the genealogy puzzle here, it will take us a long way towards finding the murderer. Briggie has a theory that whoever killed Philippa thought she could prove Joe Cuendet *wasn't* Joseph Borden. I want to see if that's true."

Etienne considered her words and then turned to Briggie. "You think this is a possibility?"

Alex's partner looked straight into the Frenchman's eyes. "Our evidence that Joseph Borden and Joe Cuendet are one and the same is all circumstantial. Philippa may have had some hard evidence that disproves it."

"Ah!" Etienne nodded briefly. "Now. What other plans do you have?"

"I would like to meet Dr. John Cuendet. He should be returning to his clinic sometime this afternoon. I'll try to arrange to meet him after work. He's the other Cuendet authority on family history. Philippa may have told him something."

"And this John is the one with whom you think I am plotting?"

"Well, not really. But we think he must have been the man you met in Bar-le-Duc. You know, the bicyclist."

Etienne nodded. "I am supposed to have remembered him all of these years and telephoned to him from France to tell him that he has an American cousin on the way and that he is going to be rich?"

"It does sound rather ludicrous," Alex allowed. "You never met Philippa, I suppose?"

"I was in England when Philippa was in France. Until the funeral last week, I hadn't been home in more than a year. I can prove it, if necessary."

Briggie was regarding the Frenchman, her head to one side. "And you, Etienne. What are you going to do?"

Smiling his lazy smile, he told her, "I am going to sleep. I was awake all during the night. But now that I know what we are going to do, I can perhaps relax."

After breakfast, they parted from the Frenchman and returned to their room to discuss the situation. "What do you think, Alex?" Briggie asked.

"My instinct says to believe him, but logic says he must be involved in some way. I'm surprised you didn't challenge him about Genevieve and Joe Cuendet."

"So am I. But he seemed different this morning, didn't he?"

"Yes. He'd shed the charm. For the most part he was the ruthless man of business. I think I like him better this way, actually. Did he intimidate you?"

Briggie grinned. "Maybe he did. I must be losing my edge."

On calling at Judge Cuendet's chambers, they were told he was not in owing to a death in the family. There was no answer at the house on Woodstock Road. Thus denied access to Philippa's research, they decided to proceed to the next item

and phoned Antonia Lamb, who urged them to come right
over.

Antonia's home was out of a storybook—a vine-covered
cottage built of golden Cotswold stone, set in the middle of a
well-kept garden still blooming with purple and yellow chrysanthemums.

She greeted Alex with a kiss on the cheek. "We were just
discussing Philippa's funeral arrangements. Charles is here.
And Philip."

Inside the cottage was bright and cozy. The walls were
white, wainscoted in dark wood. The low ceiling had heavy
exposed beams, and the furniture was covered with flowered
tapestries in shades of rose. Ferns, ivies, and African violets
adorned the sitting room, together with an enormous silver-
haired Persian cat.

Charles and Judge Cuendet stood as the women entered,
and Antonia bustled off to get the photograph albums they
had told her they wished to see.

"When is Philippa's funeral to be?"

"Thursday. Tomorrow is the inquest," Charles answered.
"We just got off the telephone with Inspector Hubbard. I imagine he'll be ringing you, as well. You don't happen to know
where that Frenchman lives, do you?"

Briggie had gone over to the cat and was attempting to
make friends.

"He's staying at the Randolph, as a matter of fact."

Charles regarded her closely. "I thought the man had a job
in London."

"He does, but he doesn't take being a murder suspect
lightly. He's determined to catch the murderer himself."

"Catch the murderer himself?" the judge repeated blankly.
"How the devil does he think he's going to do that?"

Alex pulled herself up quickly. Darn Charles. "I don't know
that he has a concrete plan. But he objects strongly to being
'the scapegoat,' as he puts it."

"Seriously, Alex," Charles said, putting a hand on her shoulder and looking her in the eye. "He's got to be involved. I don't think it's safe for you to go about with him."

She shrugged, and he removed his hand. "He says the same about you," she told him. "I can take care of myself."

Antonia reentered the room holding a short stack of three photograph albums. "I've found some really good snaps, I think." The three women settled on the sofa with Antonia in the middle and began leafing through the books. Charles and the judge resumed discussion, presumably about the funeral.

"Now here's Father with my mother, about . . . oh, it must be thirty-five years ago," Antonia told them. "It was taken on their wedding anniversary."

Alex's heart bumped in her chest. Here was the mysterious Joe, at last. But the man's face was tiny in the photograph. Too tiny to make out any resemblance to her grandfather who had died twenty years ago. Her memory of him wasn't that precise, and her parents had, for reasons of their own, destroyed all pictures of him.

"Well, Alex?" Briggie demanded.

"I'm not sure," she murmured. "He's medium height like Grandfather, and has the same thick head of hair, but I'm not certain I can really make out any resemblance. Are there others?"

There were—photographs of tea parties on the river, trips to Switzerland, holidays by the sea. Alex took them all in hungrily, but a positive resemblance eluded her. "Did they ever go back to France?" she wondered.

"If they did, I don't remember. Mother was a little peculiar about her family. I don't think they can have been happy about the marriage."

"Do you think she missed her home?"

"The only time I remember her talking about it was during the war. I was a young bride when France fell. I thought Mother's heart was going to break. She simply couldn't believe it. She had lived near the front in the First World War, you know. Well, of course you know. That's where she met my father. Anyway, she simply couldn't believe France would fold without putting up more of a fight."

"Speaking of the war," Alex said thoughtfully, " did you ever notice a scar on your father's temple?"

"You mean his head wound?" Antonia responded. "I remember it well. He used to tell us that his memory had all shrunk into that tiny little scar. I remember being terribly intrigued by the idea."

Wasn't this confirmation? Alex's heart was pumping double time. At the very least this was another foothold. "Do you happen to remember which side the scar was on?"

Closing her eyes, the older woman concentrated. Her eyes fluttered open. "Right. It was on the right temple, I think. Philip!" she called to her brother across the room. "What side was Father's scar on?"

"Scar?"

"You know—his head wound."

The judge ran his forefinger across his upper lip. "It was on the right, I think."

"Good," Alex breathed, suddenly triumphant. "That's what Joseph Borden's military records say."

"Oh! I hadn't even thought of them!" Antonia exclaimed. "What else do they say?"

"They give his eye color."

"Moss-colored," Antonia told her. "Just like mine. I have his eyes."

Alex peered at Antonia. "Hazel. You're two for two. That checks out with the military records, too."

Charles, who had taken little notice of this exchange, broke in, "What was that reading you thought of, Mother?"

"The Wordsworth, dear. 'Ode: Intimations of Immortality.' Philippa was very fond of it."

Charles sighed and pinched the bridge of his nose. "Yes. She was, wasn't she? I don't think I could manage it for anyone else. Did you want me to read the whole thing?"

"Well, no. I don't suppose you need to read the whole thing, do you, Philip?"

"I should think mainly the part about 'trailing clouds of glory.' That bit would suffice," her brother responded.

Looking at the family striving to contain their grief, Alex felt suddenly overwhelmed with guilt. "I'm so sorry," she murmured. " This horrible inheritance. I thought you would all be so glad . . . This is all my fault!"

Antonia patted her hand, "How could you have known, dear?"

"I must say," Charles intervened with unmistakable bitterness, "she could have been a bit more circumspect in France."

"Now then," Briggie responded, "just what are you accusing her of?"

The judge had his nephew by the elbow. "Easy, Charles. Alex was only doing her job. It's not every young woman who would volunteer to do what she has done, when it was a matter of disinheriting herself."

"She had no business speaking of it to Etienne Guison."

Charles's accusation had the contrary effect of chasing away her feelings of guilt. "What will you do if Etienne Guison can prove he had nothing to do with this, Charles? You are so convinced he did it, your mind is completely closed."

"Who else could have done it? I think it must be you who has the closed mind."

"Now hold on . . . ," Briggie began. Alex silenced her with a motion of her hand.

"Just what are you implying?"

"That you've fallen for Monsieur Guison. Did the moment you met him, probably. I know his type."

"You do, do you?" Alex said. "And just what type is that?"

"I've spent plenty of time in France. Enough to know the attraction that seductive Frenchmen can have for impressionable American females. I can tell you exactly how it happened. You were sitting in a little bistro. He held a cigarette between his lips and looked at you through half-closed lids." Charles performed an incredibly accurate imitation of the Frenchman. "He hinted at things and flattered you. And you bought it. You told him everything."

"Really, Charles," the judge remonstrated, "Your behavior is indefensible. Philippa wouldn't have countenanced it for a minute."

The younger man gave a sour grin. "You're right. She would have given me the devil."

"I know this is a difficult time for you," his mother said coolly, "but please have the grace to remember your manners."

Running a hand over his head in the self-restraining gesture Alex recognized, he took a moment to compose himself. Then, looking at Alex, he said, "Forgive me. What you feel is certainly none of my business."

It was said grudgingly, and Alex had the impression of a small boy made to apologize by his elders. "You've got the wrong idea entirely," she told him shortly. Turning to Antonia, she said, "Richard Grinnell, the probate lawyer who is handling the estate, will be arriving tonight. I'd like everyone to come to dinner at the Randolph tomorrow night to meet him. He'll be able to answer your questions and give you more details about the estate. He can also let you know what he needs from you."

"That'll be jolly, coming on the heels of the inquest," Charles remarked.

"Charles!" Antonia protested.

"I'm sorry, Mother, but this entire estate business is going to prove our undoing, I promise you. It's already cost Philippa's life. I want no part of it."

"Fine. You needn't be present tomorrow night."

"We're not pressing the money on anyone," Briggie intervened. "I'm sure Alex and her mother could find plenty of uses for it."

"Your sentiments do you credit, my boy," the judge said. "But Philippa would be the last one to . . . "

"It's not Philippa! It's the money itself! It's going to set us all against each other. We're already suspecting one another of murder."

Surprisingly, Alex found herself in sympathy. "I do understand, Charles. I'm afraid the money certainly corrupted my family."

Sitting down, Charles put his head in his hands.

"What do you mean, Alex?" the judge wanted to know.

"My father was murdered three months ago. It's a long story, but it all had to do with the money."

Charles raised his head, his eyes questioning. "Your father was murdered?"

"Yes," Briggie told him, her eyes flashing. "And Alex was very nearly murdered herself, but she got to the bottom of it anyway. Coming here was the next step in clearing up the mess. She sure didn't expect another murder, but now that it's happened, she's bound and determined to catch this murderer, too. She doesn't deserve what you've been dishing out, Charles."

"My goodness," Antonia murmured, "I should think not."

"You would appear to be a very enterprising young lady," the judge told her. "Don't mind Charles. He was devoted to Philippa. This is especially hard on him."

"It's hard on everyone," Alex agreed. "It's a very bad situation. I only hope some good will come of it sometime."

During this conversation, Charles had been regarding her uneasily. Now he said, "I'm sorry about your father, Alex. I'm afraid I've become a bit self-centered in my grief." He tried a grin, but it was a tired one. "Forgive me, if you can."

Sensing the depth of his feeling, she was oddly touched. "I understand more than you think," she said quietly. Then, getting to her feet, she turned to the judge, asking, "Could you tell all the others about tomorrow night? Except John and Olivia. I'm going to try to see him this afternoon after he's through at the clinic, so I'll tell him then."

The judge agreed.

"And one more thing. Would it be possible for us to go through Philippa's research?"

"I think that's an excellent idea. I know she thought she'd made a breakthrough recently."

Briggie was stacking photo albums. "That reminds me, Antonia, do you have any letters of your father's or anything of that sort? We have an old will Joseph Borden wrote at the beginning of the war and his signature on his military records. We'd like to compare the handwriting."

The older woman sat back and shut her eyes. Her weariness was suddenly obvious, and Alex was reminded again what a strain they were all under.

"I don't think I do have anything. I did have a little collection of things I'd saved, but I gave it all to Philippa some years ago."

"Well," Briggie stood up, "I guess the next step is to look at what Philippa was doing, then."

Alex consulted her watch. It was lunchtime. They'd overstayed their welcome. "Would it be possible to meet you at your house sometime this afternoon?" she asked the judge.

He nodded. "Why don't we go along there, now?"

Correctly interpreting Alex's glance at her watch, Briggie objected, "You need to eat first, Judge. You can't afford to miss meals when you're under such a strain."

Looking at Briggie, he seemed amused rather then affronted by her proprietary interest in his well-being. "I breakfasted late," he told them. "But you probably didn't. Go ahead. I'll meet you there at half past one."

"That'll be great." Alex shook hands with the man heartily and found herself hoping he was her cousin. It would be very comforting to have a presence like the judge's in her life.

Antonia saw her to the door. At the threshold she paused and said, "Charles was very close to Philippa. He loved her very much, and he's not coping well." She pressed Alex's hand. "Try to understand."

"I do," she told the woman, summoning a smile. "Tell him that, won't you?"

Owing to their own late breakfast, Alex wasn't the least interested in lunch. Briggie contented herself with fruit and a candy bar. They also used the interval to phone Olivia.

"John will be thrilled to meet you!" the actress assured them. "Why don't you just come round when the clinic is closing. About five o'clock. He's seeing patients up until half past four. Do you know where Somerville College is? It's just up the road from the Randolph."

"Yes. I know it."

Olivia proceeded to give her careful directions to the clinic from Somerville. Alex wrote them down, read them back, assured Olivia that she was looking forward to seeing her again, and then hung up.

Deciding to walk rather than take a taxi, Alex and Briggie made their way along St. Giles' Street to the point where it became the Woodstock Road.

"At least there's one Cuendet who's totally indifferent to the inheritance," Alex commented.

"You mean Antonia?" Briggie queried.

"I meant Charles, actually."

Her partner nodded. "He's definitely hot-blooded. It makes me feel friendlier towards him. I wonder why they never married?"

"First cousins," Alex reminded her. "Why is it necessarily better to be hot than cold?"

Briggie pondered this. "It means he feels *something*. When people are cold, you have to wonder if they have any feelings."

"I think you've been conditioned by romance novels, Briggie. The brooding hero syndrome."

"Doesn't Charles have a good reason to brood?"

"I just wish he'd get this Etienne thing out of his head. What do I have to do to convince him I'm not in love with the man?"

Briggie laughed. "You know, I think he's just jealous."

"Jealous!" Alex was incredulous. "You just finished telling me how broken up he is about Philippa!"

"I don't mean jealous in a conscious sort of way. I think he genuinely suspects Etienne. It drives him crazy when you stick up for him. He's fighting an attraction for you. It's obvious."

Alex shook her head. "Briggie, we've really got to wean you off Georgette Heyer romances. That's the craziest thing I ever heard."

When they arrived at the judge's house, he was putting his key into the lock.

"Welcome, ladies."

Philippa's study was a bright, cream-colored room on the south side of the house with french doors leading out into a garden. At this season there were yellow and white daisy mums lining the flagstones beneath the bare branches of what appeared to be miniature fruit trees.

The cherrywood Sheraton desk was neat and tidy. Hidden unobtrusively in a closet was a gray steel filing cabinet.

"I'll just leave you to it, if you don't mind," Philippa's father said, his voice subdued and sad as he looked around the room.

"Fine," Briggie said heartily.

"Thank you," Alex added.

"I'll take the file cabinet," she told Briggie once he had left. "You take the desk."

Philippa had been a considerably tidier genealogist than Alex was. Her file drawers were neatly packed with hanging folders labeled in precise capitals: BEAULIEU, BELLE-FONTAINE, CUENDET, LEGER, etc.

On checking these, Alex found that they all pertained to Philippa's grandmother's line. Pulling out the next drawer, she saw another collection of hanging files, these unlabeled. Looking inside them, she found that they were empty.

NINE

"This is weird," she told Briggie as she examined the last of the folders. "I wonder what happened to all this stuff."

Her partner straightened up from her examination of the desk's bottom drawer and joined her.

"Do you think the judge would know?" Briggie asked.

"Maybe. Let's look in the other drawers."

The two bottom file drawers proved to contain personal files, completely unrelated to genealogy. Several fat folders contained letters in the same fiercely jagged handwriting. The first one was dated thirty-five years before, from a school called Summerfield, the last the previous month from Ireland. They were all signed, "Charles." Alex stuffed them away before she could be tempted to read them. Another file contained news clippings—Charles's theater columns in the *Times*. Still another file contained more news clippings, but these were of a different sort. They showed a smiling Charles receiving a £100,000 check from a large industrialist on behalf of AIDS research. Another picture showed him in a benefit cricket match. Still another pictured him with a man and his seeing-eye dog, doing a charity walk along the Isis towpath on behalf of the blind. Charles a philanthropist? This was a new slant. Nothing that could help in her investigation, however.

"Anything in the desk?" she asked Briggie.

"If there is, I missed it."

"But Marcelle Cuendet's letters should be here somewhere, and all the stuff Antonia gave her . . . "

Alex began opening desk drawers herself. In the top

drawer was a collection of pens and pencils, paper clips, rubber bands, stamps, and some snapshots of what appeared to be a dog show. The other drawers were surprisingly empty—a checkbook, stationery and envelopes, a telephone directory, bills and receipts, a broken china figurine.

"I really think someone has beaten us to it," Alex said grimly. "It looks like you were right, Briggie. She must have known something someone didn't want us to find out."

"Let's talk to the judge," her partner suggested.

When confronted with the contents of the desk and file drawers, Philip Cuendet just shook his head. "This was Philippa's preserve. I didn't come in here much. But I know she had been corresponding with someone about Father. It's odd that those letters aren't here."

Alex had an idea. Excitedly, she searched the desk one more time. "Nope," she said finally. "Whoever did this took the address book, too."

"How would they get in?" Briggie demanded.

Judge Cuendet caressed his upper lip with a forefinger, supporting his chin with his thumb, and pondered.

"Everyone in the family has keys," he said finally. "Philippa and I go abroad every August. They all take turns watering Philippa's plants and checking on the place. You think the murderer did this, I gather."

Briggie said, "Yes. Probably directly after the murder, while you were in your chambers. Someone obviously didn't like the way Philippa's research was going. With her dead, there's nothing to tell us what it was she'd found."

"Except that she must have had some kind of proof that Joe Cuendet was someone other than Joseph Borden. Otherwise, why would they take it?" Alex sighed and put her hands on her hips. "This is incredibly frustrating. Judge, can you remember anything else? The slightest little clue might help us."

"I only know she was writing this chap from the States . . ."

"The States!" Briggie and Alex chorused.

" . . . and he seemed to have turned up something solid.

She'd just had his letter that morning . . . yesterday morning. She was just opening it when I left."

"I wonder if her correspondent was a researcher," Alex mused.

"Dollars to doughnuts he was!" Briggie opted.

Alex wandered over to the french doors and looked unseeingly out at the garden. "I wonder what she had him doing."

"We're not likely to find out now," her partner said dejectedly.

"If only I'd known!" The judge was obviously distressed.

"I'll bet John knows what she was doing," Alex said suddenly.

Briggie snapped her fingers. "No takers. I'll bet you're right. Can we call him?"

"He's right in the middle of his office hours. Let's just wait. I'm going to see him tonight."

Taking leave of the judge, who promised to inform Chief Inspector Hubbard of this latest development so he could have everything fingerprinted, they made their way to the Eagle and Child, where Alex intended to have a late lunch.

She introduced Briggie to her favorite pub, where, after ordering their soup, they settled next to a cozy fire at a scrubbed oak table in an empty inglenook. Today the soup was potato.

"Well, Charles won't be happy about this latest bit of evidence," Briggie said. "It pretty much narrows it down to the family. Etienne couldn't have gotten into the house, even if for some strange reason he cared what Philippa was working on," Briggie said.

"Unless he's working with someone in the family," Alex answered thoughtfully. "We did tell him we were going to look at Philippa's research this morning. And if he's descended from Joe Cuendet, too, it's to his advantage for Joe to be proved to be Joseph Borden."

"True. But Charles still isn't going to like it."

"I don't think he's thought of me as anything but trouble from the first moment he saw me," Alex said. He's scared to death someone in his family committed the murder. He *wants* it to be Etienne."

Briggie nodded. "And now we know that it couldn't be unless he's working with a Cuendet. Who do you think it is, Alex?"

"I don't know. Edward Cuendet would be the most satisfactory suspect. He's even ruder than Charles."

"You're right. But still, there was something about him that sort of reminded me of Mr. Rochester . . ."

"Briggie! That's exactly what I thought. I can't believe it."

"So *Jane Eyre* is okay? It's not a trite romance novel, too?"

Alex laughed. "Touché." She paused, looking at the doorway in surprise. "Speak of the devil. There he is now."

Alex waved to him. Raising his chin in silent acknowledgment, the artist walked over to their nook.

"So you've discovered the Eagle and Child," he said, pulling out a chair, sitting down, and crossing his legs.

"It was my husband's favorite pub. We used to come here all the time when we were in Oxford."

Edward looked at her hands. She still wore Stewart's gold band. "I didn't realize you were married, for some reason."

"Widowed."

"I'm sorry to hear it," he replied perfunctorily.

Alex decided to change the subject. "Did your father call you about tomorrow night?"

"He may have done. I've been painting all morning. Didn't answer the phone."

"We're meeting for dinner at the Randolph. The probate lawyer is coming tonight." Alex went on to explain what would take place at the dinner.

The artist removed a pocket knife from his jeans, opened it, and began scraping magenta from underneath his index fingernail. "Any idea how long it will take to settle the estate?"

"I wouldn't hold my breath," Alex said. "It's really complicated. Remember, we haven't even proven identity yet."

He raised his eyebrows. "There can't be two Americans

who were wandering around Bar-le-Duc with no papers and no memory."

"That's not enough for the probate court, I'm afraid. And then, even if identity is proven, the judge will probably have some fairly lengthy deliberations about how to divide the estate between my family and yours."

"Yes? And what will the arguments be?" He started on his thumbnail.

"That although my grandfather assumed the inheritance in error, he did so with no intention of fraud. It would probably speed things up if your family and mine could come to some sort of an agreement out of court."

Edward appeared to meditate on this. "I can see we're going to need someone to advise us."

"I imagine your father will be able to do that."

"Father's too cut up about my sister at the moment. I think I'd better take it in hand. My landlord's a solicitor. He'll know what to do." Looking vaguely about him, he glanced at his watch. "Sorry. I can't stop much longer. I have to teach some little beasts about art this afternoon. I just stopped in for a sausage. Catch me up on the news. Am I still suspect number one?"

"You seem to have taken it in stride," Briggie remarked.

He glowered. "I should have expected it. It's about par for the way my life is running. I didn't do it, actually."

"Well, the inspector doesn't take us into his confidence," Alex told him.

Turning to Briggie, Edward asked, "Just what do you make of this mysterious Frenchman, Mrs. . . . Poleman, is it?"

"Poulson," Briggie corrected. "I think he's determined to get himself off the hook."

"And how is going to accomplish that?"

"By finding the murderer himself."

"What do you think?" The artist turned to Alex. "Did he do it?"

The waiter with the jeweled nose brought their soup.

Tasting it, Alex delayed answering. It was delicious. She wished Edward would go away so she could enjoy it.

"Not unless he had some help," she said finally.

Looking thoughtful, Edward drew circles on the tabletop with a forefinger. "What is that supposed to mean?"

"There have been new developments," Alex told him. "Someone gutted Philippa's study. Etienne doesn't have a key."

"Why does that have to be connected to the murder?"

"We think Philippa had some evidence that your grandfather was someone other than Joseph Borden," Briggie said. "Did she ever say anything to you about an American researcher?"

He shook his head wearily. "Philippa never said much of anything to me. We didn't see eye to eye."

Changing his position in the chair, he remarked, "I understand that the sainted John wasn't really in Norway."

"Do you suspect him?" Briggie wanted to know.

"He ran into this Etienne fellow in France. Spent some time there. They could have struck up a friendship, kept in touch."

"I think it unlikely," Alex said. "I don't think Etienne ever would have told us about meeting him if that had been the case."

"It's pretty obvious now that someone killed Philippa to keep her from telling about her research," Briggie said. "Someone who wanted the money badly."

Edward considered. "Well, unless he wants to get free of Livy for some reason, John's got plenty of money for that clinic of his. She had a five-million-dollar contract for her last film. But there is the fact that John's the one person in the family who would have known exactly what Philippa was up to. She could have known he was in London, too. Could have called him there."

"Well," Briggie said, "Alex is going to see John this afternoon. Maybe she can find out something."

The artist appeared not to be listening. "I say, Alex."

"Hmm?"

"You didn't see anything, did you? I mean, you must have noticed who the Frenchman was standing next to."

"I just recall two women in white. He sort of stood out next to them. I assumed one of them was Philippa, because of her white dress."

"Then either he did it or he knows who did."

Pondering Edward's scenario, Alex sipped the last of her soup. He was right, of course. She had better lead him away from that line of thinking or he would be on to Etienne's plan. "I would have noticed if Etienne had pushed her," she insisted. "I was looking straight at him. His eyes were on me until the bus came between us. He would have had to push her before the bus came."

"You're determined to defend him, aren't you?"

"Not necessarily. But I'm well aware that some in the family would like nothing better than to saddle him with this. I'm playing devil's advocate, that's all. From what I saw, I think you're wrong."

"Who knows," Edward said coolly, "the two of *you* could be in league together. It would make a perfect plot. You'd been in touch with Philippa, telling her you were coming. Then you and the Frenchman set the whole thing up between you."

"Why on earth would I do a thing like that?"

Edward smiled one-sidedly. "The inheritance, of course. You thought Grandfather had died without heirs. When you inconveniently found some, you hired the Frenchman to help you discredit us. Before long I expect you'll come up with some 'evidence' that says Joe Cuendet was some poor chap who had nothing to do with Joseph Borden."

Alex stared at him in disbelief.

Briggie just shook her head. "I thought you had more sense, Edward. That's pure spleen, and it doesn't become you at all. Alex would never do anything that crazy."

"My mind isn't quite as convoluted as yours, Edward," Alex added levelly.

"Then, of course, there's Frederick," he mused, as if he hadn't heard them.

"Why Frederick?" demanded Alex.

Edward looked from one of them to the other. "I think I've impugned enough reputations for one day." Rapping the table sharply with one hand, he stood up. "Thanks, ladies. This has been most instructive."

As they watched him go out the door, Briggie shook her head. "He didn't even get anything to eat."

"Briggie! Is that all you can say? The man just accused me of murder!"

Her partner shook her head. "He was just saying it. He didn't believe it for a minute."

"You're too old for him, Briggie. And besides, he may still be married."

"So was Mr. Rochester."

"I wonder what he has on Frederick?"

Briggie stood. "Since he wouldn't tell us, it was probably something pretty damning. Let's go."

Alex followed her friend out into the street. "You know, I think we ought to go visit that school where Joe Cuendet taught. Who knows, they may still have old personnel records or something that will help us. The British keep everything."

"What a nice little mess we're going to have for Richard when he comes," Briggie said with obvious anticipation.

"He'll love it," Alex agreed, grinning at her friend. "He'll deny it, of course, but I know he's secretly dying to play detective again. This time, considering you're in a foreign country, it might be best if the two of you tried to keep within the bounds of the law."

When they returned to the Randolph, Alex placed a call to her mother.

"Alex?" her mother answered. "Richard called! He said he's going over, that you already have everything figured out!"

"Well, not everything," Alex temporized. Richard wouldn't have told her about the murder. "But things are going fairly well. I think probably I've found Joseph's heirs. There are a lot of them. How are you feeling? Have you had any spells?"

"My one arm is pretty weak right now, but I'm managing. How is Oxford, dear? As wonderful as you remembered?"

"Every bit. Is Jean Solari keeping an eye on you?"

"I've been a good girl, Alex, don't worry. I'm not about to fall into that hellhole again, MS or no MS. I'm going to live to see my grandchildren. Have you heard from Daniel?"

Her mother's thought pattern was distressingly obvious. "Yes. It seems he was a Rhodes scholar at one time, so we had a cozy little chat about Oxford. Briggie sends her love."

"Let me talk to her, dear."

Alex put her partner on, glad as always that the two of them had developed such a close relationship. Briggie had been a tremendous help in the early days after the death of Alex's father when Amelia was emerging from her alcoholism and she and Alex were trying to put the pieces of their relationship together.

When Alex set off from the Randolph to meet John at his clinic, it was already dark. Unlike the night before, the air was cold. Buttoning up her peacoat, she grimaced as she headed into the sharp wind that was blowing down St. Giles' Street, carrying with it dust, leaves, and all the debris that had collected on the busy thoroughfare during the day. This wasn't going to be a particularly pleasant walk.

Would John be able to tell her anything about Philippa's research?

A bicyclist swerved to avoid her, and Alex realized she hadn't been watching where she was going. Thrusting her hands in her pockets, she looked resolutely ahead of her, but soon her mind was back on her problem, teasing it this way and that.

She truly did not think Etienne guilty. Would he recognize one of the Cuendets tomorrow night at the dinner?

Chief Inspector Hubbard had left Alex a message at the Randolph, asking her to attend the inquest tomorrow to give evidence. Presumably Etienne would be there, too. Maybe he would identify the murderer in the courtroom. But with Charles and Edward doing their best to implicate him, how much credence was the inspector going to give Etienne's word? What they needed was something indisputable—what they called hard evidence. A third party, perhaps. Someone totally disinterested in the Cuendet family and its inheritance.

Alex saw that she had arrived at the mass of buildings that made up the hospital next to Somerville College. Unfortunately, there were no streetlights or street signs to the little alleyways that she must traverse in order to reach the clinic. Praying that she had chosen the right one, she turned into a tiny cobbled street that resembled a tunnel between two high windowless buildings. This alley was surely never intended to accommodate an automobile. It was scarcely wide enough for a normal-sized car, and on account of Oxford's lamentable lack of parking, several small cars hugged the side of the building, making it necessary for her to walk down the middle of the road.

A black phantom streaked silently across her path, sending her heart into her mouth. A cat. Surely it had been a cat. Why was she so jumpy? Possibly because of the quiet. As she progressed down the alley, the sounds from St. Giles' receded steadily into a muffled monotone. The moon was not yet up, and so she walked in darkness that was becoming more absolute by the moment. Soon she must find the turning Olivia had told her about. It was supposed to be on the right.

Suddenly she heard the squeal of tires behind her as a car turned into the alley at high speed. "My gosh," she thought instantly, realizing she was dressed entirely in navy blue, "how will it see me?"

She heard the racing of the engine and saw the long shadow her form cast in the car's approaching headlights. It was coming straight at her.

Looking frantically from right to left, she saw no place to take shelter. Unless it stopped in time, the car was going to smash her flat. Terrified, she began to run. There was a little Mini Cooper parked hard against the building on the left. If she could just reach that car . . . The oncoming car accelerated, its roar filling her ears.

Adrenaline screamed through her body, and she put on a burst of speed born of pure terror. There it was. She had reached the Mini. Throwing herself on it, she scrambled up onto the roof and held on as the careening car whizzed past her, missing the Mini by centimeters.

Alex began to shake violently. The car had nearly run her down. She had almost been killed. Who but a criminally negligent idiot would drive like that through here? Easing herself off the roof, she found her legs unsteady. Her race to the little car had used every reserve of energy she had. What she wanted was a chair. But first she had to get out of the alley.

Before she had gone far, however, she heard another squeal and was suddenly blinded by a pair of headlights approaching her from the opposite end of the alley. She froze. Could it be the same car? She must think. Think! But her mind wouldn't work. She stood staring, mesmerized by the headlights.

TEN

Up the road from Alex, a man in a white doctor's smock appeared out of the side of the building. Spotting the car, he immediately stepped back. Then he saw Alex in its head-lights.

"Run!" he yelled.

The shout galvanized her. There must be a doorway there. If she could make it, she would be safe. She ran straight towards the headlights, but this time her legs felt like lead. She wasn't going to make it.

At the last moment, the stranger in the smock darted out into the alley, grabbed a handful of her jacket, and yanked her into the doorway and out of the path of the car.

Collapsing against him, Alex clutched at his clothes and breathed hard into his chest.

"Bloody idiot!" the man cursed the driver. "You might have been killed."

"Twice," she panted, gasping for air. "That was the second time."

The man led her inside the building to a dimly lit corridor. "Are you all right?"

"I need to sit down." Abruptly, she lowered herself onto the cold concrete floor.

"Put your head between your knees," her Good Samaritan advised. "You look faint."

She felt faint. Waves of nausea rose inside her, and every muscle in her body quivered. "Thank you," she murmured. "You saved my life."

"I think I did, actually. That was the second time he came at you?"

"Yes. The first time . . . I jumped on top of a car. But this time . . . I just couldn't move."

"Shock," the stranger diagnosed. "You were suffering from shock. We had better get you into the emergency room."

"I'll be all right," she told him. "I don't want to move yet."

The man squatted down next to her and, taking her hand in his, turned it over so she could see the bloody scrape on the back of it.

"Yes. I remember. My hand was wedged between the car and the building so I could hang on."

With professional competence, her rescuer looked into her eyes and felt her pulse. "We've got to get you into a bed. Come along. Stand up. That's the way . . ."

After a nightmarish journey through a maze of corridors, Alex was finally put to bed on an emergency cot, and wool blankets were tucked tightly around her. A nurse administered an I.V.

"I'm Dr. Lasswell," her rescuer told her. For the first time she noticed that he had bright red hair, which stood on end.

She tried to smile. "Thank you very much. I'm afraid I've caused you a lot of trouble."

Sitting on a wheeled stool, the doctor glided to her bedside. He had freckles and a kindly face. "Do we need to telephone the police?" he asked.

Alex scarcely heard him. She felt as though she were floating through space. It was extremely pleasant. She had no desire to come down.

"Look here. Are you in some kind of trouble?"

With a heavy sigh, she told him, "Perhaps you had better call Chief Inspector Hubbard. CID."

"Criminal Investigation Department?"

"I witnessed a murder yesterday."

Dr. Lasswell stared as though not certain he had heard her right. There was something else she needed to tell him, but she didn't want to think. All she wanted to do was float—up to the

ceiling, through the room, up into the sky. She was safe . . . safe
. . . she hadn't been killed.

"What were you doing in that alley?" the doctor
demanded.

John. She must make an effort. "Do you know Dr. John
Cuendet?" she asked.

"Certainly. He's a colleague of mine. He has a clinic just
down from here . . . oh, were you on your way to see him?"

"Yes. He may be my cousin. He'll be expecting me."

―――――――――――――

"Alex?" Stewart with his black beard was bending over her
in the dim light. Was she dead? "What's happened to you? Dr.
Lasswell says you were nearly run down!"

Not Stewart. "Who are you?"

"John Cuendet. I'm most awfully sorry about this."

"He saved my life," she murmured. "I'm all right."

"But this is absolutely frightful. I just heard about Philippa
this afternoon. What can be going on?"

She shut her eyes wearily. She really didn't want to talk.

"Forgive me for badgering you," the doctor said sadly. "I
know you're in rotten shape. It's just been such a shock. Dr.
Lasswell seems to think it was intentional."

"I think it must have been." Alex allowed him to take her
pulse and examine her pupils.

"You didn't hit your head or anything, did you?"

"No. I'm sure it's just shock. I've never been so scared in
my life." Remembering how she had stood mesmerized by the
oncoming headlights, she began to tremble.

At that moment, Chief Inspector Hubbard strode into the
emergency room, his high forehead creased with concern.
"Mrs. Campbell! What's this I hear?"

In as few words as possible, Alex told him her story, remembering to introduce John at the end.

"How many people knew you were coming to meet the
doctor this afternoon?"

She didn't want to think. She just wanted to float—out and

away, beyond John, beyond the chief inspector and his demands. She closed her eyes.

"Mrs. Campbell, I realize you are ill. But you simply must see how important this is. Someone has tried to kill you. How many people knew of your appointment here?"

Forcing her mind back over the morning's activities, she tried to remember. "I was at Antonia's house this morning. The judge and Charles Lamb were there. I told them."

"Yes?"

"Then I ran into Edward Cuendet in a pub. I told him, too."

"And the Frenchman?"

Alex struggled to think back to her discussion with Etienne at breakfast. "I think I probably did tell him. He wanted to know what we were doing today."

"So." Inspector Hubbard turned back a few pages in his notebook. "That covers just about all the suspects as far as I can tell. Charles, or his mother, or the judge, for that matter, could have easily communicated with Mr. and Mrs. Frederick Lamb."

"But why would anyone want to hurt Alex?" John demanded.

"She was a witness to the murder," the inspector said flatly. "The murderer probably thinks she saw something."

"But I didn't!" she protested. "My eyes were on Etienne the entire time. And all he was doing was looking at me."

The policeman surveyed her speculatively. "How certain are you that he did nothing?"

Head pounding, Alex twisted under the blankets that were binding her to the bed. "Nearly positive."

"And Monsieur Guison knows this? You have discussed it with him?"

"I don't know. But he knows I don't suspect him." Looking fleetingly at John, she realized that he was studying her intently. "Besides, I think that the theft of Philippa's research pretty well eliminates him. Obviously, someone didn't like what she had found out. John, what was she working on? Do you know?"

"She had a researcher in the States studying military records. Had she found something, then?"

Alex pinched the bridge of her nose. Military records? If only she didn't feel so dull and hazy. "Her father said she had received a letter yesterday morning. It's missing."

"That's a bit of a facer. Did you find an address or anything?"

"No. Someone completely cleaned out her files and her desk. There's nothing."

The doctor thought this through. "I think you're right. It sounds like Philippa must have found evidence of some kind about Grandfather. Something that would have disproved your theory."

"When can I get up?"

John looked at her chart and then took her pulse again. "Your pulse is still a bit weak. It would be best if you stayed here for a while."

Now that she knew he wasn't Stewart, Alex studied John Cuendet objectively. He was another very handsome man in a thoughtful sort of way. He had the essence of Stewart—the piercing eyes, the beard, the broad shoulders and narrow hips. Considering Olivia's fame, he wasn't nearly as extraordinary as she had expected. But she sensed he was kind.

"Then someone must call Briggie. She's waiting for our lawyer at the Randolph. They'll wonder what's happened to me."

"And who, pray tell, is Briggie?" John asked, apparently amused.

"My partner. Brighamina Poulson."

The inspector closed his notebook and said, "I'll take care of it. Where's that doctor who pulled you out of the alley? I'd like to talk to him for a minute."

"He's about somewhere, probably taking care of Alex's paperwork. He wanted to check her once more before he went home. I'll see if I can find him."

As soon as the doctor had retreated a safe distance away, Alex said, "Chief Inspector!"

"Yes?"

"About Etienne. Did he tell you about our plan for tomor-row night?"

"Yes. I spoke to him this afternoon. He told me of the arrangements."

Alex relaxed. "Good. I just wanted to be sure you knew."

Hubbard smiled his tobacco-stained smile. "Don't worry about the Frenchman, Mrs. Campbell. He's taking very good care of himself. By the way, I'll need to take your fingerprints along with Mrs. Poulson's for purposes of elimination. My crew has spent the better part of the afternoon in Miss Cuendet's study. Perhaps tomorrow morning before the inquest?"

Alex agreed to this and added, "Now that we know it was military records she was looking at, maybe I can figure out what it was she found. Give me a little while to think about it. It could be important."

"Not important enough for you to get murdered over. If it's not asking too much, I'd like you to keep a low profile. You're in danger, young woman. Someone knows what you can do, and that someone wants you dead."

"Not according to Edward Cuendet. He thinks I'm behind all of this, trying to keep the money for myself."

"That's a bit thick."

"Briggie thinks he didn't really mean it. She's fallen for him."

"I beg your pardon?"

Alex gave a little grin. "I think I'm a little punchy. Don't pay any attention to me."

The policeman smiled his great yellow-toothed smile. "As soon as I leave here, I'll be off to check alibis for the time you were in the alley. You'll be all right?"

She nodded, and the floating sensation returned. She closed her eyes.

"You need to take good care that you stay in safe company." He paused. "It probably wouldn't be a good idea for you to be alone with the doctor or any of these Cuendets in an isolated spot."

"Oh." Alex opened her eyes. She hadn't thought of that. In fact she had given surprisingly little thought to who had nearly run her down. She was too busy being grateful to be alive.

Biting her lower lip hard, she looked up into the chief inspector's face. "It has to be one of them, doesn't it?"

"I don't suppose there's any chance you could identify the car?"

She shook her head. "None. It was dark, and the headlights blinded me."

Returning with Dr. Lasswell in tow, John excused himself. "I'll just go telephone to Olivia, then I'll be back, Alex. We can have a nice, long talk."

For once, Alex had absolutely no desire to discuss family history.

"Could we leave it 'til tomorrow, John? I really just want to get back to the Randolph and into my own bed."

Dr. Lasswell was taking her pulse. "I'd say that was a very good idea. There's no reason why you shouldn't do just that."

"I'm sorry. I should have realized . . . " John smiled a bright, professional smile. "We must talk soon. After all these years of trying to put the puzzle together, I'm anxious to learn about this Joseph Borden."

"We can do it tomorrow." Alex said. "You're invited to dinner at the Randolph to meet the lawyer who is probating the estate. Bring Olivia. I believe we're going to start about seven-thirty." Alex looked at the chief inspector. "How about a police escort back to the Randolph?"

"You're on."

───────────

To say Briggie was concerned was a serious understatement. Turning dead white at the inspector's news, she wordlessly gathered Alex in her arms and squeezed her tight. Alex hugged back. Dear, dear Briggie. Comfort seeped through to the cold place inside her, bringing tears to her eyes.

"Richard has arrived at Heathrow," her partner said as she whisked Alex upstairs, leaving Chief Inspector Hubbard to follow. "I told him about the Airport Link bus to Oxford. He ought to be here in another hour. You're not going to be in any shape to see him if you don't get right to bed. What have you done to your hand?"

Sensing Briggie's obvious competence, Hubbard left them at the door of their suite, after admonishing her, "Obviously, it would be a good idea for you to keep your eye on Mrs. Campbell until we arrest the person who did this thing."

"Don't worry, Inspector. She's not going to leave my sight."

Alex had been settled in bed no longer than five minutes when a call came up from the front desk.

"It's Charles," Briggie told her. "He insists on seeing you. Says it's very important."

Curiosity worked through her muzziness. What could he want?

"Let him come up, Briggie."

"Are you sure? You're still awfully pale."

"Sparring with Charles is sure to have a beneficial effect on my blood pressure."

Dressed surprisingly in disreputable Levi's and a faded black sweatshirt, Charles entered the room, looking harried. His blond hair was less than perfectly combed, and his eyes darted restlessly from Briggie to Alex in the bed.

"What's wrong?" he demanded.

"Alex just missed getting murdered, that's what's wrong," Briggie told him tartly. "And if you carry on like you did this morning, you're out of here."

Charles stared at Briggie. "You're serious? She was almost murdered?"

"A car tried to run her down."

"Where?"

"In the alley near John's clinic," Alex told him. "It's okay. I'm all right."

Pulling a chair up to the bed, he searched her face. "Are you sure? You look pretty done up."

"The doctor said it was just shock. I'll be okay in the morning, I think."

Charles gently touched the bandaged hand. "And this?"

"I scraped my hand. But it's nothing serious, really. Just a graze." Pulling her hand away from his, she said, "You've made me curious. What's so important?"

"Did that Frenchman know you were going to see John?"

Alex rolled her eyes in exasperation. "Yes. And so did you, your mother, your uncle, and your cousin Edward."

"You think one of us did this?" His face went suddenly hard.

"Someone did."

Standing up, he began pacing the room. "I came here to apologize for my behavior this morning, Alex. I was an officious idiot. What you feel for that Frenchman is certainly none of my affair . . ."

Alex covered her ears with her hands. "Charles, will you kindly shut up?" He broke off and looked at her in surprise. "It is you who have hypothesized that I am madly in love with Etienne. It is absolutely not true."

He sat down on the chair next to the bed. "Then why do you defend him when it is so obvious he is implicated in this?"

"I *don't* defend him! I simply don't assume he's guilty! There's a difference."

Briggie had been sitting on the vanity stool surveying the proceedings with a grim look on her face. "Haven't you got any sense?" she accused Charles. "Alex was nearly killed tonight! Why do you have to go on at her like this?" Standing, she walked in front of him, looking directly into his face. "And I'll tell you something else, Mr. Charles Lamb. You've got cotton for brains. You think just because Etienne happens to be good-looking that's she's bound to fall for him. What kind of sexist claptrap is that? It so happens that Alex had a terrific husband. She loved him in a way I doubt you could ever understand. He was killed by terrorists. She has had a terrible time. Falling for a guy like Etienne Guison would be the last thing Alex Campbell would be likely to do." Briggie paused for breath.

Alex intervened, "Briggie . . ."

"No." Charles stood up and ran a hand through his hair

before turning to face Alex. "Terrorists? Is there any brutality you've been spared?"

Alex squirmed uncomfortably. "It's all right, Charles. I'd prefer not to talk about it."

"Briggie's right. I've been abominably chauvinistic. I was angry. I guess it's because . . . well, never mind."

"Sit down, Charles," Alex told him. "Briggie, could you call down and order us something to drink? I'm suddenly parched."

Her friend moved to the telephone, "What does everyone want?"

"I'll have mineral water," Alex said.

Charles studied her for a moment. "The same for me," he told Briggie.

Alex raised an eyebrow.

"I won't drink whisky alone," he said with the beginnings of a grin. "That's a sorry habit to get into."

When Briggie had given the order, she came back to the bed and began fussing with Alex's covers.

Taking her by the elbow, Charles said, "Briggie, I understand why you're angry with me. Can we call a truce?"

She stood up and looked directly at him. "Until the next time," she replied with obvious reluctance.

"Why don't you like me?" he asked her.

"You're too darn good-looking," she answered shortly. "You've gotten your own way all your life, and you think it's your natural right."

"No," he said in a low voice. "Now it's your turn to be wrong."

There was a painful silence for a moment. Then Alex spoke, "Philippa?"

Charles appeared to be studying the pattern of the rug. "There was some unfortunate history in the Cuendet family about cousins marrying one another."

"Why don't you tell us what she was like?"

Charles thought for a few moments. "Let's put it this way. I tend, like most of my peers, to be a cynic. I fight it, but there it is. Unlike my brother or cousins, I have no obsessions to bury myself in. I play the game, drive the car, write my column . . . but I've never been able to care about anything that much. It seemed so pointless. Unless I was with Philippa. In her eyes the world was still a good place. She was tremendously . . . enthusiastic, alive, full of wonder at the smallest things. I was always afraid she'd become disillusioned, but she was amazingly tough." He passed a hand in front of his eyes and left it there. "With Philippa there was always hope. It's all wrong that she died this way. It's an insult to everything she was."

"I know," Alex whispered, reaching out to touch his sleeve. "I know."

"You understand? It nullifies her. It silences hope."

ELEVEN

"I do understand," Alex told him. "Believe me, I do. And I'm hurting for you. But there *is* hope. It doesn't feel true right now, but believe me, it is."

Briggie stood looking at the pair of them for a moment and then moved discreetly into her own room.

"I guess I can't tell you much about grief," he said, removing his hand from his eyes and looking at her. "I'm very sorry about your husband. When did it happen?"

"Almost three years ago. It doesn't help when it's something violent that takes them away. It makes you crazy, like the universe has gone berserk."

"My universe wasn't any too stable to begin with." Charles focused on her face thoughtfully. "How ever did you get through it?"

Taking a deep breath, she said, "I don't really know what would have happened if it hadn't been for Briggie. My husband and I lived in Scotland, and none of Stewart's Scottish relatives were the least comforting. They wouldn't talk about their grief, and they didn't want me to talk about mine. I thought it was going to destroy me, it was so violent."

Alex noted the hastily hidden flash of understanding in Charles's eyes. She remembered how dreadful it had been to feel so full of sorrow that no one seemed to share. Perhaps that's how Charles felt. Smiling at him faintly, she continued, "Briggie was a distant relative of Stewart's. I met her when she came to Scotland to do genealogy. I guess she could tell how lost and depressed I was. I didn't see much to recommend being alive. The next thing I knew, she had scooped me up and taken me home to the States to live with her. I was so listless, I think I went just to avoid arguing with her." Alex grinned suddenly and put her hand lightly over Charles's. "Briggie's my miracle, you see. Because of her I eventually began to hope there might be a God."

Charles nodded for her to go on.

"You have to understand, I had absolutely no one left in the world when Stewart died. My parents hadn't spoken to me in fifteen years. There was nothing but pain, and I couldn't see any purpose in it. Life seemed totally futile."

"And Briggie changed that?"

"At first, I thought it was just Briggie. That she was one of those special people. Like Philippa. Hope personified. I suppose I clung to her for dear life. Then, little by little, she showed me that it wasn't her, that the source of what I was feeling came from beyond her. She was only an agent, as I suspect Philippa was."

"An agent? You're talking about God, I suppose." Charles's face was bleak, but his eyes continued to focus on hers closely.

"More specifically, about Christ. To me, he had always been some remote, tortured person on a cross. I saw no hope in that. Or even in a resurrection, if all we had to look forward to was more of the same."

Charles nodded emphatically, running a hand through his hair. "Exactly. Irrelevant."

"Other men have been crucified, vilified, tortured, killed. What makes Christ different, Charles, is the first part of what he suffered, in addition to the Crucifixion. The Garden. The Atonement. *That* is relevant to me personally. That's my source of hope."

Leaning forward, he asked, "What do you mean?"

"He knows it all, Charles. He's been to the depths and triumphed over them as only he could. If you think about it, that means not only does he understand every vestige of sin but he understands *us*. He was sinless; he didn't need to atone for anything. He did it because even knowing all there is to know about you and me, he still loved us enough to help us. I know that part's pretty hard to swallow, but how else can you account for his sacrifice?"

"I don't need to account for it if I don't believe it happened."

"All he asks is that we exercise a particle of faith to begin with. Just think, Charles. Here is someone who *knows* despair as we've never known it. He *knows* injustice."

"Even if I grant you that, I still don't see that it helps me much."

"You've got to carry it further. You've got to go on to the resurrection and the promises he made to us. He won! We don't have to do this all by ourselves, Charles. He doesn't want us to."

Putting his head in his hands, he looked as though he were struggling to make sense of all she had said. Alex was suddenly weary.

Finally, raising his head, he said, "Supposing I believe he has that kind of power. That he really knows every naughty deed I've committed and still thinks I'm worth something. What do I do? Where do I begin to work with this, so it has some relevance, some meaning, to me?"

"On your knees," she answered with a sigh. "There's no other way."

He recommenced his study of the floor.

There was a sharp rap on the door. Briggie came back into the room to answer it. It proved to be room service with their mineral water. Charles rose to tip the bellhop.

He drank his water absently and then insisted on ordering dinner for them all.

"I'm not really hungry," Alex told him.

"You will be when you catch sight of some food. When was the last time you ate?"

"A pub snack with Cousin Edward," she said wearily. "Incidentally, he's got a theory. I'm behind the murder."

"The man's mad," he said grimly, dialing room service. "It would be forgivable if he could paint, but he can't."

He had no sooner placed the order and reset the telephone when it rang.

"For you," he handed the instrument to Briggie.

Alex could hear the booming voice all the way across the suite.

"Richard!" her friend exclaimed. "Are you downstairs?" Briggie was unconsciously preening herself as she looked in the mirror.

"He's here!" she said triumphantly, hanging up the telephone. "I'll just run down and get him. Oh!" She looked at her baggy blue Royals sweat suit as though seeing it for the first time. "Do you suppose I ought to change?"

Grinning, Alex assured her, "You look fine, Briggie. I don't imagine Richard looks like he's stepped out of a bandbox after a transcontinental flight, do you?"

His charcoal-gray suit was a bit crumpled, but Richard looked surprisingly alert. His eyes went first to Alex in the bed and then alighted on Charles.

"Richard Grinnell," he said, offering his hand.

Charles took it unhesitatingly. "Charles Lamb."

"Yes." Richard set down his travel bag. "Hope you don't mind if I set this here, Brighamina. I'll take it along to my room in a few minutes." Turning to Alex, he said, "She tells me it was an automobile this time."

"A nearly lethal automobile. Hello, Richard." To her surprise, the lawyer leaned down and kissed her lightly between the eyes.

"I'm relieved you're in one piece. Daniel would skin me alive if I let anything happen to you. What's Brighamina thinking of, letting you wander off by yourself when there's a murderer loose?"

"Believe it or not, most of the time I manage to take care of myself fairly well . . ."

The lawyer grunted his doubts and turned to face Charles. "So you're one of the alleged heirs?"

The younger man frowned in distaste. "So Alex tells me. Right now, I'm more concerned with finding my cousin's murderer."

"Yes," Richard looked Charles over speculatively. Then he turned to Alex and Briggie. "Playing detectives again?"

"Well," Briggie temporized, "a little, maybe. Things just sort of . . . happen."

Puffing out his chest, Richard heaved a sigh and said to Charles, "I don't know if they've told you, but these two have just come through some pretty harrowing escapades in the States. Between you and me, they don't always exercise the best judgment . . . "

"That's a little much, coming from you," Alex said with a short laugh. "Who was it who broke and entered . . . "

Richard raised a hand. "Forgive me. Let's just say that the two of you form a rather dangerous combination. You attract trouble."

"We go a long way towards ending it, too," Briggie reminded him. "It wasn't you who found Alex's dad's killer . . . "

Charles, Alex could see, was beginning to be amused in spite of himself. She beckoned to him to sit next to her on the bed. "You must make Richard see that we've been behaving with prudence and circumspection."

Charles took the place offered him. "They've been models of decorum. It's the cursed fortune that's the problem."

Nodding, Richard seated himself in a wing chair next to the mammoth stone fireplace. "I was afraid it might be," he said seriously. "Large estates have a nasty effect on families."

"I'm not at all convinced the murderer is within the family, *per se*," Charles told him. "Although I'm not denying the money has brought out the worst in some of us."

"Who do you suppose murdered your cousin, then?"

"The Frenchman, Etienne Guison."

"And why would he do such a thing?"

"There's some thought that perhaps he's an illegitimate connection, but I admit we haven't any evidence."

Briggie intervened. "Actually, there is some new evidence since we saw you last. If Etienne's guilty, he has an accomplice in the family." Briggie explained about the theft of Philippa's research. "Etienne wouldn't have had access to a key, and the house wasn't broken into," she concluded.

Stricken, Charles objected, "I still can't believe it! No one in my family would want to murder Philippa!"

"Our theory is that someone thought she could prove Joe Cuendet was someone other than Joseph Borden," Alex said gently. "Whoever it was killed her and destroyed all the evidence."

"But . . . she would have told someone about news of that kind! I mean, she would have been tremendously excited if she had found out who Grandfather was!"

"She tried to tell your uncle at breakfast, but he was in a hurry to leave for the courts. Presumably she did tell someone else, and that someone killed her."

"Wait," Charles put up his hands. "Why would anyone need to kill her? We didn't even know about Joseph Borden until you told us last night."

"Someone must have known."

"The Frenchman knew."

"Yes, but he didn't have a key."

Rising, Charles began to pace the room. "John. It would have to be John. He knew Etienne. He's also the person Philippa would have called."

"But John doesn't need the money," Alex objected. She explained to Richard about Olivia's enormous income. "Unless he's planning on leaving his wife."

Charles looked uncomfortable. Sitting down in a chair some distance from Alex, he lapsed into silence, his arms folded across his chest.

"You have no problem accusing him of murder, but when it comes to a little hanky-panky you have to stick together, isn't that right?" Alex challenged.

He scowled but didn't answer.

"An Englishman's conscience is a thing of wonder," Alex remarked. "How was the flight, Richard?"

The lawyer was leaning forward in his chair. "Can we go back a bit?" he queried. "Why would this Etienne Guison want to murder Philippa Cuendet?"

"As Charles said, there's the theory that he might think he's descended from Joseph Borden, too, on the wrong side of the blanket," Briggie told him.

"If it's true, there ought to be evidence somewhere," Alex elaborated. "You know, a premature birth recorded in the parish register, that sort of thing."

"It seems like a trip to France is in order," Charles said decisively.

"Just so you understand there's no way Etienne could have acted alone," Briggie cautioned, looking up from the descendancy chart she was making for Richard.

Charles sighed wearily. "Look, ladies. I don't think I'll stay for dinner after all. I'm no longer hungry. Richard, be a good chap and eat my lamb chops, would you?"

———————

It took the entire mealtime to bring the lawyer up to speed, and when they had finished, he remarked, "Well, you two certainly didn't waste time setting the cat among the pigeons."

Briggie objected. "It's not our fault they're inclined to murder each other. I don't like this case. These aren't the kind of people I understand."

"Why is that?" Richard wanted to know.

"Briggie is feeling a little threatened by Oxford," Alex told him.

"I'm out of my element," Briggie complained. "These Cuendets make me uneasy."

Richard reflected. "I think Charles is a bit high-strung."

"You're on the wrong track there, Richard," Alex assured him. "Apparently, the murdered woman was the love of his life."

The lawyer looked at her, obviously amused. "You seriously

underestimate your charms, my dear. Now, tell me. Who did it?"

"I really haven't the least idea, " Alex replied, sighing.

"That's what I mean about this case," Briggie said. "No one seems like a murderer. And yet, they all have a motive. It's dangerous. Like someone sneaking up on you."

Richard folded his napkin and laid it neatly beside his empty plate. "So the idea is, we stage this little dinner tomorrow night, and the Frenchman sits at a nearby table, waiting to recognize the murderer?"

Nodding, Alex went over to the vanity where she inspected her still-white face. "But first there's the inquest to be gotten through. I wonder if they'll call Etienne as a witness? Maybe he'll recognize someone right there in the courtroom."

"That would be suitably dramatic," Richard said.

After the lawyer had gone to his room, and Briggie retired to bed, Alex lay awake, trying to absorb what had happened that day. Whenever she closed her eyes for just an instant, she flashed back to the moment when she had been trapped in the headlights of the would-be murder car. As her mind replayed the terror, her heart slammed into high gear, and she felt a cold sweat break out on her body. Then, mercifully there was the saving grip of Dr. Lasswell, and relief engulfed her in a wave of sweetness. She was going to live. By the grace of God, she was going to live.

Rolling over onto her side, Alex stared at the moonshadows that wavered in the silver light coming in through the window. Since Stewart's death she had known that life was unbelievably fragile, but this was the first time since then she was glad to be alive. The feeling of being left behind was gone. She was going on alone.

TWELVE

The surroundings for the inquest were a surprise. Alex had expected a dark, paneled courtroom with a steep gallery, reminiscent of the Old Bailey. But Oxford's legal setting was streamlined and modern. In a room of subdued grays and pale woods, the coroner sat on a very modern bench and presided over a disappointingly dull proceeding.

Alex was called to recount her story. She told it briefly and was not asked to elaborate.

Then another witness, a short blonde woman with a refined BBC accent, gave her account.

"I felt someone push her from behind. Miss Cuendet was standing shoulder to shoulder with me. I felt the impact. Then I saw her pitch forward. But I was so shocked when she fell under the bus, I didn't think to look for the person who pushed her until too late. When I turned around, all I saw was a crowd of horrified people."

"And you have no idea who pushed her?"

"None. There was a crowd around us, waiting to cross. The only one I remember was a tall dark man in a business suit." She scanned the courtroom. "I don't see him here, but he went along with me to the police station. I believe he was French."

Following the blonde, there was a hushed conference between the coroner and Chief Inspector Hubbard. Etienne was called but failed to appear. The chief inspector left the courtroom briefly, only to reenter it, shaking his head. In the end, the inquest was adjourned without proffering a verdict.

"I wonder where the Frenchman got to," Hannah mused. "I certainly hope the police haven't lost him."

Alex wondered, too, but she said nothing.

"Why don't I take you and your friends back with me to the house for lunch? Nothing formal, of course, but how do sausages and omelettes sound?"

"Delicious," Alex told her.

"I have the Range Rover, so there will be plenty of room."

Hannah and Frederick's house was not right in Oxford but up a high-hedged lane on a hillside overlooking the university. Alex reflected that there must be lots of money somewhere in the family. Covered with vines, the old stone farmhouse looked centuries old, and obvious pains had been taken on the inside to foster that feeling.

"We have done a lot of restoration work since we moved in," Hannah told her. "At first, I didn't think I'd even get Frederick to allow me a modern kitchen. That's the worst of being married to an archaeologist!"

Briggie was examining the diamond-shaped panes of the leaded glass windows. "These look like they're out of a fairy tale," she said.

"Yes. They're original to the house. As a matter of fact, I think it was the mullioned windows that seduced Frederick."

Richard examined the bookshelves. "Who is the E. M. Forster fan?" he inquired.

"Oh, that's me. I can safely say that I have everything he wrote and everything that was ever written about him. I read modern literature at Somerville, and Forster was my speciality."

"The greatest writer in the twentieth century," Richard pronounced. "Seriously overlooked until Merchant Ivory Productions took him in hand. Did you see *Howard's End?*"

"Yes. I loved it. It's not often a film will live up to the original material. Of course, Emma Thompson is a genius. Now," she said, holding up a photograph, "I must acquaint you with my children."

Alex took the framed picture and looked at the three children in it. They all wore white shorts and sweaters as though they had just come in from a game of tennis. Long and lanky like Hannah, the two boys had her chestnut hair and dark eyes. The girl was nut brown like her father, squinting into the sun and grinning for all she was worth.

"They look like a happy crew," Alex remarked. "They play tennis?"

"Yes. We have a grass court in the garden. In the holidays this house is packed to the rafters with their friends. They're at school now, of course. I'm afraid I miss them terribly, which is rather un-British of me."

"It's only natural that a mother should miss her children," Briggie told her.

Hannah shrugged. "Most women seem to get along."

Because Frederick had a tutorial, there were only four of them at lunch. Over the omelettes, Hannah broached the subject of Alex's near miss. "The inspector knocked on our door at about ten o'clock last night. Frederick had scarcely gotten in from his lecture. I couldn't believe it when he told us someone had tried to run you down! What kind of a car was it?"

"Fast," Alex told her.

"It's insane! Are you absolutely certain it was connected to Philippa's murder?"

"Unless you have someone in Oxford who enjoys mowing down tourists in dark alleys."

"How do you know the driver saw you?"

Hannah's stare was so intense it made Alex uncomfortable. "Because when he missed me the first time, he turned around and tried again."

Hannah bit her bottom lip in consternation. "You didn't get a look at the driver?"

"No. I was blinded by the headlights."

"It must have been quite dreadful." Hannah returned to her lunch.

"It was. But I survived, at least. Philippa didn't."

"No. It's been a terrible shock about Philippa, enough to make me wish we'd never heard about this ghastly estate."

Alex nodded. "Charles agrees with you."

"Yes. Poor man. I think it's a case of not realizing what was before your nose until it was gone. A lot of his anger is with himself, I think."

"Her brother doesn't seem too grief stricken," Briggie interjected, breaking a roll and buttering it.

Hannah frowned into her cider glass. "You have to make allowances, I suppose. Edward has always been the *enfant terrible*. He's frightfully talented but unfortunately still unrecognized. He's a super-realist, you see, and most people think his paintings are no better than blown-up photographs. The worst part is that he minds terribly. He doubts himself, you see. He's not one of those cocky geniuses who can thumb his nose at the world. That's why he puts up the front."

"Is it only a front?" Alex wondered.

"I'm sure of it. Edward is actually a lot more thin-skinned than the rest of us." Hannah selected an apple from a fruit bowl in the center of the table and began to peel it. Alex imagined Edward's skin spiraling onto her hostess's plate. "He and Philippa didn't see eye to eye because she thought he ought to get a job and support his family. He interpreted that to mean that she doubted his ability to succeed. Nothing she could say reassured him. And she was doubly upset about the divorce, of course. With one brother dead and never having married herself, she was very close to Edward's children."

"He talked to us yesterday," Briggie recounted. "He didn't mention his sister once."

"He wouldn't," Hannah sighed. "I suppose he just went on about the estate, didn't he? He's in denial about Philippa. That's why he's concentrating so hard on the money, of course."

Richard was enjoying his omelette. "I am only beginning to master the ins and outs of this family," he said. "Tell me what you think of John Cuendet. He seems to be the dark horse."

"Yes. Charles told us he wasn't in Norway. Imagine constructing such a dodge to avoid telling your wife no! But they're like that, Olivia and John. He just wants to go his own way and do his research. She wants him to be famous, recognized. He was at one time. Before Victoria got sick, he was a prominent surgeon in London. He gave that up to go into AIDS research." Hannah shrugged. "Not that Olivia regrets that. If anything, she's more passionate about it than he is. More driven. She wants him to get publicity so he can get grants and so forth."

"Was she famous when they married?" Briggie wanted to know.

"Beginning to be. She's positively brilliant, isn't she? Every bit as brilliant as Emma Thompson, and she could be married to just about anyone, I suppose. But the only man she's ever loved is John. He doesn't smother her or try to tell her what to do. I think it rather intrigues her that he's so wound up in his career. It's a challenge for her, if you know what I mean."

"I thought her eyes looked terribly tragic," Alex said. "She reminded me a little of Jeanne Moreau in *Mata Hari*."

"Fancy your saying that! Moreau is her idol. Although I think she's surpassed her altogether. Victoria's death nearly killed her, but since she's gone back to the stage, she's been better than ever." Hannah paused to eat a sliver of apple. "It's John I worry about. Since Victoria's death, he's worn himself to a thread with his research. I think he feels he must single-handedly defeat this terrible disease. It's become a kind of one-on-one combat with him. I know grief is a normal process, but there's something a little unhealthy about John's grief."

Alex tried to imagine what Hannah would term "proper grief" and failed. She felt a sudden kinship with the doctor. After Stewart's death, his aunts had been convinced that the extent of her own grief was pathological.

"How is it unhealthy?" she inquired.

"They keep the child's room as a shrine. Olivia can't face it, but he spends a lot of time in there."

"Perhaps it helps him to cope. With the clinic he seems to be doing something healthy with his obsession. In time, that should help heal him."

"Perhaps," Hannah allowed. "But how can this continual probing of his sore spot be good for him?"

Alex sighed. How could she explain it? "Grief is a peculiar thing. It's hard to know what's 'good' for a person. The important thing right now is that he is still feeling, that he hasn't shut off his emotions. That can lead to severe depression. It's better to hurt."

"It's the injustice," Hannah said fiercely. "That's what was so hard for Olivia. Why should an innocent child die because some depraved drug addict polluted the blood bank?"

"It would make anyone tremendously angry."

"We were really worried about Livy for awhile. She feels everything so intensely, being an actress. Her rage was rather frightening."

"Was she hospitalized?" Briggie asked.

Hannah seemed to emerge from her memories abruptly, looking rather coldly at her guest. "Yes. I believe that's not unusual in the circumstances." For a moment Hannah was silent, and then once more she subjected Alex to her peculiarly intense scrutiny. "At the inquest Charles told me about your father and husband. It sounded quite horrid." Her deep voice was empathetic. "How on earth have you survived?"

Alex was irritated. Was Hannah a crepe hanger or something? She seemed to delight in discussing misfortunes. "A day at a time," Alex told her. "Tell me about Frederick's work. Do you go with him on his digs?"

Though she obviously didn't wish to leave the subject of Alex's grief, Hannah began talking about last summer's dig in the Middle East.

After luncheon, she led them into the sitting room where they arranged themselves on oversized couches that looked as though they were covered in burlap. "All this suspicion is really rather unfortunate, Alex. We're actually quite a nice family. I hope the children aren't going to suffer because of this. They're my chief concern. I've telephoned to their school, of course. But heaven only knows what the newspapers will say."

Richard, who had been uncustomarily silent, sympathized.

"The press can be rather irresponsible, I'm afraid. At least in England, the courtroom is still considered off-limits."

"Speaking of courtrooms," Hannah said, "I can't help thinking Monsieur Guison must be the guilty party, especially since he didn't turn up. I was anxious to get a look at him."

"Yes," Richard said. "That was strange. I confess I'm anxious to meet the fellow, too. Everyone's wishing this murder onto him, but Alex is convinced he didn't do it."

Hannah looked surprised, her eyebrows arching in her pale Madonna face. "I didn't know that."

"I had my eyes on him until the bus went by," Alex explained. "He didn't push anyone. Besides that, there's the break-in, or rather the un-break-in. Someone with a key got into Philippa's study and made off with all her research."

Winded, as though someone had just delivered her a body blow, Hannah was speechless for a moment. Then, "I didn't know about that." As she thought this over, a frown creased the skin between her eyes. "That changes the picture entirely, doesn't it? It *had* to be one of us. How utterly grim!"

Alex thought that of all those concerned, this woman seemed to be the only one who could accept that a member of her family might be a murderer. She looked from one of her guests to the other, clearly expecting more information.

"I know it's a bit odd under the circumstances, but you are going to join us for dinner tonight, aren't you?" Alex asked. "Richard is going to explain to everyone all the details about the estate."

"But I thought the identity wasn't proven yet. And doesn't this theft of Philippa's research give you pause? I mean, this break-in rather proves Briggie's theory, doesn't it? Philippa must have had some kind of proof of who her grandfather was. If that proof pointed to Joseph Borden, why would anyone steal it?"

Alex decided the best way to counter this question was with one of her own. "Did you ever meet Frederick's grandfather?"

"No. Frederick was just seventeen when he died."

"Do you happen to know the preparatory school where he taught?"

"It was Somerset Hill. Near Blenheim. Quite exclusive nowadays. Charles and Frederick both went there."

"I think we'll go down there this afternoon. There's a chance they might have some employment records or something else that can help us," Alex told her.

Their hostess sat back in her chair, folding her hands in her lap. "You never answered my question. What is the purpose of this dinner tonight?"

"I just want to meet the players, Mrs. Lamb," Richard said affably. "We may all be working together a long time."

"But that hasn't in fact been determined, has it?"

Alex had to hand it to the woman. Though fragile and ethereal-looking, she was as tenacious as a bulldog. Did Frederick ever find this an uncomfortable trait?

"Let's just call it a social occasion, then."

Hannah raised an eyebrow. "In rather poor taste, under the circumstances."

"Well," Briggie said, "You know Americans."

––––––––––

When Hannah dropped them at the hotel, Briggie talked Richard into taking a nap to fortify him against jet lag. "You'll want to be on your toes tonight, Richard. This bunch is really something. You look kind of green around the gills."

"Thank you, Brighamina," Richard said a little huffily. "I take it you don't want my company at this school you're going to visit."

"It's not that we don't want it. It's just that it might turn out to be a wild goose chase. There's no need for you to come. We'll bring copies of whatever we find."

Rather surprisingly, Alex thought, Richard allowed himself to be shooed upstairs by her partner. This marked a significant departure in their relationship. Richard was accustomed to being the "shooer." He had never been the "shooee" to her knowledge.

Consulting the concierge about the best way to get to Somerset Hill, they were told that a bus left hourly for Blenheim and vicinity from in front of the American Express office on St. Aldates. Alex went upstairs for her briefcase and insisted on calling Etienne's room before they left. No answer.

"I wonder where he is," Briggie mused. "I wouldn't have thought he'd miss the inquest for the world."

"He's a dramatic type, Briggs. He's probably reserving his appearance for tonight when he can finger the murderer *à la* Hercule Poirot."

They set out on foot, walking down the oak-lined St. Giles' Street with St. Mary Magdalene's church sitting in its center like a dark medieval jewel. Soon they came to the intersection with Broad Street, where the thoroughfare changed character along with its name. It became the twentieth-century Cornmarket Street, alive with the whoosh of red and blue city buses, green and yellow open-topped tour buses, and swarms of shoppers laden with string bags dodging in and out of the chemist, the stationer, and the grocer. The modern store fronts always jarred Alex. There was even a McDonalds. As if to counteract all this unfettered modernity, looming over the next intersection was the ancient gray Norman keep, tall, crude, and solid, calling to mind knights and imprisoned princes. This corner—Carfax—had been the busiest place in Oxford for twelve hundred years. Presently it was a collision of ancient stone and modern steel, businessmen with their rolled umbrellas and students with backpacks, zigzagging cars and bold pedestrians. The air was rich with diesel fumes and something else—a sweet smell peculiar to Oxford that Alex could never identify.

From Carfax on, the street was called St. Aldate's and assumed an important character as the residence of banks, the golden neoclassical structure of the Oxford Town Hall, and the post office. It was the building next to the latter that housed the American Express. Alex and Briggie stood dutifully at the bus stop, observing the bustle around them.

"What do you think of Hannah after our lunch today?" Briggie asked.

"There's money somewhere," Alex remarked. "Old farmhouses like that cost a fortune to buy and remodel. Not to mention maintenance. I'd never have thought a professor of archaeology could afford a place like that." After a moment's silence, she continued. "I hate this investigation. Here I've been looking for family all my life and I meet some perfectly charming people I'd be delighted to call cousins, and I'm forced to suspect all of them not only of murdering Philippa but of trying to murder me!"

Briggie sighed. "I think this is our bus."

————————

Somerset Hills looked like something out of a landscape by Turner—a handsome house of Cotswold stone set on a hill surrounded by several noble cedars of Lebanon against a dramatically clouded November sky. A shaft of light shot through the clouds directly onto the golden façade, giving the school a magical appearance. It had obviously been a very grand home at one time.

A maid in apron and cap answered the front door and directed them to the administration wing, where a competent redhead in a forest green suit introduced herself as Miss Cooper and inquired about their business.

Alex explained, "We're professional genealogists, and we're trying to prove the identity of a man who was once employed here. His children and grandchildren may have a claim on an American estate. The man was American, but he had lost his memory and never recovered it. We thought perhaps that if the school retained any personnel records, we might be able to have a look at them to see if there is any clue there."

"Fascinating," the woman remarked. "You have identification, I assume?"

Alex fished in her briefcase for a business card and the contract Richard had prepared hiring them to make inquiries on behalf of the Joseph Borden estate. The woman glanced at them briefly and then returned them to her.

"When would this Joseph Borden have been employed here?"

"If he is who we hope he is, he came after the First World War. He went by the name of Joe Cuendet."

"Excuse me for a moment." Miss Cooper left them to enter a room that opened off her office. They heard file drawers being opened and shut. Briggie wrinkled her nose. The room smelled strongly of stale cigarette smoke.

The woman returned. "This is all we have," she told them, handing over an old reddish-brown cardboard file.

THIRTEEN

The file consisted of a series of memos:

Memorandum
10 Oct 1920
To: Headmaster
From: James Craddock
Re: Cuendet
The man is obviously a gentleman, albeit an American. His French is impeccable, with little trace of an accent. He has married into an old and respected French family in Lorraine. I have been in touch with them, and they have nothing to say against him.

Aside from his amnesia, caused by a very obvious head wound on his right temple, he appears to be in good shape mentally. No apparent shell shock or other physical or mental disorders. I recommend we hire him, as he is the best applicant who has presented himself. As you know, sir, there are few to choose from.

Memorandum
12 Oct 1920
To: Craddock
From: Rupert Collins, Headmaster
Re: Cuendet
I appreciate your evaluation. One thing concerns me. How do we know this fellow wasn't a deserter? I would hesitate to hire anyone who would in any way lower the moral tone of the school.

We have a responsibility to the parents of our charges not to subject them to potentially harmful influences. If there is any defect in this man's character, it would be far more serious than a defect in his French grammar.

Memorandum
10 November 1920
To: Headmaster
From: James Craddock
Re: Cuendet

The applicant does know his military unit, it seems. The Moreau family, who took him in when they found him wandering without papers, says he was part of Company I, 167th Infantry, which was billeted in their village. He wore the uniform of a private. I have written to the Moreau family to ask where and how they found him. Translated, their reply reads, "He was wandering in a fever by the side of the river. He was in a state of collapse. His uniform was dirty, his head bandage had obviously not been changed in many days. All the Americans had left a week before. He had no papers. He was so ill, we took him home to nurse him. When he was well, he tried to find out from the war office who he was, but all was in confusion. Soon he fell in love with Marcelle Cuendet. Her parents were against the match, of course, because they did not know his identity. They tried to correspond with the war office and were likewise unsuccessful. There were many people missing and taken prisoner in the final days of the war. They suggested the family should wait for a year until things should sort themselves out. Joe and Marcelle did not want to wait, so they took the only part of her dowry they could get their hands on (a pre-war silverware setting for sixteen) and eloped to England where we presume they were married. Eventually, we sent the rest of her dowry to them. As far as we know, that is all the money they have in the world."

I have a letter on its way to the American war office now. There may be a delay before we hear from them, but I recommend that we hire Cuendet at once. Men like him are few, and we have not interviewed anyone nearly as competent.

Memorandum
12 Nov 1920
To: Craddock
From: Rupert Collins, Headmaster
Re: Cuendet

I am aware that we are in urgent need of a French tutor. However, I should like to wait until we hear from the American War Office.

I should feel much better about the situation had he been an officer. Also, his willingness to live off his wife's dowry is a strike against him in my book.

Memorandum
12 Dec 1920
To: Headmaster
From: James Craddock
Re: Cuendet

I have just received a communication from the war office. They have informed me that they do not have the personnel to do a search as you suggest. It would entail searching the records of all the privates in Company I and trying to locate them. They tell me Cuendet's story is a credible one; as you know, there was great confusion during the demobilization. We have no alternative but to hire a researcher in the States, or to believe Cuendet's story. I strongly advise the latter course.

As for his willingness to live on his wife's money, the man is most desperate to remedy the situation as soon as possible. Not working at a job clearly runs against the grain with him.

Memorandum
14 Dec 1920
To: Craddock
From: Rupert Collins, Headmaster
Re: Cuendet

We will hire Cuendet on a per course basis to begin with. If he should prove satisfactory, we will offer him a contract.

There followed a carbon copy of a contract to teach French at Somerset Hill School, dated 7 Jun 1921. Unfortunately, the signatures did not appear on the copy.

"Blast!" Briggie said. "I thought for certain there would be something in his handwriting."

"Briggie," Alex said thoughtfully as she dug through her briefcase for Joseph Borden's military records, "I think this may help anyway . . . Yes," she said. "That's the right unit. Joseph Borden was in Company I, 167th infantry. The only problem was that he was a lieutenant, not a private."

"Hmm," Briggie responded. "Do you think we could have a photocopy of these records, Miss Cooper? They may be extremely important in the probate case we're working on. We'll be happy to pay for them."

Obviously interested, the woman's blue eyes were alive with questions she was too well bred to ask. "I'm glad we could help. I love mysteries. You two are rather like detectives, aren't you?"

Briggie laughed. "Some days we're pretty sharp. It's a lot of fun except when someone's trying to kill us."

Miss Cooper's eyes widened. "Kill you?"

"Briggie," Alex said, shaking her head. "It's time to go."

They discussed their find in the bus on the way back to Oxford.

"Philippa had hired a researcher to look at the military records. What would you have done if you were in her shoes, Briggie?"

"If she knew Joe Cuendet's company and rank, she probably would have asked them to search for anyone who went AWOL at the end of the war."

"Exactly." Alex looked at her watch. "It's four thirty. The St. Louis Personnel Records Center will just have opened. Let's give them a call when we get back to the hotel."

The Records Center referred them to Will Mahoney, a twentieth century military historian in Washington, D.C. Placing a call to him, Alex outlined their problem.

"The best thing to do," Mr. Mahoney told them, "would be

to access the morning reports for the unit. They're in the public domain and that would be the only record of an AWOL soldier that I know of for the American Expeditionary Force. Do you have his unit?"

"Yes. I'm in England at the present time. Could you give me the name of a researcher who could do this for me?"

"I'd get Morris Truebody. He's a military records researcher here in town."

"Could you please give me Mr. Truebody's telephone number?"

"His home number is all I have. He does research all day in various places. You can probably find him home tonight." He gave the number. Alex thanked him and hung up, punching the air with her fist. "With any luck we'll find out who Philippa's man was in a day or two. Poor Joseph Borden. They didn't have historical archivists in 1920. You can imagine what the army records must have been like . . . "

"Well, call this Mr. Truebody, for heaven's sake," the older woman commanded.

"I'll try. But Mr. Mahoney said he'd be out researching during the day."

He was. There was only an answering machine. Rather than trying to tell the machine her complicated tale, Alex hung up. "Let's see, there's five hours' difference between here and Washington. When we get through with our dinner tonight it's going to be about . . . say ten o'clock. It'll be five o'clock there. Let's try again at eleven, and if he's still not in, at eleven thirty."

"Sounds good. I think we should celebrate. Do you think they have hot fudge sundaes on the room service menu?"

Alex wore the one and only skirt she had with her for the dinner party. It was an old denim one, and she wished for the umpteenth time that she had known the kind of company she would be keeping when she packed her duffle. At least her white turtleneck was clean. Running a long-fingered pick through the tiny ringlets of her hair, she suddenly decided to pull it back off her face. That at least would give her a more formal look. Twisting it into a ponytail, she called through to Briggie, "What are you going to wear?"

"My cranberry thing. I don't have anything else."

Dinner had been set for seven-thirty, but by the time all her cousins had arrived, it was nearly eight o'clock.

"My dear, I understand you had a near escape last night," the judge said at her elbow.

Turning, she saw the concern in his gentle brown eyes. "Yes. It was pretty awful."

"If you'd gone the way of Philippa . . ."

Alex put a restraining hand on his arm. "Let's not even talk about it."

"Do the police have any ideas?"

"No. I didn't give them much to go on. I couldn't see anything. The car's lights were too bright."

Antonia had joined them. "Alex, I have a very sensible suggestion. Why don't you just go back to the States and let Mr. Grinnell handle the whole thing now that he's here?"

The older woman was very matter-of-fact, even serene. It occurred to Alex that her suggestion made of lot of sense . . . from the murderer's point of view.

"Then the murderer would just have to get rid of Briggie, wouldn't he?"

Seeing the stricken look on Antonia's face, Alex repented immediately.

"Thanks for your concern, Antonia, but I'm not going anywhere," she said, trying to smile. "Excuse me, will you?"

As she introduced Richard to those who hadn't met him, Alex kept a sharp eye out for Etienne. Either he wasn't there yet, or he was being extremely discreet. Her heart accelerated as her anxiety level bumped up a notch.

"So," Charles asked her, "How did you spend your afternoon?"

"I thought you weren't going to come," Alex replied.

Extremely charming in a white dinner jacket, he looked at her with a gleam in his eye and took hold of her elbow. "Someone has to make sure no one puts poison in your soup."

Alex grinned. "I feel much safer already."

Turning to Olivia who was still bundled in her wool overcoat, she asked, "Are you cold? Are you not feeling well?"

The woman looked pinched and miserable. She rolled her large brown eyes. "I'm coming down with some beastly bug or another, I think. John insisted that we come. I'm glad for him if your man should turn out to be his grandfather, of course. But I don't really care about all this."

"Did you have a performance scheduled?"

"My understudy has taken over for me since Philippa's death. After the funeral, I'll go back." She laid a hand on Alex's arm and her deep, sad eyes registered concern. "I understand you had a close call last night. I must say I feel as if it's my fault, Alex. I should have sent the car for you. It never occurred to me you'd be on foot."

"And you certainly couldn't have known there was a maniac lying in wait."

"Have you any idea who it was? What about Monsieur Guison?"

Alex shrugged. "It could have been anyone. Why don't we talk about something else. What are you performing at the moment?"

"*Hamlet!*" Her face lit up and transformed. "You must come and see it before you go. The director is mad, of course—they all are, trying to get a new slant on poor old Shakespeare after five hundred years. The lead plays a positively psychotic Hamlet, running around in dirty pajamas, but you won't want to miss my King Claudius."

"You're Queen Gertrude, I assume?"

"Right. And Timothy Dalton is my dearly beloved. Have you heard of him?"

"Ummm," Alex replied. "My favorite 007."

John joined them then, laughing. "He's much better in

Shakespeare. Livy detests *Hamlet,* but she couldn't pass up a chance to play opposite him. I must say, I'm a bit jealous."

Olivia glowed.

"What's he like?" Alex asked.

"Difficult, but absolutely marvelous." The actress related an anecdote with some passion. "He's tremendously intense. Of course, one gets used to that in this business, but with him it's not narcissism as it so often is. He genuinely worships Shakespeare."

"How are you feeling today?" John inquired of Alex eventually.

"Completely recovered. And I have two bodyguards now that Richard's come, so I'm certain I'll be safe from harm."

"Any luck on the great ancestor hunt?"

"We're a step closer, I think. We made some inquiries today at the school where your grandfather taught. He was in the same unit as Joseph Borden in the war."

"It's looking better and better then, isn't it?"

Richard came up to her. "Is this everyone, then?"

Alex ran a quick eye over the family. Yes. They were all here. She nodded.

"Let's just go into the dining room," the lawyer suggested to everyone in his well-modulated courtroom voice.

Bringing up the rear, Alex was amused to see Richard play the host. He couldn't help it. He just naturally took control of every situation he found himself in. She was relieved, actually. By the end of the evening, one of these people would be in police custody, God willing. Playing hostess seemed suddenly hypocritical to her. After all, one of them had tried to kill her.

John managed to seat himself at her right. Charles was sticking close on her left. After they had studied the menu and given their orders, John began quizzing her.

"So you're getting really close, it sounds like. What's next?"

"Tonight we're calling a military researcher in Washington, D. C. We were very lucky to get on to him."

"Does it look like Grandfather was Joseph Borden, then?"

"Well, there is a discrepancy, actually. When your grandfather was found, he had on a private's uniform. Joseph Borden was a lieutenant."

"Hmm. That doesn't sound good."

"But Joseph Borden's record also shows him as invalided out, not AWOL. There's a mistake somewhere."

There was a pause in the conversation while the waiter placed bowls of soup. When they returned to their discussion, John asked, "What about this Frenchman everyone's talking about? The one who didn't show up at the inquest?"

Charles broke in at this point, "The ubiquitous Monsieur Guison. Tell us, John, did you do a bicycle tour near Bar-le-Duc? Are you the one who met him?"

John unfolded his napkin and placed it in his lap. Tugging slightly at his beard, he answered, "Yes. Olivia asked me about that. It must have been me, although I can't say I remember him at all." He gave a short burst of laughter. "Fancy him remembering me after all this time!"

"He was impressed by your bicycle gear," Alex told him.

The doctor grinned. "Bicycling is great fun. But Olivia's much too fragile to do anything like that. We generally do a cruise or something that's meant to be relaxing. She gets completely burnt out in her work, but I can never relax, unless I'm doing something physically demanding. Too much adrenaline, I guess."

"Did you enjoy your visit to the chateau?"

"Very much. Uncle Roland was charming to me. What's this fellow's name who claims to have met me?"

"Guison. Etienne."

"He's a connection of the Cuendets?"

"Not for certain," Charles answered. "But he may be. Hannah hypothesizes that he might be illegitimately descended from Grandfather. Alex doesn't know whether she buys it or not. Did you bring it up with Monsieur Guison, Alex, or did you find the subject too delicate?"

"I haven't seen him," she answered shortly.

"The police haven't found him yet?"

"Oh, don't worry. He hasn't disappeared. He's probably just been in London. He has business there, you know."

At that moment, a waiter approached her. "Pardon me, Madame, but you have an urgent telephone call. You may take it in the lobby."

Surprised, Alex excused herself. When she got to the lobby, however, she found Chief Inspector Hubbard waiting for her and decided the telephone call must have been a convenient fiction. Pacing the Persian carpet, he looked harried and preoccupied.

"Mrs. Campbell, when was the last time you spoke to Monsieur Guison?"

"Isn't he in the dining room?"

"No."

She frowned. "The last time I saw him was yesterday morning. I've telephoned him, but he hasn't been in."

"He was in," the inspector contradicted grimly, "but incapable of answering the telephone."

"What do you mean?"

"I'm afraid your Frenchman is dead."

FOURTEEN

Stabbed to death," the inspector told her. "More than twenty-four hours ago."

Alex pulled at the turtleneck that seemed suddenly to constrict her throat. "No," she whispered.

The inspector steadied her with a firm hand. "Suppose we sit down." Leading her to a nearby couch, he sat down beside her. "Now, I realize what a shock this must be, but we need your help. When you feel like it, I'd like you to go back to your dinner party."

"How can I?" she demanded flatly. "This is horrible. One of them murdered him!"

Her thoughts were spinning out of control. How long was this going to go on? Someone had to make it stop. She squeezed her eyes shut.

He patted her shoulder clumsily. "We'll see this through, Mrs. Campbell. Steady."

"I just can't believe it."

The inspector was silent. She felt clammy all over. She had to pull herself together.

"One of those Cuendets killed him," she said dully. "Whoever did it is in there now. In the dining room. Eating. Knowing he's upstairs. Dead."

"Yes."

Suddenly, Alex was filled with rage. It started in her jaw and spread to her whole body until she was rigid with it. "This has got to stop! I'm going to burn that horrible money!"

"It would be far more satisfactory if you were to help us catch this murderer."

Alex made her way back into the dining room. The rage had passed, leaving her numb. She felt as though she were in a dream, struggling against a heavy current. Nothing seemed real, but it all seemed terribly difficult.

Charles greeted her with a raised eyebrow. She chose to ignore it. One of these people was a double murderer. Taking her seat, she scanned their faces.

Edward was deep in discussion with Richard at the head of the table. She had no doubt of the subject of their conversation. Money.

Briggie was regaling Frederick and Hannah with a lively bout of genealogy war stories. At the foot of the table sat Antonia, conversing quietly with her brother Philip. Alex, seated in the middle, could not hear their conversation. Olivia had lapsed back into her pinched silence. John was merely eating.

It all seemed perfectly normal, perfectly innocent. It was impossible that one of these people could have tried to run her down, could have pushed Philippa under a bus, could have quietly disposed of Etienne. Whoever it was must lead a double life. That seemed the only explanation.

"Well, Alex," Charles said, "you're looking grim. Trying to decide which one of us is a murderer?"

"It's not a joke," she told him.

She faced him squarely. Charles had made no bones about hating Etienne. Had he killed him in a rage, believing him to be Philippa's murderer?

No. This man beside her couldn't have done that. Those long, sensitive fingers could never stick a knife into anyone.

His look was mocking, bitter. A new thought sailed perversely into her consciousness, startling her with its clarity. *Charles had been in the hotel last night, in her room talking to her.* Had he gone from her room to Etienne's? No, he wouldn't have been carrying a knife around with him. Whoever did this had planned it all out ahead of time. It couldn't have been Charles.

Swallowing with difficulty, she answered. "Let's not talk about this anymore."

"You're worried, aren't you? What was that telephone call?"

"I'll tell you later," she said. "I don't want to talk about it right now."

After another quizzical look, Charles returned to his dinner.

John resumed their conversation. "Olivia and I were just talking about taking you and your partner to dinner Friday night after *Hamlet*. Do you think you can manage it?"

"I don't know, John. Something has come up . . . "

Olivia urged, "You must come. I was just telling John that I'm virtually certain I can talk Timothy into joining us."

The glass Olivia was holding slipped from her grasp and overturned on the table.

Deftly, John set it aright. "You mustn't get so excited over the fellow, Darling. You'll start a rumor in the tabloids."

Olivia laughed immoderately, causing Alex to wonder whether she'd had too much to drink.

When the main course had been cleared away, Alex stood. "There's coffee waiting for you upstairs in our suite. Richard can discuss the estate with you there in more detail."

She led the little crowd up the wide staircase to her room, her palms damp. Etienne's plan to identify the killer and his subsequent murder had put this evening's concerns on the back burner. They hadn't really planned on getting as far as a legitimate discussion. They had thought Etienne's identification of the murderer would break up the evening. What on earth was Richard going to say?

On entering the room, Alex saw that room service had complied with his request. Two silver coffee pots sat on a silver tray. Cups, spoons, sugar, and cream had been laid out neatly on the table. There were even extra chairs. Reminded of her mother's bridge parties, Alex stationed herself behind the coffee pot and began taking orders. It was steadying to have something concrete to do. When everyone was seated, she nodded to Richard, who began.

"As you know, Alex's father recently died, leaving a considerable estate. I am counsel for that estate. In her efforts to find his murderer, Alex uncovered the fact that her father actually had no clear title to his inheritance. His father, Edward Borden, had succeeded to the original estate when Joseph Borden was presumed dead. I won't go into the details of how this came to be—it's an extremely complicated story. Suffice it to say that Alex, as a professional genealogist, volunteered to go to France to try to find evidence of Joseph Borden's death. You know what she found: You.

"Now, in order for us to prove that Joseph Borden was in fact Joe Cuendet, we will need help from you. Anything you have that might be written in Joe Cuendet's handwriting would be very valuable. For instance, does anyone know what became of the marriage license?"

Richard was extemporizing brilliantly. Briggie must have coached him, Alex reflected.

Judge Cuendet spoke. "I have been wondering about that myself. In the event that identity is proven, we'll need all the vital documents, won't we? Marriage licenses, birth certificates, everything."

"That's true. Do you have any idea where your father kept his important papers?"

"In a safety deposit box, which I emptied at his death. I was his executor. The signed original of his will is at the solicitors, I suppose. All the rest of the things I gave to Philippa to help in her research. They've been taken."

"The will is gone, too, I'm afraid," John told them. "I collected it from the solicitor about a year ago, and Philippa was keeping it. We had the same idea about handwriting. Even then we were trying to figure out how to get to his military records. We had considered the idea of flying to the States and going through the records of everyone in his company to try to get a handwriting match."

The discussion of genealogical detail had drawn Alex out

of her preoccupation. "I have an idea," she said suddenly. "I think it will be possible to get a sample of his signature, Richard."

"How?" John demanded.

"On second thought, I don't believe I'm going to say anything," Alex replied. "Too much evidence is missing already."

She felt Charles's eyes on her, and she looked down at her lap.

At this point, the door of Briggie's bedroom opened, and Chief Inspector Hubbard entered the room.

"What is this?" Charles demanded.

"Mrs. Campbell is not responsible for my presence," the inspector said, holding up a hand. "I am here because there has been another murder. A murder committed by one of you."

This was the scene Alex had been asked to orchestrate. For a moment the room was absolutely silent. Chief Inspector Hubbard, accompanied by the freckled Sergeant Higgins, stood surveying the Cuendet family. Each policeman shifted his gaze from one face to another.

"The Frenchman," Charles spoke finally. "That's why he wasn't at the inquest."

The heavy silence following this remark was broken by a shrill laugh. Olivia, her face a caricature of horror, was hysterical, staring at Charles with blank eyes. John quickly took her in hand. Going to her chair, he knelt by her side and took her face in his hands, "Livy . . . " She shook him off, looking down into his face as though she didn't recognize it.

The policeman chose to ignore the outburst. "Correct, Mr. Lamb. If I'm not mistaken, you knew that Monsieur Guison was staying in this hotel?"

"Yes. As a matter of fact, I did." Charles returned the Inspector's scrutiny coolly, likewise ignoring the actress.

"Did you tell anyone else?"

"My mother and uncle knew, but surely . . . "

"Mrs. Lamb," the inspector cut in, "Did you tell anyone of the whereabouts of Monsieur Guison?"

"Why," Antonia began, white-faced and flustered, "I believe I mentioned it to my son, Frederick."

"Mr. Frederick Lamb? Did you communicate Monsieur Guison's whereabouts?"

"To my wife . . ."

"And I told John," Hannah contributed.

"Who presumably told his wife?"

John nodded. Olivia's face was drained of color.

"Judge Cuendet?"

The judge hesitated. Finally, he said, "I told my son, Edward."

Inspector Hubbard sighed. "So. Everyone knew the man was staying here."

"But why would anyone murder him?" Olivia demanded shrilly.

"Because Etienne Guison was standing next to Miss Cuendet when she was pushed. It is more than likely he could have identified her murderer as one of the people who stood around him on the pavement. He had arranged to do just that. He was to have been in the dining room tonight."

Alex felt Charles's eyes on her. She looked at him squarely. "Yes. We arranged it together," she told him. Then she faced the room in general. "I hope this finally convinces you that Etienne was not Philippa's murderer."

She felt the family draw away from her in a body. All except Hannah, who stood up and came to her. "My dear, this is positively beastly for you."

"You all know that the murderer also made an attempt on Mrs. Campbell's life last night, presumably with the same intent," the chief inspector continued.

"I didn't see anything," Alex said tightly. "So whoever you are, you've got to believe that. If I had, you'd be in jail by now."

"It's that damned money!" Charles expostulated, looking at her bitterly.

Standing behind her, Hannah put her hands firmly on Alex's shoulders. "Alex has been through quite enough without your temper tantrums, Charles. It's a horrible thing, but it is clear now that this murderer is in our family. I think the best thing to do is to find out who it is before he or she kills anyone else."

"Yes," agreed the judge sadly. "Please, let's bring all this horror to an end. How was the man killed?"

"Stabbed."

Alex felt Hannah's hands convulse, clutching her shoulders.

"I can't believe anyone in this family would stab someone to death!" Antonia exclaimed, looking from one member of her family to another.

Seeing the sudden pallor of the judge's face, Alex reflected that in the last five minutes he seemed to have aged ten years. "He thinks Edward did it," she thought. Some of her anger died as pity leapt inside her.

Edward, she noticed for the first time, was sitting in an unobtrusive corner, sunk in a profound melancholy, nursing a drink he had apparently brought along from dinner. Surprisingly, he said nothing.

"When was the man killed?" Frederick asked.

"He's been dead more than twenty-four hours, at least since nine o'clock last night when we began trying to contact him to establish his alibi for Alex's accident. We won't have a more precise time of death until after the postmortem. I have your alibis from five o'clock on because of the incident with Mrs. Campbell. Now I want your actions from noon until five."

Alex knew she needed to pay attention, but all at once she felt weary and sick. She couldn't bear the tension for another moment. Standing, she walked into Briggie's bedroom, closed the door, and lay down on the bed. Muffled voices filtered through to her, but they were indistinct.

Another death. And someone in that room—someone she had sat with, talked with, eaten with—was a murderer. Someone had taken a knife and brutally stabbed Etienne. That same someone had attempted to murder her with an automobile.

Her mind refused to take it in. It was like a lead shield had gone up. Dissociation, Daniel called it.

It was just as well. She didn't want another battle with her *Weltschmerz* now. Her life depended on finding this murderer.

Where had all this started?

With Philippa. Someone had told Philippa she was coming. Who? Etienne? If he had told someone, that could be another motive for his death. But why would he tell anyone? It didn't make any sense. He never would have told her the story about meeting John on the bicycle tour if he had been trying to keep his connection with the family a secret. And surely when he found out he was suspected of murder himself, he would have talked! One would think so, anyway. But perhaps it had been more complicated. They would never know what had gone on in Etienne's mind now. Did he think he was descended from Joe Cuendet? Or was he playing some convoluted game of his own?

The door opened slowly and Charles walked in. Alex sighed heavily and turned her face away from him.

"Alex, look at me."

"I hope you're satisfied," she said dully.

"Of Guison's innocence? Oh yes." His voice was hard. Sitting up, Alex faced him reluctantly. His features were grim and forbidding, a double crease marring his forehead. "Why did you come in here?" she demanded.

"Because I wanted to talk to you—to try to make some sense out of this. I simply can't believe anyone I know well . . ."

"Could be a murderer," she finished for him.

"Yes. It was abominable for me to blame you in any way for all of this. You have been nothing but generous with us."

"But if it weren't for me, Philippa would be alive," she continued harshly. "I know that. It hurts me every time I look at your face and realize what my coming here has done to you."

He reached out and cupped her set jaw in his hand. "Don't, Alex. We've each of us got to make our peace with this thing. The money was a catalyst. The evil was already there."

"But how is it possible for someone to be evil enough to kill and for no one to have any idea of it? All of you seem perfectly normal to me."

"I don't think we're going to get anywhere by analyzing personalities. I've been thinking. The key to this whole thing is that someone told Philippa you were coming."

"Right. I've gotten that far myself. If it were Etienne, maybe that was an additional motive for his murder. But I would have thought that as soon as he knew he was suspected, he would have told us if there had been a connection. He was desperate to prove his innocence. That was why I cooperated with him over tonight's program."

"I see that. Whom did you talk to in France besides Guison? There must have been someone. John knew everyone in the chateau."

"Yes, but the only person we met there was Simone. She would have been an infant when John visited. While we were there, her parents were in Paris and her grandfather was in Italy."

"But surely she would have communicated with them? You had gone a long way toward solving the family mystery, after all!"

"Of course!" Alex struck her forehead. "And everyone in the chateau knows your family! Briggie did mention something like this in the first place when she concocted her theory. We've been working on the genealogy end when we probably should have been paying more attention to the living."

Briggie entered the room, concern furrowing her brow. "Are you all right?" she asked Alex.

"Fine," she told her. "At least better. We were just about to decide to get in touch with Simone. Remember the original idea you had about someone in the family over there contacting someone over here?"

"As I recall, you hardly gave it a second's thought. Charles kept insisting it was Etienne who was the link," Briggie said. "I think we half believed him."

"Briggie, we've called another truce. I've apologized," Charles told her. "I think a trip to France is in order."

"Don't you think a telephone call would suffice?" Alex asked.

"There are other things that need explaining that we should attend to here," Briggie agreed. "We need to find out what it was that Philippa had found out about Joe Cuendet. That would give us our motive for sure. It will also help us with our original job, which keeps getting lost in all of this. We could put through our call to the States right now, Alex."

"Then there's Etienne's story," Alex mused as though she hadn't heard. "Do we accept that he came here on account of my blue eyes, or did he have another motive?"

Charles remained silent. Briggie shrugged. "We probably *would* have to go to France to check that one out. Look in the parish records and so forth. Do you think it matters now?"

"Briggie! Etienne was just murdered!"

"Because he could identify Philippa's murderer," she reminded her.

"We don't know that for certain. He could have been playing some kind of game of his own. I think it's important that we find out."

Briggie got her notebook out of the desk. "Let's make a list."

"Number one: Call chateau re Philippa's informant," Charles suggested.

"Number two: Call the military researcher in the States re who went AWOL from I Company," Briggie added. "Number three: Get specimen of Joe Cuendet's handwriting. You said you had an idea about that, Alex."

"Yes." She looked at Charles. "When is Philippa's funeral?"

"Tomorrow at half past ten."

"We'll go down to London afterwards, Briggie." She glanced at Charles again.

"Are you going to tell me what's in London?" he asked.

"Can we rely on you to keep it to yourself?"

He frowned and stood up. "I forgot. I'm in the enemy camp, aren't I?"

"Charles, someone tried to murder Alex last night.

Someone did murder Etienne. And on top of that, someone's made off with all the genealogical evidence. It's not that we suspect you. It's just that you might let something slip. We'll tell you what we find when we find it," Briggie promised.

"Do you think you could negotiate the call to France for me now, Charles?"

"I think you should talk to them, Alex," Briggie countered. "You had the last contact."

"I'm not up to directory assistance and all that. If Charles will manage that, I can talk to Simone."

"Trying to make me feel useful?"

"Just do it, Charles, please."

Without further argument, he initiated the process of ascertaining the chateau's telephone number and placing the call. Soon Alex found herself holding the receiver to her ear, listening to the ring of a distant telephone without having given any thought to what she should say.

When the telephone was answered, presumably by a servant, she asked in English for Simone. After a delay of several minutes, she heard the French girl pick up the telephone.

"Simone, this is Alex Campbell calling from Oxford. I called on you a few days ago about Joe Cuendet?"

"Oh yes! How do you do, Alex?"

"Well, as a matter of fact, things aren't going too well here. One of your English cousins, Philippa Cuendet, was murdered the very day I arrived."

"No! How horrible!"

"We think it has something to do with the inheritance, but there is one problem. I had not contacted the family yet, so we don't see how anyone could have known about it. We were wondering if you or your parents or grandparents had talked to anyone in England after I spoke with you."

Simone was silent for a moment. "I didn't, but my parents are still in Paris. I told them your news when they rang me from there. I'm trying to think when that was." She paused. "Yes. It would have been the day after you were here. Sunday."

"That would have been the day before I arrived at Oxford. Do you have a number in Paris where I can reach them?"

"Certainly. Here it is." She read the number, and Alex copied it down. "This is a dreadful thing you have been telling me. You must take care, Alex."

"Yes," she told Simone. "I will. Thank you so much for your help."

When they dialed the Paris number, they were informed by a servant that Monsieur and Madame Cuendet were out. Alex left a message for the Cuendets to get in touch with her at the hotel.

"Well," Charles said thoughtfully. "It looks like we might be on to something."

"Maybe," Briggie agreed, "but most likely they won't call back until morning."

"Are you telling me it's time for me to leave, Briggie?"

She yawned. "It's been an awfully long day."

Alex rose and walked with Charles to the door, slipping out into the corridor with him. "The funeral's bound to be tough on you, Charles," she murmured.

He looked soberly into her eyes. "Don't worry about me, Alex. I'll be fine. It helps to have something else to think about."

"What about your work?"

"They've got someone covering for me at the newspaper for a few days. I canceled this week's tutorials. Are you sure you don't want some company when you go to London tomorrow?"

"You won't be in the mood for a trip to London. I wouldn't expect too much of yourself tomorrow."

He gazed at her a moment and then squeezed her shoulder. "I know I've behaved like an ungrateful whelp, Alex, but the truth is, I wouldn't be doing half as well as I am without your help. Good night."

Returning to the room, she swiftly stifled a tiny glow and found that Richard had entered from next door. Everyone else, apparently, had gone.

"Time for the two of you to go home," he announced. "This is getting far too dangerous."

"No," Alex told him. "We're going to see this through, Richard. We're going to London tomorrow and possibly France later in the week."

The lawyer raised his eyebrows.

"We've got to solve this thing now. Two murders and one close call are too much," she said grimly. "It's all part of this Cuendet-Borden puzzle."

"What's the trip to London for?" he asked.

"They have a nationwide index of marriages down there. If we get the name of the church where Joe and Marcelle were married, we should be able to see their signatures in the parish register."

Seating himself in the wing chair, the lawyer put his feet up on the ottoman. "Wouldn't John and Philippa have figured that out?"

"They already had handwriting samples. They had the original marriage license." Alex sighed, thinking of all the wonderful documentation that had now very likely gone up in smoke. "We'll have to make sure we take the camera."

"And France?" Richard queried.

"That depends on what we find out from the Bar-le-Duc Cuendets." Alex explained about the telephone call they were expecting from Paris. "If that doesn't lead anywhere, then we're going to look into Etienne's background and family and see if he did have some sort of vested interest in this thing. We've got to establish some link between here and Bar-le-Duc. When we do, we'll know how Philippa knew I was coming. That should lead us to the murderer."

Richard let out a gusty sigh. "I really don't understand why you can't leave France to me. I need to go over there anyway to interview Madame Guison."

Thinking of that formidable lady, Alex felt another wave of futile sadness. How would Genevieve react to Etienne's death? It had been clear how proud she was of her handsome great-grandson.

"I feel as though I owe it to the family and to Etienne to see this through, Richard. I started it all with that horrible money."

"That's enough of that," Briggie said tartly.

"Everyone had an alibi, I presume?" Alex asked Richard.

"Oh yes. Hannah and Frederick Lamb went to London yesterday. John was working. Olivia was at home with the ubiquitous housekeeper. The judge was on the bench, and . . . " Richard shut his eyes a moment in concentration. "Edward was in his studio. Apparently someone was sitting for a portrait. Antonia was in her garden without any witnesses, but then I can hardly see her stabbing anyone."

"Who do you think did it?" Alex asked.

"Frederick Lamb," the lawyer pronounced.

"*Frederick?* Why on earth . . . ?"

"Because he's the most unlikely?" Briggie guessed.

"No. Antonia is the most unlikely in my book. I think there are hidden depths to Frederick, though. He has the classic self-centeredness of a murderer. Does he always act as though the world's his oyster?"

"Well, yes. More or less." Alex admitted. "But if by some stretch of the imagination Frederick were guilty, that would make Hannah an accomplice if she's his alibi, and that I cannot accept."

"Because she's been kind to you?" the lawyer asked. "Don't be fooled by that, Alex. I think everything Hannah does is carefully calculated. She's an extremely intelligent woman."

"What does intelligence have to do with it, Richard? A woman can be intelligent without being dangerous."

"There's a certain cold-bloodedness about Hannah's intelligence . . . "

"Exactly!" Briggie pounced.

Alex regarded her friend in puzzlement. "What makes you say that? I think she's by far the warmest of all the Cuendets."

"The most outgoing, maybe," Briggie said. "But there's something not quite right. Have you noticed how willing she's been to tell us everyone's life history? That doesn't square with my idea of the British. Not that I know everything about them, of course."

"I don't think she's cold-blooded," Alex said. "I think she's simply realistic. What do you think she would do if she found out her husband was the murderer?"

Briggie pondered.

"Turn him in," Richard replied. "You're right, Alex. Whether you call it cold-blooded or realistic, she probably wouldn't tolerate Frederick's guilt."

"Under the right circumstances, she would," Briggie disagreed.

"What do you mean, Brighamina?"

"I think her children are the sun, the moon, and the stars to Hannah. I can't see her turning Frederick in when it would do them so much harm. No. I think she'd concentrate on muddying the waters, which is just what she's doing."

"While we're at it, is there anyone else you suspect?" Alex wanted to know.

"I think it's got to be John," her partner answered. "He doesn't have an alibi for the first murder. And if he thought you'd seen him on the pavement next to Philippa when he was supposed to be in Norway or London, that would give him a motive for murdering you before you ever met him. Olivia would give him an alibi like a shot for the second murder, and he's the one we know for certain has contacts with the chateau."

"Except for a complete lack of motive, that's fairly convincing," Alex agreed thoughtfully. "Very good, Briggie. I was going to say Mr. Rochester, but I think you've got me beat.

"Mr. Rochester?" Richard queried faintly.

"Briggie's got a thing for Edward," Alex explained. "He reminds her of a brooding gothic hero."

The lawyer looked at Alex's partner in some surprise. "I never suspected you of being a romantic, Brighamina."

Smoothing her hair, she grinned at him. "I'm sort of complex," she told him. "I have hidden depths."

Richard merely raised his eyebrows. "Speaking of brooding heroes, there's always Charles."

"Charles?" Alex repeated dumbly.

"You've got a soft spot for him, haven't you, Alex?" the lawyer asked, his eyes speculative.

"Are you kidding?"

"I may be wrong," Richard allowed, "but he strikes me as quite a romantic figure, speaking of brooding heroes."

Alex just rolled her eyes. "Are the two of you ganging up on me, or what?"

"I think Charles is fond of you, Alex," Briggie agreed. "But I think playing with Charles is playing with fire."

"Oh, please," Alex said with an elaborate sigh. "This really isn't a Barbara Cartland romance. It's a murder mystery if it's anything. And back to your original point, Charles is the last one who would have murdered Philippa. He didn't kill Etienne either. This is not *Clue*. These are real people we're talking about, not game pieces. They've got minds and hearts . . ."

"Okay, okay," her friend said. "We're all dead on our feet. Let's put that call through to the States and get to bed."

Morris Truebody answered on the first ring.

"It might take me a couple of days to search the muster rolls, depending on how easily I can access them," he told Alex. "Fortunately, I finished up a job today, so I'm free."

They settled on his fee with the understanding that Mr. Truebody would call or fax the information to the Randolph as soon as possible.

FIFTEEN

Alex woke to rain and gloom the following morning. It wasn't until she began dressing that it occurred to her she was going to have to buy a dress for the funeral. There was a Laura Ashley store close by with ruinous prices, but she didn't have the time to scout for bargains.

She certainly wasn't looking her best, she thought, pulling her Northwestern University sweatshirt over her head. Her eyes looked like they had deep mascara smudges underneath them.

The telephone rang.

"Madame Campbell? This is Maurice Cuendet returning your call from Paris. In what way may I help you?"

Alex took a deep breath. "Thank you for calling me back, Monsieur Cuendet. Has Simone told you that there has been a murder here?"

"Yes. I spoke with her this morning. We were greatly disturbed. She said it was that nice English girl."

"Right. Judge Philip Cuendet's daughter, Philippa. The circumstances are rather odd. She was murdered outside my hotel the day I arrived, but I hadn't told her I was coming. To put it briefly, the police don't think it was coincidence. They believe that she knew I was here and was murdered by someone in the family who also knew I was here. I was just wondering, did you tell any of your English Cuendet relatives that I was coming?"

There was a pause as Maurice digested this. "Why, yes," he answered finally. "Yes, I did. I telephoned my cousin, Antonia Lamb. Years ago, she brought her sons to the chateau. For some time we have been corresponding. I knew she would be thrilled at the news you brought us. I suppose it was selfish, but I wanted to tell her myself. It bothered her terribly, you know."

"What did?" Alex asked dumbly.

"That she never knew her real name." He paused, but Alex found she was speechless with shock. "You must see of course that it is absurd to suspect Antonia of committing a murder!"

Her chest hurt as though someone were squeezing her heart. "I see," she replied when the silence had stretched out too long. "Do you remember when you called her?"

"Hmm. Yes. It would have been on the Monday morning. I tried to reach her on Sunday without success."

"Thank you very much, Monsieur."

Suddenly unable to continue the call, she hung up the telephone and sat staring at it, her hand still on the receiver.

Antonia. How was she ever going to tell Charles?

Alex was completely unaware of the funeral service. Sitting between Briggie and Richard in the old church, she stared straight ahead at the back of Antonia's head.

She wouldn't have imagined the woman had it in her to be deceitful. Alex simply could not absorb it all. How could she wreak any more havoc on this family? Should she leave now? Should she simply get on a plane and leave Briggie and Richard to pick up the pieces?

Her coming here had been like hurling a huge stone right into the middle of a serene pond. The result wasn't ripples but waves that were threatening to engulf everyone.

But to go would be cowardly. If she had learned anything since Stewart's death, it was that you just had to face things straight on. Trying to avoid them only made you neurotic.

The cemetery was truly miserable. A fine mist now, the rain clung to everything. With its droopy evergreens and gray slab headstones, the old churchyard seemed as desolate as something out of a Dickens novel. They were putting Philippa in the ground. In the cold, black ground.

As though reading her thoughts, Briggie put an arm around Alex and squeezed her tight.

———————

All through the funeral, Alex had avoided looking at Charles. He was in so much pain already, how could she add to it?

But she owed it to him to tell him before she told Chief Inspector Hubbard. He had to find out from her, not the police.

As they straggled out of the churchyard, she walked up beside him. His face was white and set. At first he didn't seem to notice her.

"I'm sorry, but I have to talk to you, Charles."

It took him a moment to focus. "I thought you were off to London."

"I want to talk to you first."

"Don't worry, Alex," he said wearily. "I'm perfectly fine. Don't feel a blessed thing, as a matter of fact."

"It's not that," she murmured. "It's something else."

Finally he stopped walking and turned to face her, his eyes questioning. She had told Briggie and Richard to go ahead, and the rest of the family were just getting in their cars.

"Let's get out of this beastly rain," he said suddenly, taking her arm.

When they were sitting in the XKE, he said, "What we need is something hot. Mother has a spread on."

"In a minute, Charles. I've got to tell you this. I don't want to, but I don't want you to hear it from anyone else." She took a deep breath. "Maurice Cuendet called your mother from France to tell her I was coming."

It was a moment before Charles could take it in. Then he merely stared at her, horrified. Frozen.

Taking his hand, Alex held it fast between her own. It hurt to see the blank horror in his eyes.

"Charles, think. It doesn't mean your mother is a murderer. All it means is that she knew I was coming. She could have told someone else."

"But why wouldn't she say anything?" he demanded. "Why wouldn't she immediately call her brother . . ."

"He was on the bench . . . "

"Or me?"

"You were out. She probably couldn't reach anyone . . ."

". . . but Philippa. Philippa knew. And the murderer knew."

As he groped for understanding, Charles clamped his jaw. A muscle jumped in his cheek while his eyes studied the dashboard, looking for the answers he needed.

"There's only one thing to do," she said firmly. "Instead of sitting around here speculating, you should ask her."

He didn't answer.

She tried to infuse her voice with a heartiness she didn't feel. "You don't really think she's guilty, do you?"

Closing his eyes, Charles took a deep breath. "Of course not. It's just the shock. And the fact that she said nothing. It's so . . . dishonest, somehow. So unlike her. I can't understand it."

Seeming to come out of his daze, he squeezed Alex's hand and then started the car. "Have you told the chief inspector?"

"I wanted to talk to you first."

"Thank you. Of course, Mother must be made to call him herself. It will look better that way."

By the time they arrived at Antonia's, the rain had let up, but there was still no sun. It was cold and damp. Instead of its golden, shining self, Oxford looked bleak and almost menacing. Charles had driven in complete silence. Now he turned off the car and sat back in his seat with a heavy sigh.

"I'm sorry, Charles," was all she could say.

Reluctantly, he opened his car door and came around to let her out. When she greeted them at the door, Antonia's words died as she saw the grave look on her son's face.

"There hasn't been another murder?" she queried bleakly.

"No, Mother. May we come in?"

"Of course. Everyone's around the fire getting warm. What a hideous day!"

"We need to talk to you alone."

"Alone?" she repeated.

"Alone."

Looking from her son to Alex, she finally led them into what appeared to be a study and closed the door. There was no fire, and it felt damp and cold.

Charles waited for his mother to sit and then seated himself on the edge of a wing chair next to hers. Alex sat at the desk, feeling as though she shouldn't be there.

"Mother, whom did you tell that Alex was coming?"

Antonia stared at her son and then, seeing the knowledge in his eyes, averted her gaze to look out the window. "What makes you think I told anyone?"

"Someone murdered Philippa. I'd rather like to think it wasn't you."

The woman looked back at them, changed in those few seconds almost beyond recognition. Her serenity was gone. Her eyes had lost their luster; they looked haunted, hollow. "I didn't murder Philippa, Charles."

"I never thought you did. But you must have told someone. Whom are you protecting? Frederick?"

"I didn't tell anyone, Charles. You must believe me!"

"You're asking a little much, Mother!" Charles said, his voice as stern as though he were talking to a recalcitrant child. "You are the link. We've been trying to find out how Philippa knew about Alex. We thought it was the Frenchman, but now he's been murdered. If you're not protecting someone, why didn't you say something?"

"Because I was afraid. You all were so sure that whoever knew Alex was coming was the murderer that, well . . . I just panicked."

Charles looked at her hard and then stood and began to walk around the room. "It's not like you to panic," he said roughly.

Antonia studied the arm of her chair, picking at the pattern with her fingernails.

"What time did Maurice Cuendet ring you?" Alex asked.

"I've been trying to recall. It was before I went to the meeting. I think it must have been about half past nine. I did try to call Philip, but he was in court. I was running late, so I thought I would tell the rest of you later. Then we got the news about Philippa, and that completely put it out of my mind. I never thought of putting the two things together until we were sitting in Philip's drawing room and the Inspector began to question us."

"Mother, you can't be telling the truth," Charles insisted, controlling himself with obvious difficulty. "Think of it. Whomever you're protecting is a murderer, even if it's Frederick."

"Frederick never murdered anyone," Antonia said, pulling herself up and facing him squarely.

"But you did tell him?"

"No, I did not."

"They're going to suspect him. They're going to suspect me, for that matter."

"Is that what all this fuss is about?" Antonia sighed. "You're worried they'll suspect you?"

Alex began to feel exceedingly uncomfortable.

"You know me better than that, Mother!" Charles expostulated. "I know I didn't do it. My point is that the police are going to suspect that you're protecting someone. I am your son. So is Frederick. *Someone murdered Philippa, and someone murdered Guison.* You're the key. You have the missing piece, Mother."

"I don't," she said quietly. "You must believe me, Charles."

Was she lying, or was she telling the truth? Her quiet dignity was uncomfortable. It suggested martyrdom.

"The police aren't stupid, Mother. They're bound to put two and two together eventually. They'll call Maurice and find you out. Don't you think it would look better if you told them yourself that you talked to him?"

The little woman studied her fingernails. "Yes, I suppose you're right."

When she made no move, Charles exploded. "This is just so unlike you!"

"Perhaps you just don't know me as well as you thought you did," she remarked.

"Of course I know you! You're my mother, aren't you? You brought us up never to cheat and always, no matter how uncomfortable the situation, to tell the truth." He paused but continued pacing furiously. "Is that it? Are you waiting for Frederick to turn himself in?"

"Why are you so ready to condemn your brother, Charles?"

"Because I can't think of anyone else you'd perjure yourself to protect."

"I haven't perjured myself," she said softly.

"Yet!"

Antonia said nothing. Charles's hot eyes went from her to Alex and rested there. He began again. "Whoever it was who murdered Philippa tried to murder Alex as well. Have you forgotten that?"

Turning troubled eyes on Alex, the woman merely nodded. "Of course, I haven't."

After one more exasperated look, Charles picked up the receiver of the telephone on the desk. He dialed in silence.

"I'd like to speak to Chief Inspector Hubbard, please."

"Who would she protect but Frederick?" Charles demanded later as he returned Alex to the Randolph. Chief Inspector Hubbard had been to the cottage and gone. It had been easy to see that he shared their suspicions.

"Do you think Frederick really would have murdered Philippa?" Alex asked.

Charles was silent. Finally, as he pulled into a parking place several blocks from the Randolph, he answered, "I wouldn't have thought so. But Frederick is a strange chap. I've never felt that I knew what was going on in his head. I suspect the only one who really understands him is Hannah."

"What do you mean 'strange chap'?" she asked as they began the walk to her hotel.

"He has these passions that totally isolate him from the rest of the world. Even when he is surrounded by chaos—his children, for example—he can completely shut them out and concentrate on his work. And he seems so amiable when you meet him, you'd never believe that he could be passionate about anything."

"They have a lovely home," Alex reflected. "Is there money in Hannah's family?"

"Heaps. And she's an only child. I imagine they've run through most of it restoring that old house. That's another of Frederick's passions. I've never really been able to understand how he can waste so much psychic energy on something so totally inanimate."

They walked in silence. It was very cold, and Alex pulled her jacket more closely around her. Charles gathered her fiercely to his side with one arm. "I'd much rather it weren't Frederick."

"Well?" Briggie demanded. She and Richard had apparently been whiling away their time with the newspaper and the London *Times* crossword.

Charles had gone. Alex threw herself into a chair and outlined the encounter with Antonia. "I feel so sorry for all of them," she said. "Only one of them is guilty, but until they find out who it is, they are all going around suspecting one another. Imagine having to wonder if your own brother is a murderer."

"Have they set a date for the Guison inquest yet?" Richard wanted to know.

"It's going to be tomorrow morning, Inspector Hubbard said. I guess we'd better get a move on if we're going to go to London this afternoon, Briggs."

Her friend stuck her pencil behind her ear and tossed the crossword onto the table. "What do you think, Alex? Is she protecting someone?"

"It's the only thing that's consistent with her character. She certainly didn't murder anyone."

"But, assuming it's Frederick, why would he murder Philippa?"

Putting her feet up on the coffee table, Alex replied, "I think Charles worries that maybe it has something to do with his work—money for an expedition or something like that. Apparently, he's pretty intense."

"He didn't seem that way to me," Richard objected.

"Me neither," she agreed. "Charles says he can get passionately involved with things."

"That doesn't surprise me," Briggie put in. "It's a trait he shares with his brother."

"Do you still suspect Charles?" Alex asked, amused.

Her friend stood up and began folding the scattered pages of newspaper. "It would be a pretty clever move to take you to his mother's like that. Sort of a bluff."

"It wasn't like that, Briggie, honestly. What *do* you have against Charles? He wouldn't have murdered Philippa. He of all the Cuendets had no motive whatsoever."

Exchanging a look with Richard, Briggie said, "I don't think you can afford to ignore the possibility, Alex. All his righteous indignation about the money could be an act. Look at the car he drives. From the beginning I've thought he was self-centered, and I've seen no reason to change my mind."

"You're crazy. He worshipped Philippa."

Richard and Briggie exchanged a glance.

"Remember the comment Hannah made yesterday at lunch?" Richard asked.

"Which comment?"

"The one about Charles not appreciating what was in front of his nose until it was gone," Briggie reminded her. "That doesn't square with the way he's been coming across. According to him, it was the great tragedy of his life that he couldn't marry her."

"So the two of you have been discussing this, have you?" Alex challenged.

Richard cleared his throat. "We can't really afford to eliminate anyone, Alex."

Trying to remain cool, Alex walked over to the window, her fists bunched at her side. "You . . . neither of you really knows Charles. If you did, you wouldn't be saying these things. Besides, it was Charles's idea that we call the chateau! And you weren't there to see how shocked and upset he was when he found out it was his mother who was the link."

"That would have emerged in time, Alex. It was bound to come out. This way he had the whole situation under control. He had his reaction ready. His mother had her reaction ready . . ."

Remembering the anguish of the scene in Antonia's sitting room, Alex could only stare at her friends. *"You think he was acting? You think Antonia was acting?* I repeat: You weren't there. You don't even know what you're talking about!"

"Maybe you're not the best person to judge their reactions, Alex," Briggie told her.

Alex exploded. "What is it with you two? You're sickeningly smug, do you know that? Charles is not a playing piece. He is a real human."

"Antonia would only have kept quiet if she were worried about one of her sons. We're agreed on that," Richard said soothingly. "That means there's a fifty percent chance that the murderer was Charles."

"That's right!" Alex cried. "Reduce it all to an equation. Don't allow for human feeling. Especially not *my* human feeling. We all know Alex is unreasonable."

"If Charles is guilty, he's using you," Briggie said flatly. "He's manipulating your emotions." She bent over and began putting her Nikes on, carefully tying the shoestrings in double knots.

Richard straightened his tie.

"Look, Briggie, I appreciate all you've done for me," Alex continued, her voice flat and deliberate, "but when will you learn that I lived in this world quite capably a lot of years before you came along?"

"Just keep an open mind, Alex. That's all that I'm asking."

"I don't think so. I think you're asking me to doubt my own mind!"

"Has it ever occurred to you how much Charles is like Stewart?" her friend asked shrewdly. "Handsome, sure of himself, sure of the world and everyone's place in it . . ."

"Charles isn't as sure of things as he appears. Besides, I always thought you liked Stewart!"

"No one could help but like Stewart. He was mesmerizing."

"And trustworthy down to the ground!"

"Exactly. Now, what I'm afraid of," Briggie told her, "is that you're drawn to Charles because they seem alike. That you think because Stewart could be trusted, Charles can be trusted. It doesn't necessarily follow, you know."

Alex stared at her friend. "First of all, no matter what you may think, I'm not in love with Charles. But he is having a difficult time. I understand what that's like. Second, his resemblance to Stewart is superficial. They're very different underneath. Charles is capable of thinking on a completely different plane. And third, I think I can figure out for myself whom I can trust. Your logic is completely skewed. When the two of you get together, you're totally unreliable!"

The atmosphere between them was strained on the bus ride to London. Richard had elected to get in touch with Daniel's old tutor at Balliol. They were dining together, and Richard intended to pump him about Frederick Lamb.

Alex's anger with Briggie was not a new phenomenon. Her friend was capable of making her see red frequently. She was so doggoned stubborn! What made it worse was that she was very often right.

But her accusations against Charles were absurd. Though individually sound, when Briggie and Richard got together, they were inclined to warped judgment and fantastic theories. *No one could be that good at acting.*

Could they? Granted, it would have been an ingenious trick—getting her to uncover his mother's complicity and then accompany him to her house. She was an A Number One witness to his mother's denial. Antonia's scrupulous refusal to name anyone would be bound to cast suspicion. And none of it would fall on Charles, of course, as he was supposedly demanding that she tell the truth.

It was too absurd. Too convoluted. Charles would never have murdered Philippa, for starters. And his mother would never cover up for him. Briggie and Richard were prejudiced against him because of Daniel. Which was ridiculous. She wasn't in love with either man.

One thing interested her, however. In her anger, Alex had heard herself acknowledge something she hadn't even admitted privately. Charles *was* capable of thinking on a higher plane than Stewart. Already she had had conversations with him she could never imagine having with Stewart.

The thought made her squirm a bit. Wasn't that disloyal to Stewart? After all, he had never had the chance. She had been a different person in those days.

But could she, in reality, see him on his knees? His theme had always been the words of "Invictus":

> *It matters not how strait the gate,*
> *How charged with punishments the scroll,*
> *I am the master of my fate:*
> *I am the captain of my soul.*

Stewart would never surrender control to anyone, she realized suddenly. Rather than be indebted to Jesus Christ, he would pay for his own sins.

A weight seemed somehow to detach itself from her and drift out into space, now light as a helium balloon. She wasn't responsible for Stewart. He *was* the captain of his soul. That was how he had chosen to live his life. It was self-deception for her to believe she could change him in retrospect and fit him into her present context. She must go on with her life, with this path she had chosen. That was what Stewart would want. Here, looking at these roads they had traveled together, she was suddenly absolutely certain of it.

Alighting from the bus at Victoria coach station, Alex consulted her map. They walked the two blocks to the Underground and took the tube to the part of London referred to as the City. There another map consultation was followed by a short walk until they reached St. Catherine's House, the British repository of birth, death, and marriage records recorded since the mid nineteenth century.

Alex had never been there before and was surprised at the crowd of people on such an inclement day. They stood in a medium-sized room filled with bookcases that housed large red volumes dated by the quarter for each year.

Dividing up the work, Alex took the volume for the first quarter of 1920, giving Briggie the volume for the second quarter. The names were written alphabetically in longhand on thick parchment paper that had withstood the passage of time remarkably well.

It was Briggie who found it.

"Here! On the twenty-fourth of May. Joe Cuendet and Marcelle Cuendet. It doesn't give the church, though, just the district."

"I know. We have to copy the index entry down on a form and give it to a clerk. Then someone looks it up and gives us a certificate with all the details."

Obtaining a form, Alex filled it in carefully and then walked into another room and stood in line for the clerk.

"That'll be five pounds," the small man with rimless glasses told her.

Obediently, she handed the money over. "Can we get the certificate today?"

"I'm afraid not. It'll take a few days at least. You're an American?"

"Yes. Do you mail it, or what?"

He studied her form. "You're staying in Oxford. We'll mail it there."

"This is actually important evidence in a probate case. Would it be possible to speed it up? There's a murder involved."

The clerk adjusted his glasses on his nose. "That would be the Cuendet murder, then? I wondered if there was a connection. I read about it in the newspaper."

"Yes. It's the same case."

"Well, I'll see what I can do. Perhaps I can get some special handling on this. Maybe we could telephone you with the information."

Alex beamed. "That would be wonderful. If we're not in, please just leave a message with the desk."

Their errand complete, Alex asked Briggie what she wanted to do.

"Have tea," she said, looking at her watch. "Someplace where they have herbals."

The meal, eaten in a small tearoom Alex knew of in Kensington, restored them to more comfortable relations. When they took the tube back to Victoria station, they were almost amiable. The sky was clearing, and the setting of the sun had made it even colder. Alex dug her hands deep in the pockets of her peacoat.

"I wish we were here under other circumstances," she said. "I love London. It would be nice to see a play or something, but I don't feel like it today."

"Not surprising," Briggie sighed. "But never mind. This business will be over soon."

"It's looking grim, though, Briggie. I can't imagine a happy ending to this one. Someone we know and like is guilty."

They had just come up the escalator and were walking into the street towards Victoria Coach Station when Briggie grabbed Alex by the arm and pulled her behind a kiosk.

"What is it for heaven's sake?" Alex asked.

"Look!"

Peering around the kiosk, Alex observed Dr. John Cuendet on the pavement just in front of them, apparently meeting a strange woman in a long camel-hair coat. She was kissing him.

SIXTEEN

W hat should we do?" asked Alex.

"Say hello, of course." Briggie moved from behind the kiosk and, Alex in tow, hailed the doctor.

The embrace had broken, and John nervously put his hand to his tie to straighten it. Obviously he was unsure how much they had witnessed. He forced a grin. "Briggie! Alex! What a coincidence."

"We're just on our way to the coach station," Alex explained.

"And I've just come from there. Meet my colleague, Dr. Sandra Brown. Sandra, these are the genealogists I told you about on the telephone. Brighamina Poulson and Alexandra Campbell."

"One of you might be a cousin?" the petite redhead inquired, her eyes round with curiosity. She was pretty, but not devastating like Olivia.

"That's me," Alex answered

"Well, I guess we should shove off," Briggie said, looking at her watch. "Did Olivia go back to the theater tonight?"

"Tomorrow," John told them. "The funeral was too shattering. She's home in bed. I've just come down to read a paper to a society who's thinking of funding some research. Sandra arranged it."

Alex nodded. Briggie stuck out her hand. "Nice to meet you Sandra. Good luck, John."

"Yes, good luck," Alex added.

They waited until they had boarded the bus to discuss the meeting.

"She's the 'colleague in London,' obviously," Briggie said with evident satisfaction.

"Yes. That's why Charles clammed up on us when we were asking about it. If John's looking for outside funding, and if this Dr. Sandra Brown is setting it up, he won't be as dependent on Olivia for money anymore."

"If he wants a divorce, I suppose that gives him the best motive of the bunch."

"Yes," Alex mused. *A far better motive than Charles could possibly have.* "I think I'll phone Olivia when we get back and accept her dinner invitation for tomorrow night. I want another opportunity to observe them together."

When they returned to the hotel, there was a message awaiting them from Morris Truebody, the American researcher. "Got lucky. Have the information you requested. Sorry I couldn't catch you. Call me at home after six Washington time."

"Drat!" Briggie expostulated.

"That's eleven o'clock our time," Alex looked at her watch. "It's only six now. What are we going to do for five hours?"

Without answering, Briggie led the way upstairs to their suite. As soon as they entered, the telephone rang.

"Alex? Charles here. How did things go in London?"

"Okay. We won't have the information we need for a couple of days, though. Maybe not until Monday."

"Bureaucracy, I take it."

"Yes. We got a call from our American researcher, however, and he's got something for us. We think it must be the evidence Philippa had. We can't get in touch with him until eleven, though."

"What're you two going to do in the meantime?"

"I don't know."

"How about keeping me company?"

His voice sounded artificially hearty. She remembered the

day of Stewart's funeral. The rest of her life had seemed to stretch forward endlessly, totally empty.

"I'd love to," she told him. "I'm afraid Briggie won't be able to come, though. She wants an early night."

Her friend looked at her indignantly.

"I'll pick you up in twenty minutes."

"What did you say that for?" Briggie demanded after she had hung up.

"I thought you might be feeling a little tired," Alex lied.

"Alex! I really don't think you should be alone with him."

Alex turned on her. "And I happen to think you're wrong. Charles needs company tonight. Sympathetic company. In your present state of mind, you hardly qualify."

"I just try to keep an open mind."

Alex rolled her eyes in exasperation. "Concentrate on John, why don't you? Or Mr. Rochester. We haven't dug up any new dirt on him."

"I'm only thinking of your safety."

"What's Charles going to do? Murder me?"

Briggie let out a long sigh and went through to her bedroom.

Richard Grinnell had heard a lot about Dr. William Chaplain from Daniel. It was due to Chaplain's influence that his son had made psychotherapy his career. He was somewhat surprised, therefore, to find that the man was blind. Daniel had never mentioned it.

They had arranged to meet at the don's rooms at Balliol, from whence they set off on foot for a small French restaurant above the covered market. Amazed at how well his host and his dog knew the streets, Richard still couldn't resist taking hold of his elbow.

"It's not necessary, really," the tutor told him. "Sabrina knows her way."

The restaurant was cozy, warm, and full. Nevertheless, the

headwaiter steered them to a corner table, whisked off its reserved sign, and bade Sabrina welcome.

"You come here a lot?"

"Nearly every night. It's pleasant. Now. Tell me. How is your son doing? I haven't had a letter from him in a while."

The lawyer embarked on a pleasant discussion of Daniel's career and then the tutor entertained him in turn with spirited anecdotes of Daniel's Oxford doings. This conversation carried them through until the dessert.

"I've just met a colleague of yours, Frederick Lamb. He's involved in a probate matter I'm here to deal with," Richard remarked after they had made their selection from the pastry tray.

"Ah yes, Lamb. Is it true his cousin was murdered the other day?"

"According to the police, she was pushed under a bus."

Chaplain appeared to consider this. "Have they any idea who is responsible?"

"No. There's a large fortune involved—the estate I'm probating. It's a complicated case, but the upshot of it is that the motive was apparently greed, which isn't surprising."

"And you want to know my opinion of Lamb."

Surprised at this directness, Richard cleared his throat. "Well, yes. I suppose I do. I know you must feel a certain loyalty towards the fellow. I mean being colleagues, and all that, but murder is a serious business."

"Don't know the man well," the blind tutor told him, reaching down to scratch Sabrina behind the ears. "All I can really give you is college gossip, I'm afraid."

"That would be a help," the lawyer said encouragingly.

"Rumor has it that he's made some sort of terrific find. He's terribly close-mouthed about it. You know how these things are. He's got to go to all the right people for permission and then raise a packet of money. It's hard to do that without arousing suspicion. And if anyone else were to get wind of it, they might beat him to the punch. Apparently, things are a bit sticky on the money end of things. He's not having much luck."

Richard considered this. "Do you think he'd commit a murder?"

"As a psychologist, I know everyone has his flashpoint, but nevertheless, I can't imagine anyone I know committing a murder. That includes Frederick Lamb."

"What about his brother?"

"Hmm. Christ Church, isn't he?"

"Right. He's a theater critic for the *Times,* also."

The blind man abruptly ceased scratching his dog. "Charles Lamb. Yes. Psychologically speaking, a very interesting type. I cooperated with him on an intercollegiate committee once—a charity for the blind, as a matter of fact. Charismatic fellow. A lot more ruthless than his brother. I believe Charles would have had the money Frederick's looking for months ago."

"Why is that?"

"He seems to have a particular talent for raising money. The man's an absolute wizard at it."

"But you say he's ruthless?"

"Yes. It's an odd thing to find in a man involved in charity work, but he seems to have very few scruples."

Richard considered this and weighed it against what he knew of the man. "Why *was* he involved with the blind charity then? He seems far too narcissistic for anything on that order."

"A complex type. I wouldn't call him narcissistic. I don't think you can classify him that easily. As a matter of fact, I wouldn't be surprised if he secretly cherished a passion or two that no one knows about. Blind people might be one of them. I understand he's thrown himself into AIDS fund-raising now."

"Really?"

"Yes. A young relative of his recently died of it, I heard."

"And there was never any hint that he . . . uh, well, misappropriated funds?"

"Never." Chaplain looked suddenly as though there were a bad smell in the room. "Perhaps I've given you the wrong impression. He's not that type at all. He'd not steal unless it were for a cause of some sort. A Robin Hood, if you like. He's the complete pragmatist—the end justifies the means."

Left alone in her suite, Briggie spent several minutes kicking herself mentally. Why on earth had she let Alex out on her own? Should she and Richard have kept their suspicions to themselves and just not let her out of their sight? She was so doggoned stubborn.

Well, no sense brooding about it now. She might as well do something useful. Picking up the telephone book, she looked up the number for Edward Cuendet.

He answered after several rings.

"Edward? This is Brighamina Poulson. I'm at loose ends tonight, and I wondered if I could buy you dinner."

"Me? Why would you want to do that?"

"I thought you might be feeling a little down after the funeral."

There was silence on the other end of the telephone.

"Edward?"

"What made you think that?"

"Let's just say I'm a student of human nature."

"I can always use a free dinner," he said finally. "The Eagle and Child?"

"You sure you don't want something fancier than a pub snack?"

"A pub will be just fine."

Briggie felt odd sitting all alone in the pub with people drinking beer all around her. She didn't know why it was that pubs were so different from bars. It had never occurred to her before, but she would never meet anyone in a bar back home.

Edward arrived, dressed in his chrome yellow silk shirt and paint-spattered jeans. He *was* fascinating looking. If she had more imagination, she might have said that his eyes actually smoldered.

"Hello, Briggie. What's happened to Alex and your legal friend?"

"Alex has gone out with your cousin Charles. Richard is having dinner with his son's tutor. Daniel Grinnell was a Rhodes scholar about fifteen years ago."

"Ah!" the artist nodded in understanding.

After ordering soup, bread, and cheese for the two of them, Briggie told him, "If you want beer, you'll have to buy it yourself. I don't do beer."

Edward laughed. "I don't need it, believe it or not."

"I was wrong about you, then."

"You thought I was an alcoholic, I suppose. Did the good Charles tell you that?"

"No. I deduced it. I made a mistake. You were under a big strain when I met you for the first time."

Avoiding her eyes, Edward looked at the table and traced a scratch with his fingernail.

"Tell me about Dr. Sandra Brown," Briggie instructed him.

The artist glanced up, his eyes puzzled. "Do I know her?"

"Maybe not. She's a doctor in London. A friend of John's."

"Ahh," Edward nodded. "The other woman?"

"Is she?"

"I've wondered. Philippa was worried about it, as a matter of fact. It's one of the few things she discussed with me."

"She knew about Dr. Brown?"

"I suppose it was the same woman. She and John are both AIDS researchers. She's very upper class and has access to all sorts of people with money. Princess Di included."

"Does Olivia know about it?"

Edward shrugged. "Philippa didn't know. She didn't even know if there was really anything going on. She was just worried there was."

Briggie nodded. "How would Olivia react if there *were* anything going on?"

"That's a fascinating question, actually. I don't believe anyone really knows. We don't really *know* Olivia, you see. She's so many different people. It all depends on the part she's playing."

"She must have *some* basic personality."

"She must, I agree. But nobody knows what it is."

"Not even John?"

"I don't know. I've never really been able to figure out why he married her, if you want to know the truth. They haven't a thing in common, and she wasn't rich or famous in those days."

"That's a pretty cynical comment."

Their food arrived, borne by the waiter with the jeweled nose.

Edward dug right in. It occurred to Briggie that he probably hadn't eaten all day.

"Go on," she prodded him after he had taken several bites. "Explain yourself."

"John's a passionate sort of guy. Intense. We all are, as a matter of fact." He paused to bite off some buttered bread. "Now I could understand it if Charles had married her. His passion's the theater. But John's is medicine. Always has been."

"Maybe she swept him off his feet."

"I think she must have done. There's no other explanation. Their daughter really was the only thing they had in common."

Briggie nodded. "And Charles? What do you think of Charles?"

"Not a great deal. Nor he of me. In particular, I don't appreciate his holier-than-thou attitude about this Borden money. He'll be just as glad of it as the rest of us."

"Any particular reason why you say that?"

"Charles is a bit of a mystery," Edward reflected. "He drives a Jag, decorates with antiques, travels a bit, all on what shouldn't be that much money."

"You think he's dishonest?"

"Either that or a brilliant investor. He's fond of his comforts, is Charles."

Charles and Alex were sitting in a tiny French restaurant outside Oxford on the Thames. In the dim light of candles reflected off starched white linen, they pretended to eat the magnificent food. Charles's eyes looked bruised, evidence that he had not withstood the days' battering well. She felt she ought to know the words that would comfort him, but she was not very confident of her own ability.

As he spoke, striving valiantly to keep his end up, entertaining her with stories of his rowdy undergraduate days, she listened with only half an ear.

Why am I such a chicken? she demanded of herself. Probably because she felt the weight of seven hundred years of Oxford tradition on Charles's side of the scale, and her own fragile, new testimony on the other.

When he got to the end of his anecdote, she cleared her throat, looked him squarely in the eye and asked, "Have you tried it yet?"

Charles raised his eyebrows. "What?"

"Kneeling. Praying."

Extending a hand across the table he laid it over hers, a sheepish smile on his face. "I'm still trying to get up the courage. At the moment, you're all I seem to need."

"I'll fail you, Charles."

"And what, pray, do you mean by that?"

"Just that I'm only one very human being. I'm no substitute for God."

Sighing, Charles moved his hand and settled back in his seat. "I guess I have a difficult time believing there's anyone out there."

Alex decided to risk a small probe. "Haven't you felt Philippa near you today? When Stewart died, it seemed for months as though he were only in the next room. I felt the comfort of his being there."

Nodding slowly, Charles looked at her thoughtfully. "Actually, when I was a boy, I did have one experience . . . "

He looked down at his lap and refolded his napkin.

"Are you going to tell me about it?"

"I've never told anyone. I didn't think they'd believe me."

"Try me."

"When I was a boy, my father died. It wasn't sudden or anything. A very peaceful death. He'd been ill for some time."

"Were you close?"

"As close as any English schoolboy ever gets to his father, I suppose."

"What does that mean, exactly?"

"Oh, well, we're sent away to school at eight, so after that it's mostly just the holidays. He was a doctor. He used to take me to the clinic with him. I enjoyed that."

"How old were you when he died?"

"About fourteen. A very young fourteen. There had been nothing in my life to prepare me for his death. I'd never even lost a pet. Both the grandparents I knew were still alive."

"So what happened?"

"I'd been taught to pray by my mother when I was little. If I thought of God at all, I thought of him as a very rational, understanding sort of person. I stopped praying when I went away to school. One does."

Alex nodded. She could picture the scorn he would have had to endure otherwise.

"Well," Charles switched his gaze to an empty table near them. "One day during the long vacation, I missed my father very much. I took the bus out to Blenheim the way I used to do with him, and went for a ramble in the park. I came to a really secluded spot, and . . . well, I knelt down."

"And?"

"Well, I've never really been sure what happened. All I know is, I *felt* my father there. But instead of soothing me, it frightened me. I guess I didn't really expect it. It was so unorthodox somehow. I jumped up and began running. I've never prayed since!"

"Because you're afraid you'll get an answer?" Alex grinned.

"I think it frightened me to realize there might be a realm I couldn't see. I mean, I know these things happened in the Bible, but, well, why should they happen to Charles Lamb?"

"So you chose to limit your reality to what you could see?"

"Well, more or less. I guess I did. When I think of God, I just think of stone cathedrals and stained-glass windows. He doesn't seem to have anything to do with today."

"You mean you don't want him to have anything to do with today. In fact, Charles, you're still frightened."

The man across from her considered this seriously. "I guess I am a little afraid of losing control, of becoming dependent on something outside myself."

"You have to want to open up to new possibilities, Charles," she said gently. "It does take a special kind of courage. It's called humility."

Reflecting on this, he leaned back in his chair, stroking his upper lip like the judge. "I think Americans are inherently better at that than Englishmen."

"We aren't hampered by tradition," she agreed. "Stewart used to say we are always reinventing ourselves. That we have a perpetual identity crisis."

"Tell me about Stewart."

Settling back in her chair, Alex ruminated. "He was sure of himself, cynical, strong-minded. He was a draft-dodger from the Vietnam War. When I met him, he was living in Paris. He couldn't go home, because amnesty hadn't been declared yet." She smiled briefly, remembering the speeches she had endured in Left Bank cafés. "He was a student at the Sorbonne, waiting tables at night. Eventually, he graduated and, because of the kindness of a clear-sighted Frenchman who became his patron, he was able to set up for himself as a photographer. He became famous in a small way. He did photo-essays, travel books, travel posters, that sort of thing."

"Sounds as though he led a charmed existence."

"He always said you make your own luck. I think he did, too. He was the most determined person I've ever known, except for Briggie, maybe. But then they're distantly related, so maybe that accounts for it."

"When were you married?"

"About thirteen years ago. We went to Scotland to find his extended family. Stewart fell in love with the country. Briggie always told him it was the voices in his blood. We were married there, in the village kirk."

Charles looked down at his hands. "He's been dead how long?"

"Three years, next month."

"Have you let go of him yet?"

She considered the question carefully. "I think I've made some progress. For a long time, I didn't want to let go. But I've made a new life for myself. He's never really been part of it. If I had stayed in Scotland, it would have been harder."

"Alex."

"Yes?"

"Can you picture Stewart on his knees?"

Sighing, she said, "Not really. But you're not Stewart, you're Charles. And you're hurting. I think you'll get there eventually."

It was eleven o'clock when they returned to the hotel, and Briggie and Richard were waiting impatiently. Charles insisted on remaining to hear the American researcher's news.

Alex picked up the telephone and dialed.

"Mr. Truebody? This is Alex Campbell. You have some news for me?"

The others watched as she listened and finally broke into a broad grin.

"So that was it! Thank you! That explains everything!"

Hanging up the phone, she turned to Briggie. "We should have figured it out, Briggs. Guess who the only soldier in I Company was who was AWOL at the end of the war? Harold Simpson!"

"Harold Simpson!" Briggie and Richard cried together.

"Who the devil is Harold Simpson?" Charles demanded.

SEVENTEEN

Alex endeavored to explain. "Do you remember when we told you that first night that someone else had turned up in the States with Joseph Borden's papers? Well, that someone was Harold Simpson. We assumed that he had taken them off the dead body of Joseph Borden. But there was no proof of Joseph's death. Now it looks like Joseph must have been delirious or something and Harold must have known he'd lost his memory. Harold was a private. Joseph was his commanding officer, and Harold knew he was very wealthy and had no wife, siblings, or parents. There was a resemblance between the two. He must have switched uniforms with Joseph, taken his papers, and left him with none."

"I wonder why . . ." Briggie started and then said, "Oh. I was going to say that I wondered why Harold hadn't simply switched papers, but it wasn't part of his plan for Joseph to try to take up life as Harold Simpson. Harold's family would have rejected him, and then people would have wondered what had happened to the real Harold Simpson."

"Right," Alex concluded, "an investigation would have been conducted, and eventually they would have come across something. Private Simpson was pretty clever. He realized it was better to leave them with nothing to go on. Thus, the record shows that he was AWOL."

"This Harold Simpson posed as Joseph Borden?" Charles asked incredulously.

"He tried, but it didn't work. Someday, I promise I'll tell you the whole story. In the meantime, it looks like we're one step closer to proving Joseph Borden and Joe Cuendet were the same person." Alex sighed. "If the murderer had only known he had nothing to fear from Philippa's information. It didn't lead to the conclusions she thought it did. Joe Cuendet was not Harold Simpson."

Turning his back, Charles walked over to the window and looked out into the night. Alex went to him and stood by his side. Though she wanted to, she was very careful not to touch him.

––––––––––

When Alex awoke the next morning, it was with the sense that there was something she had failed to do. Lying there, staring at the ceiling, she fought the desire simply to go back to sleep and tried to recap the case in her mind. After Charles had left the night before, Richard told her of his conversation with Dr. Chaplain concerning Frederick. Briggie had reported on Edward's observations about Dr. John Cuendet and Dr. Sandra Brown.

That was it! John. She needed to call Olivia and accept their invitation for dinner that night. Turning on her side, she picked up the telephone.

"Olivia, this is Alex!"

"Oh, good morning. I was going to ring you later. Have you changed your mind about tonight?"

"Yes. If it's all right. But don't ask Timothy Dalton to join us. I'd rather just have John bring his genealogy and we can talk family history. It's looking more and more like we're going to be cousins. I promised to tell him about Joseph Borden."

"How nice," Olivia said with a yawn Alex could hear over the telephone. "But if you're going to discuss genealogy, there's no need for you to wait until I'm there after the play. Why don't you and John have dinner beforehand and get your talk out of the way? Then I can ask Timothy to join us later for dessert or something."

Obviously, Olivia was one of those people who found

genealogy as dull as ditch water. "All right. If you really don't mind."

"Not at all. John is anxious to show you his Cuendet charts. Along with everything else, he's an amateur calligrapher, so they're beautiful. What time should he come for you? The play begins at eight, and Stratford is about an hour from here. Shall we say half past five? Is that too terribly early?"

"No. That will be perfect."

"I'll look forward to seeing you after the play, then."

"Fine. I hope you're feeling better?"

"Yes. It's still a terrible business, of course, but life must go on. I can't afford to be too temperamental or my understudy might begin to get delusions of grandeur."

"Well, break a leg!"

"Thanks, Alex. I'll see you."

The inquest on the body of Etienne Guison was held in the same courtroom as the inquest on Philippa. It was eerie to Alex to realize that the last time she had been here she had been watching eagerly for the Frenchman, when all the time he had been lying dead in his hotel room.

The first witness, Chief Inspector Hubbard, pronounced his theory of how the murder was committed. The murderer had apparently knocked out a chambermaid and stolen her room keys, letting himself into Etienne's suite while the Frenchman was out. The chambermaid was interrogated but could tell the court nothing about her assailant. The murder weapon was produced—an ordinary kitchen knife. It had already seen years of service but was not from the kitchens of the hotel.

Then Alex was called as a witness. After having her state how she had met Etienne, the coroner asked her, "Did the deceased know Miss Philippa Cuendet?"

"Not that I know of," Alex said.

"There was not some theory that perhaps he had met her

in France and had communicated with her about your intended visit?"

"There was such a theory. But Monsieur Guison assured me several times it was false. He claimed he had never met her and that he could prove he hadn't been in France when Philippa was there."

"I believe that Mr. Guison was to have met you in the dining room the night after he was murdered. What was the purpose of that meeting?"

"Monsieur Guison was standing next to Philippa Cuendet when she was pushed under the bus. He thought that if he could see all the members of the Cuendet family together in the dining room, he might recognize someone who had been there, someone who might have pushed Philippa."

"I see. And you had no qualms about this? No doubt that Mr. Guison would tell what he knew?"

"I'm afraid I don't understand."

"It has been suggested by the police that perhaps Mr. Guison might have used his knowledge less than honorably. He might, for example, have contacted the guilty party privately and arranged blackmail."

"But he didn't know any of them. That was the point of the dinner. He was going to see them all together, the whole family, for the first time."

"I believe that is not quite true. He met Mr. Charles Lamb on the night following the murder, did he not?"

Alex's heart plunged into her stomach. Darting a quick, anguished glance at Charles, she saw that he was stunned.

"He did," she answered finally. "But I must tell you that he gave absolutely no indication that he had ever seen him before." Remembering the events of that dinner, Alex rushed on. "Mr. Lamb as much as accused him of murder. If Etienne had thought Charles were guilty, it seems to me that as angry as he was, he would have made a counteraccusation right then. I don't think he was in any mood to calmly contemplate blackmail."

The coroner merely nodded. "That will be all, Mrs. Campbell. Thank you."

Charles was called to the stand. Asked to recount his conversation with Etienne, he said, "I'm afraid I flatly accused him of murdering my cousin. He took great offense and left. I never saw him again."

It couldn't have been Charles, Alex told herself firmly. The chambermaids would have been at work in the morning. He hadn't been there then—he'd been at his mother's planning Philippa's funeral. Of course, she didn't know where he'd gone after that. She hadn't seen him again until late that evening— after she'd been attacked. A perverse thought occurred to her, and she considered it reluctantly. If Charles *were* the murderer, then it was Charles who had attacked her, coming later to offer her his sympathy . . . No, that was ludicrous. Charles would not do that, and besides, it had been a big car, not an XKE.

The jury failed to find enough to convince them that any particular person was guilty. They rendered a verdict of "murder by a person or persons unknown."

As the only member of the Cuendet clan who had attended the inquest, Charles joined them afterwards. Alex felt wilted by the proceeding. He studied her face, patted her cheek lightly, and then proposed that Briggie, Richard, and Alex join him for lunch at the Mitre.

"You may recall," he remarked lightly, "the Mitre was the restaurant where Lord Peter Wimsey and Harriet Vane ate on one of the many occasions when he tried to woo her."

So the mood was to be light, Alex thought. They were to pretend the accusation of blackmail had never been made. How would Briggie cooperate with this program?

"So you're a Lord Peter Wimsey fan, Charles?" Briggie asked, apparently ready to play along, at least for the time being.

"No, but he's legendary at Oxford. I worked as a guide one summer and had to commit to memory all the important locales from *Gaudy Night.* I have read several of Sayers's more serious works, though. She wrote quite prolifically on theological subjects."

Briggie raised her eyebrows. "You read theology?"

"I'm not a complete heathen, you know."

"He considers himself a pillar of orthodoxy," Alex explained with a faint smile.

"Yes. Well." Charles opened his menu. "The place has been bought out by a consortium, so it's not the same as it was when your two fictional friends supped here, but the food's passable."

Alex ordered scampi, at Charles's suggestion. It wasn't the best she'd ever had, but as he said, passable.

"Now that the inquest is over and none of us has been detained for murder as yet, I suggest that we go to France tomorrow morning," he proposed.

"What do *you* expect to find in France?" Richard asked.

"Some kind of connection. My mother still insists that she didn't tell anyone of Alex's coming. If I'm going to believe her, that means I must find some other means of communication between here and there. I still favor Guison. Murdered or not, I still think he was up to something, and I think he must have had a confederate over here. There has to be some link between his family and mine."

"Well, if there is, Briggie and Alex will uncover it," Richard assured him. "There's really no reason for you to inconvenience yourself."

Charles turned to the lawyer, one eyebrow raised. "It's no inconvenience. Someone in my family is obviously a murderer. At the moment, I appear to be the prime suspect."

"But surely that's absurd!" Alex told him. "Why on earth would you kill Philippa?"

"That remains a mystery to me, but obviously the police believe Guison was blackmailing me and I killed him."

There was silence. Richard cleared his throat. "You're taking it pretty calmly."

Charles gave a one-sided grin. "They can't prove it, because it isn't true."

From the Mitre, they returned to the hotel, where Charles and Richard made the travel arrangements. They would leave for Paris in the morning by plane and then fly from Paris to Strasbourg, where they would rent a car for the drive to Bar-le-Duc, arriving in the late afternoon.

That left them only today to prepare for the next day's journey.

"Alex and I are badly in need of a laundromat," Briggie announced. "Plus, I think it's time we brought Chief Inspector Hubbard up to speed on the Borden-Cuendet connection. He doesn't know about our telephone call last night."

Charles offered to take Alex to his laundromat in the college basement where he likewise had business. Obviously figuring that she'd be in no danger in a more or less public facility, Briggie and Richard agreed to separate from them, visiting the inspector and collecting the airline tickets.

Arriving at the police station just as Chief Inspector Hubbard was returning from lunch, Briggie and Richard managed to get his attention before he could get involved with anything else.

"Mrs. Poulson has an update for you, Chief Inspector," Richard informed the policeman in his plummy voice.

Leading them into the cubbyhole he called his office, Hubbard cleared two plastic chairs of debris and bade them be seated.

"We were in touch with an American military researcher last night. We think Philippa had found out about a man called Harold Simpson who went AWOL after the war. She must have thought he was her grandfather." Briggie attempted to explain in as few words as possible how Simpson fit into the case and the manner in which Philippa had apparently been misled.

"So," she concluded, "it's fairly certain she did think she could disprove Alex's claim. If someone wanted the Borden fortune, they had a motive for killing her, all right."

"Congratulations, Mrs. Poulson. I guess you were right

about the motive after all. Well done." Leaning back in his chair, he fixed them with a friendly gaze. "We weren't able to get anyone else's fingerprints from Miss Cuendet's study. The thief wore gloves. Now tell me, is Mr. Charles Lamb in any particular need of money, do you know?"

"Is there a specific reason you're focusing on Charles?" she asked. *"Frederick* Lamb is in desperate need of money."

The policeman gave a little smile. "My, you have been busy. Yes. I am aware of Frederick's circumstances."

"Charles seems to do quite well for himself," Richard observed. "He's a bachelor, after all. He doesn't have the expenses the others do."

"I'm having Sergeant Higgins check with his bank this afternoon."

"But he of all the Cuendet heirs has the least possible motive for murdering Philippa," Briggie said perversely. Why was she defending Charles, for heaven's sake? She found she had no intention of repeating Edward's gossip of the night before. It had been so obviously laced with envy. And this was serious. "Have there been any developments you haven't told us about?" Richard asked gravely. "We need to know. Alex is seeing a lot of Charles."

The policeman appeared to consider. "I suppose there is no harm in telling you. I intend to bring Lamb in this afternoon for questioning. You see, the chambermaid from the Randolph recognized him at the inquest."

"But she testified she didn't see her attacker," Briggie protested, her heart in her throat.

"No. This was before the attack. The same afternoon about one o'clock. She saw Charles Lamb outside Guison's door in the hall of the Randolph."

"When was the attack?" Richard queried.

"About three quarters of an hour later."

"Just enough time," the lawyer mused solemnly, "for him to go and get himself a knife."

There was something soothing about attending to a purely domestic task—perhaps an assurance that ordinary life was still there. After filling all the available washers with clothing and detergent, Alex and Charles agreed to leave the murders behind for the time being and discuss only matters connected with the laundry or their respective theories of education. Charles was intrigued to hear that Alex had been at the Sorbonne.

"It seems like every time I'm with you I find another unexpected piece to the puzzle of Alex Campbell."

"I'm still finding them myself," she said. "But wouldn't it be dull if we knew everything there was to know about ourselves by the time we were middle-aged?"

"Reinvention again." He paused, thoughtful. "I suppose you think it wouldn't do any harm for this stodgy Englishman to attempt some reinvention?"

"You're not as stodgy as some I could name. I'd say there was hope." She grinned. "There's life out there. Just try to put a little comma between yourself and that thousand years of British tradition. Give yourself a little breathing room."

"Maybe I ought to throw over my career and visit the States for a while." Though the tone was casual, he studied her face intently.

"It's a thought."

"If you're right and we turn out to be cousins, someone from the family will need to go over and attend to things."

"I think you'll have to fight your cousin Edward for that job."

Charles considered. "If I assure Edward I'll act as expeditiously as possible, I think he'll be happy to stay here and paint."

"Your attitude towards the inheritance seems to have undergone a material change," she remarked.

Instantly she regretted her flippancy. Charles scowled and concentrated on transferring his clothing from washer to dryer.

"I could be the murderer, you know." His voice was bitter. "The police have painted a very convincing scenario."

"Pushing someone under a bus isn't your style, Charles. Especially not Philippa."

"But I didn't take to Guison. Most likely it has occurred to you that I could have killed him out of vengeance. Because he killed Philippa. Perhaps I even forced him to confess before I killed him."

He wouldn't look at her now, but went on tossing clothes from washer to dryer. The jumping muscle in his cheek showed the measure of his tension.

"I think I've thought of everything," she said quietly.

"You'd be stupid not to," he agreed. "I'll bet Briggie's got money on me. Am I right?" Still he avoided her eyes.

"It's not what Briggie thinks that counts, is it?"

Wadding up a T-shirt, he threw it violently across the laundry room.

"It's not going to make for a particularly joyful *menage a quatre,* is it?"

Then, turning to her suddenly, he put his hands on her shoulders, squeezing them as though he were holding her to earth by main force. She was taken aback by the intensity of his grip. Looking at her squarely, he said, "Alex, tell me the truth. You don't really think I murdered anyone, do you?"

As his eyes bored into hers, she tried valiantly to maintain some vestige of self-awareness.

"It's important," he persisted. "More important than you realize."

Every sense screamed "No! You never murdered a soul! You're simply incapable of it!"

But was that only because of his nearness, because of the way his eyes were burning away every triviality that lay between them? There were worry lines on his face she had not noticed before. This was no marble Greek god as she had once thought. This was a living, breathing, vulnerable man.

Biting her lip, she let out a long, slow breath. "My intuition is against it."

"Are you certain?"

Marginally aware that there were others in the laundromat, she looked down in sudden shyness.

"Yes."

He did not let go of her at once but squeezed her shoulders even harder. "Good," he had said finally, dropping his hands and thrusting them into the pockets of his trousers.

Her heart was beating so hard she was trembling.

––––––––––––

She needed to get ready for her evening with John, but after Charles left her, she sat at the vanity, staring unseeingly at her reflection. She was swimming in very deep waters.

Something entirely unexpected had happened to her in the laundromat of Christ Church College. But were these amazingly powerful feelings only the product of being thrown together in a crisis? Or were they real? Could she trust herself while riding on this emotional seesaw?

And their conversation. It struck her now as ironic that she, who had once thought Oxford the epitome of civilization, should be actually urging Charles to look beyond it, to not be tied by its limitations. When had this mutiny sprung up within her? The fact that Charles might even consider taking her advice was suddenly wondrous.

Common sense tried to reassert itself. She was a love-starved widow, making far too much out of an encounter with a desperate man. Feeling the need to reconnect with her sensible Kansas City self, she picked up the telephone and dialed her mother's house.

"Alex! What a wonderful surprise!" Amelia Borden answered. "I just had Daniel on the telephone a few minutes ago. He said he was calling to check on me, but I really think he was wanting to know if I'd heard from you. Apparently, his father hasn't been in touch. He's a little worried about him."

Alex laughed. "So far, Richard and Briggie have managed to stay within the law. We're leaving for France in the morning, though, so who knows what they'll get into over there."

"And how are you doing, dear?"

"I'm not sure. I'm starting to feel things again, Mother. Things I haven't felt in a long time. I can't numb out anymore. When something bad happens, I feel it. When something good happens, I feel it."

"I know. It's the same process I'm going through, only I was the one administering the numbing before."

"And you're not tempted to do it again?"

"Of course I am. Every day. But feeling things is important. If you can't feel anything, Alex, you might as well be dead. I lost twenty years of my life. Twenty years with your father." Her voice quavered with grief. "You know, Alex, I find that I'm not remembering very much at all."

"Maybe there's not all that much to remember, Mom," she said sadly, chilled by this glimpse into the void of her mother's life.

"That's the saddest thing of all," Amelia agreed wearily.

There was a moment of silence and then, "Alex, you've just got to live for both of us," she said suddenly, her words strong and determined. "You've got to take life in both hands and go for it."

Alex smiled at her fierceness. "I'm planning to. But you've got to do the same. You've got a life, too."

"I love you, dear."

"I love you, too, Mom. Bye."

At that moment, Briggie entered the suite, "Are you decent, Alex? Can Richard come in?"

"Yes. But I have to change in a minute."

Seeing Briggie's face in the mirror, she was surprised to read sadness and dread. "What is it?"

Her friend walked into the room and put a hand on Alex's shoulder. "I'm afraid Charles is going to be brought in for questioning this afternoon, honey. He was seen in the Randolph the afternoon Etienne was killed."

EIGHTEEN

Alex turned to face her friend and Richard, who still stood at the threshold of the door.

"What?"

"It was the chambermaid," Briggie said apologetically, going to sit on the edge of Alex's bed. "Tell her, Richard."

The lawyer took a chair near the window. "I'm sorry, Alex. She saw him outside Etienne's door about forty-five minutes before she was knocked out."

Alex could only stare. It wasn't possible! Charles would have told her if he'd seen Etienne that afternoon.

"There's got to be some mistake."

"They're checking on his financial status right now," Richard continued. "They're trying to find a motive for Philippa's murder."

"They think he killed her, too?"

"It's the blackmail scenario they talked about at the inquest. They're working on the theory that Charles was being blackmailed because Etienne recognized him at the scene when Philippa was killed."

"No matter what anyone says, I can't believe he killed Philippa," she said sharply.

Sighing, Briggie got up from the bed and walked over to knead Alex's shoulders. It was something she had been doing since Stewart's death. Alex scarcely noticed. Fear was assaulting her from every direction.

"They could be wrong, you know," Briggie said softly.

Alex looked at her friend's reflection in the mirror. "This

from you, Briggie? I thought you had him cast as Suspect Number One!"

"I told you, I keep an open mind, Alex. When's John coming for you?"

Alex consulted her watch. "Fifteen minutes. But I can't possibly go out with him now! How can I sit and pretend to be interested in his pedigree charts and *Hamlet* and Timothy Dalton when I don't know if Charles has been arrested?"

"How can you afford not to?" Briggie replied. "Do you think he's guilty?"

"Of course not!"

"Then don't you think the best plan would be to proceed with the program and find out who is? The only change I suggest making is that Richard and I become part of the party. John is too good a suspect. I don't want you having dinner with him by yourself."

Taking a deep breath, Alex sat up straighter and patted Briggie's hand on her shoulder. "I won't be alone. I'll be in public. And he wouldn't try anything when he knows you know I'm with him and Olivia knows I'm with him."

"I don't like it."

"I'll be all right. I'll call you."

———————————

From the way John handled his family history, Alex could tell it was precious to him. After a light meal, they sat in the restaurant's bay window, overlooking the Avon river, as she watched him reverently unfold a wall chart of his pedigree. In spite of all her preoccupations, she forced the genealogy portion of her brain into gear and took the chart from him carefully.

It began with John Cuendet, born 1956, Oxford, Oxfordshire, England, married to Olivia Thielbault in 1978. Parents were Jean Maurice Cuendet, born 1926 at Oxford, and Elizabeth (Bit) Norris, born 1929 at Jackson Hole, Wyoming.

"Your mother's an American," Alex remarked. "I didn't know that!"

"Yes. They're over there now, as a matter of fact. Father's doing a book tour, and Mother's doing something with television. They've been gone over a month and won't be home until Christmas, I'm afraid. It's too bad you'll miss them."

"Maybe your father will go to Kansas City on his book tour. Do you have his schedule?"

"Somewhere," John replied vaguely, stroking his beard. "Look. See how far back I have the Cuendets."

With obvious pride, her cousin indicated a pedigree recorded in beautiful calligraphy going back ten generations. "If I had a definite tie-in to the nobility, I could go much further back. But the French records are so spotty that I was lucky to get back this far. Fortunately, our family didn't move around much."

"Do you suspect that they do connect with nobility somewhere?"

"That's the family tradition. But you know how reliable family traditions are. Now. Tell me about the Bordens."

Alex drew a brief descendancy chart. "So far I've only gotten back as far as my second great-grandfather, Jacob Borden, profession unknown. He had two sons, James, who was probably your great-grandfather, and Earl, my great-grandfather.

Jacob Borden

James Borden	Earl Borden
Joseph Borden (Cuendet)	Edward Borden
Jean Cuendet	Joseph Borden
John Cuendet	Alex Borden Campbell

"I got my information from the U.S. Census last August, and since then I've been too busy to follow it up. I don't really know anything about them, except that they were from Illinois.

It shouldn't be hard to get back further. Our censuses go back to 1790. What about your mother's line? It doesn't look like you've done much there."

"I was hoping to hire you to do that for me—when you have the time, of course. Mother doesn't know much about her origins. She says most Americans don't."

"That's true, I'm afraid. Look at me! It never occurred to me to wonder about anyone further back than my grandfather until long after he was dead."

"When did you take up genealogy?"

"Not until I was married and living in Scotland. My husband's family are Scottish, so I had a great time doing his pedigree. After he died, Briggie and I formed a sort of partnership called RootSearch. We do heir searches and that sort of thing. It's not tremendously lucrative, but it's fun. I just started working on my own pedigree last summer."

"That seems odd," the doctor said, "considering you're a professional."

"My family had this secret, you see, about Grandfather. They wouldn't discuss him. I couldn't get past it."

"How did you do it?"

"Luck, mostly."

John raised an eyebrow. "I've done enough genealogy to know that luck seldom has much to do with it. It's patience you need."

"True," Alex agreed.

"Let me tell you how I came up with my fourth great-grandfather, Raoul Cuendet . . ."

There was no chance of escape. She was destined to listen to every detail of John's research, accompanied by all his stories of perseverance and victory. No one, she knew from experience, could be more boring than a genealogist.

Keeping her eyes attentively fixed on his face she wondered where Charles was. Had they arrested him? Maybe she could manage a telephone call before they went to the theater.

Studying the man who was probably her cousin, she forced herself to consider the possiblity that he might be a murderer.

As he talked, his forehead corrugated with earnestness, and he illustrated his story with frequent hand gestures. Letting it all flow over her, she enumerated the points against him.

First, he had no alibi for Philippa's death. Second, if Philippa had known where he was (and Edward had said she knew of the existence of Dr. Sandra Brown), she would have called him as soon as she got the letter from the researcher. But how would he have known about Alex's theory and that she was on her way? Etienne? But Etienne presumably wouldn't have known where to contact him in London. Was there any possibility Antonia could have told John? But how would she have known where to find him?

Leaving that difficulty for the moment, Alex moved on to the next item. If he wanted to leave Olivia for Dr. Brown, he needed an alternative source of funding for his clinic. Also, he would have heard from Olivia that Alex had witnessed Philippa's murder. He would have been worried she might recognize him. It made sense that he might have tried to run her down with the car before she had a chance to meet him.

It made sense. She shivered slightly.

"Cold?" the doctor interrupted his narrative. He looked puzzled. There was a roaring fire only a few feet away.

"No. But I just remembered something. I need to make a telephone call before we go to the theater. Is there time?"

Consulting his watch, the doctor suddenly beckoned the waiter. "I'm afraid not. You shouldn't have let me go on so long. We scarcely have time to make the opening curtain."

Alex nearly panicked. Olivia had said the curtain was at eight. It was only seven-thirty. She had plenty of time. She couldn't possibly sit through *Hamlet* without knowing Charles's fate! "It's only seven-thirty . . . "

"Yes. But the theater is half an hour from here." He was stacking banknotes indiscriminately on top of the bill the waiter had handed him. "Let's go."

The drive to Stratford was accomplished at high speed. Evidently, John hadn't exaggerated. Olivia had left them tickets at the front office where they were urged to hurry as the curtain was just about to rise.

No sooner were they seated in the box than the house lights dimmed. Alex sighed deeply. *Hamlet* was an interminable play.

To her disappointment, it was performed in modern dress. Horatio in a trenchcoat resembled the spy who came in from the cold and detracted considerably from the spirit of the play—not to mention the appearance of Hamlet in dirty pajamas and socks. Nothing could take away from Olivia's performance, however. As Queen of Denmark she was superbly regal, her perfect profile, queenly carriage, and honey-blond coiffure overcoming the obvious detriment of a Queen Elizabeth II suit and hat.

It emerged that Olivia and Timothy Dalton were carrying the play. He was magnificent. Alex was almost able to forget the murders in her own life as she followed the machinations of the mythical King Claudius. On the other hand, Hamlet's interpretation was so bizarrely psychotic that no one could have the slightest sympathy with his plight.

At the interval, Alex put the play out of her mind and made a mad dash for the telephone next to the ladies' room. Unfortunately, there was a line of young mothers (obviously checking on children) already waiting. The third gong was sounding just as she made it to the phone. Suddenly, she realized she didn't even know Charles's number, and there was no time to call directory assistance. Frantically, she signaled John, who was waiting a short way off.

"Charles's number. What is it?" she demanded.

"We need to go in, Alex."

"Please just tell me Charles's number!"

He gave it to her.

The telephone rang repeatedly in the bachelor's flat. No one answered, not even a machine.

Hanging up disconsolately, she followed John back to their box. As they settled in just before the curtain was to go up, she felt she needed to smooth over the sudden awkwardness, but she had no intention of telling John her worries.

"Somehow Olivia has managed to carry off the idea of a woman cruelly wronged. I've never read Gertrude that way. She always seemed pretty silly to me."

Her companion grinned through his beard, an appreciative light in his intense blue eyes. "You've managed to put your finger on Olivia's genius. I suspect she knew this wasn't going to be a 'straight' *Hamlet*. Since everyone else was messing with the interpretation, she wasn't going to have the audience thinking her character was a silly woman."

As the curtain went up, Alex found herself thinking fleetingly that Mr. Rochester had been wrong. There was in fact some understanding between John and Olivia. He understood her art, at least. That, to an actress, would be worth a good deal.

But where was Charles? It was all she could do to remain in her seat. The words of the play didn't penetrate now as she stared blankly at the stage. What if he had been arrested?

And why was she so certain he wasn't guilty? Were these her feelings speaking, or was it her head? If Charles hadn't made such an issue of her loyalty that afternoon, would she still be uncommitted?

No. She had never considered Charles a possible suspect. Knowing the depth of English reserve, it struck her as probable that she might be the only one who knew the strength of his feelings for Philippa. But Etienne? Could he have murdered Etienne?

Squirming in her seat, she considered this possibility. The business about his being seen outside Etienne's room had shaken her. But remembering the steadfastness of his scrutiny that afternoon, she couldn't believe he had anything serious to hide. She had felt his innocence from deep within. There must have been an innocent reason for his presence outside Etienne's room.

She would prove him innocent. There was no alternative.

Looking sideways at John, she wondered again if she were sitting with a murderer.

Before they met Olivia, Alex tried the telephone once more. There was still no answer, so she tried Briggie. Her partner was probably sitting by the phone waiting to hear from her. She should have called before now.

After assuring Briggie that all was well, she asked, "Have you heard anything from Charles?"

"His uncle called," her friend said heavily. "They've got him in custody."

"They can't!"

"Apparently, his finances aren't all they should be. Oh, Alex, I'm so sorry!"

Her friend's distress after the fact only made her angry. "Do you still have an open mind, Briggie?"

"As a matter of fact, I do."

Alex hung up the phone.

"I'm sorry, John, but I just had some distressing news. Charles has been arrested. We can't possibly go on with our little party. I'm far too upset."

To her surprise, John put a comforting arm around her. "He didn't do it, Alex. I know he didn't do it." Looking into his eyes, she was surprised to see the sadness in them.

"I didn't know you were close."

"We've always been. Don't worry. It'll work out. Livy has things all arranged with Dalton, so I'm afraid we need to go along for a few minutes anyway. Charles would understand, and there's nothing we can do for him at the moment anyway."

Even under the circumstances, meeting Timothy Dalton was an overwhelming experience. He was less aloof than she expected from his reputation as one who guarded his privacy.

"How do you do, Mrs. Campbell. I understand you may be Olivia's cousin-in-law." His green eyes danced as though this were some kind of joke. He looked at Olivia and smiled his famous mischievous smile.

In spite of herself, Alex was stunned by his matinee-idol handsomeness. Obviously, Olivia wasn't immune to it either. A look crackling with electricity passed between the actress and the actor. It was clear there was a good deal of chemistry going here.

"You were both brilliant tonight," John said, seemingly oblivious to the byplay.

Dalton laughed his rich chuckle, transforming his strong-featured face into that of a wickedly naughty boy.

Olivia seemed to be watching her husband covertly, measuring his response to her flirtation. Suddenly, the actress stretched her arms above her head in a sensuous, satisfied gesture that reminded Alex of a cat. "At least it's over and done with finally. Another week and I would have killed Hamlet and saved Laertes the bother."

They were seated at a small table in an intimate, candlelit restaurant where all the waiters wore evening dress. Dalton placed his arm across the back of the actress's chair with a proprietary air. "The performance seemed to tax you more than usual tonight, Livy. Are you sure you're all right?"

"Yes, thank you, darling," she said. Then, lifting a cascade of golden hair off the back of her neck, Olivia addressed Alex. "So what did you think of the Royal Shakespeare Company?"

"I was disappointed in the modern dress," she admitted. "But I suppose Americans always are. Hamlet was a little too much of an original for me, but John's right, the two of you were brilliant."

The woman smiled the famous du Bois smile that had dazzled her fans for so long. Olivia's features were generous, almost larger than life. It was tremendously difficult to steel yourself against their appeal, even when you were trying to be objective. "I suppose it sounds almost sacrilegious," the actress confided, "but I do get so tired of Shakespeare."

Dalton laughed. "Imagine how tired he must get of us! Always meddling with his characters, taking his plays out of their proper atmosphere, mangling his moral tone!"

"Oh, I know you worship him," she said patting his hand.

Turning to her husband, she asked, "How was the clinic, darling?"

John hunched forward on his elbows. "We're getting closer. That little Baker boy is doing quite well."

Olivia's face lit up, and the mood changed instantly. Her delight was obviously genuine. "That's wonderful! We must have a toast!"

The actress summoned the waiter. "We're ready to order," she told him. "A bottle of champagne and four glasses."

Alex wanted to go through the floor. "Just mineral water for me, please," she said. Why didn't John tell her this was inappropriate? Why didn't he tell her about Charles?

When the wine and water came, Dalton took over the honors of uncorking the bottles and pouring out.

"I'd like to propose a toast," Olivia said carefully, raising her glass. "To the most brilliant doctor in the hemisphere: John Cuendet!" The effect of this tribute was slightly marred by the fact that the actress kept her eyes fixed on Dalton's and toasted with him playfully, as though it were some intimate matter of their own. Alex looked away, but at that moment, Olivia's glass fell from her hand onto the table and a small stream of champagne ran across the tablecloth and into Alex's lap.

"This is becoming a habit, darling," John said curtly, as he mopped up after her.

Olivia looked conscience stricken. "Have I ruined your dress, Alex?"

It was the new Laura Ashley—a black velveteen with a large white pique collar. "Heavens, no," she lied.

Dalton signaled for a waiter. As Alex concentrated on blotting her skirt, she wondered what had happened. Clearly there was something going on here. John seemed wearily tolerant and not at all put out by his wife's flirtation. Did he not care, or was he used to it?

What an extreme sort of person she was! At the moment, she seemed to be playing the child who was afraid she would be punished.

"I am so sorry," she was telling Alex. "I can't think what happened. I must be more tired than I thought. Such a strain, this *hideous* play."

"Not to mention the murder in the family," Dalton murmured. "You're entitled to a little temperament, Olivia. It must have been a brutal week by anyone's standards."

Alex welcomed this reference to reality. "It's just gotten more brutal, I'm afraid. Charles Lamb, John's cousin, has just been arrested."

"Charles?" Olivia looked up, her eyes large, her lips parted. "But why?"

"He was seen outside Etienne's rooms on the afternoon he was murdered," Alex said flatly. "But I don't think he's guilty."

"Nor I," John added.

"Of course he's not guilty, Alex!" Olivia laid a hand over hers, and Alex was ashamed to feel tears coming to the surface.

"This Charles Lamb," the actor was saying, "Is he the theater critic?"

"Yes," John said. "I'd forgotten, but you must have heard of him."

"He's impaled me with his pen once or twice. But only when I deserved it. He's quite respected in the profession, actually."

"He's the kind of critic who finds holes in your performance you didn't know were there," Olivia commented. "He's been a tremendous help to me on more than one occasion." Turning to her husband, she said, "Why didn't you tell me about this at once? I would never have proposed that silly little toast."

"I thought you deserved a good time after the rotten week you'd had," her husband said mildly.

Timothy Dalton put his arm around Olivia's shoulders, squeezing her gently. Actresses and actors were always doing this, of course. John seemed to take it in stride, but Alex hadn't missed the glow of enjoyment his wife seemed to direct at him as she shifted sensuously in Dalton's half embrace.

Alex cast around in her mind for a new subject that might

cut through the current generated by the performance she was witnessing. She realized that with all her preoccupations, she hadn't given John the news. "It looks like we've found what Philippa was after in the States," she told him. When she was sure she had his attention, she related the tale of Harold Simpson.

Instead of showing the jubilation she expected, John merely sighed. "So Philippa's murder need never have taken place."

"No. Unfortunately, not. But it's looking more and more like Joe Cuendet was Joseph Borden."

"When will you know for certain?" Olivia asked.

"There's a piece of evidence I'm waiting for. I'll probably get it in the next couple of days."

"What I don't understand," Olivia said, "is how anyone could possibly think Charles killed Philippa."

"Money," John said. "I think he was a little overextended."

"But Charles is always overextended," she said, throwing up her hands. "He likes living on the edge. And he has no dependents."

"This must be very boring for Mr. Dalton," Alex said finally.

"I'd much rather you called me Tim," the actor said, smiling briefly. "You seem to be some sort of detective, Mrs. Campbell."

"I'd much rather you called me Alex. And I wish we'd met under much happier circumstances."

———

Briggie was waiting up for her when she got back to the hotel. "I wanted to talk to you, Alex."

Sitting down on her bed, Alex felt incredibly weary. "Spare me. I'm not in a patient mood. I know your opinion of Charles."

"Actually, I wanted to apologize. I'm afraid I kind of went off the deep end. You know me when I get the bit between my teeth."

"But what's made you change your mind? I would think that after his arrest, you'd be more convinced than ever."

Briggie sat next to her on the bed and began to pleat the spread between her fingers. It was an oddly evasive action for the straightforward woman. Alex realized her friend was having difficulty looking her in the eye.

"When I heard about the chambermaid, all of a sudden I realized I didn't really, deep down, believe he was guilty. I tried to explain away the situation to Chief Inspector Hubbard, as a matter of fact. Later, when I thought about it, I realized I had been letting my feelings get in the way. I *wanted* Charles to be guilty."

Alex was stunned by this admission. "But why?"

"Because I could see you were getting fond of him."

"And you were worried for Daniel's sake?"

"No. Oh, that's part of it, I suppose. But there's more to it than that." Finally, she looked up, and Alex could see her brow was furrowed over troubled eyes. "I guess I was just worried you'd get carried away."

"What do you mean?"

"By all this," Briggie swept her arm in a gesture which Alex supposed indicated Oxford. "And by Charles's looks and ideas."

Alex was beginning to see a glimmer. "Do you mean you were worried about my testimony?"

"Well, yes. I guess that's what I mean."

Standing, Alex went over to the window and looked out, recalling her epiphany of the other night. "If you really believe the gospel is true, Briggie, why do you have so little confidence in it? The truth can hold its own."

"I guess I never really knew this side of you, that's all. It's different seeing you in these surroundings. And seeing you with Charles, well, I guess I was a little scared, because it seemed like you belonged together."

"And you were worried he'd talk me out of my beliefs."

Her friend nodded.

"It's not like that, Briggie," Alex said with some weariness.

"Actually, we've been making some headway in the other direction. Underneath it all, I really don't believe Charles Lamb is as much of a cynic as he pretends. At least he wasn't. Heaven only knows what this experience is doing to his philosophical viewpoint."

Briggie gave Alex one of her impulsive hugs. "Please forgive me, honey. And believe me when I say I want to help him."

Hugging her friend back, Alex said, "Of course I forgive you. But you really need to have a little more faith in me, Briggie."

"I know. I know. You're far stronger than I realize."

"Now, I've never felt less like sleep in my life, so let's get packed and make an action plan for France."

"Did you learn anything interesting from John?"

"Nothing material. Olivia was flirting like mad with Timothy Dalton, but I doubt it means anything. As a matter of fact, I got the impression she was doing it for John's benefit."

Briggie digested this. "If he's afraid Olivia's going to bolt, he has all the more reason to need the money from the estate."

"But don't forget the lovely Dr. Brown in London. No, the field's still wide open. I just hope Charles was right and that we'll find something that will help us in France."

NINETEEN

The travel arrangements worked out smoothly, and by two o'clock the following afternoon, Briggie, Alex, and Richard were in their rental car, headed west out of Strasbourg.

Their destination lay in a forested region south of the Argonne in the Marne River Valley. Before leaving home, Alex had spent a week reading up on the Battle of the Marne and knew that the region of Bar-le-Duc had seen some of the heaviest and most fruitless fighting. At one time, the countryside had been a wasteland broken by lines of barbed wire and muddy shell holes. Behind the barbed wire, there had been trenches, scars dug deep into the ground where the troops lived between pointless assaults in which more of them died each day.

Now, looking at the peaceful, bucolic terrain and the River Marne, purged long ago of blood, it was impossible to imagine such devastation.

"What are we going to do first?" Briggie wanted to know as they slowed their speed to enter the town.

"Have a snack," Richard said. It was close to four o'clock, and lunch on the plane had been light.

"There are plenty of little cafes," Alex told them. "Maybe we could get an omelette somewhere. Why don't you just drive to the center of town and park, Richard?"

Following her instructions, the lawyer negotiated the narrow streets crammed with baby buggies and bicycles. At last he found a short space that was barely large enough for the car.

It felt good to get out and stretch her legs. With the rest of her party in train, Alex led the way through the hodgepodge of crumbling old buildings and uninspired new ones until they came to a market square full of black-smocked farmers and their barrows of harvest vegetables. Mounds of pumpkin, squash, cabbage, and turnips held aloft chalkboard signs advertising their price. A very large woman in a blue and pink jersey was seated upon a bench, watching her tiny poodle sniff the gutter at the end of his leash. With a slight bow, Richard asked her for directions to a good restaurant. The woman looked blank. Alex repeated the question in French. Amid much animation and hand gesturing, she at last pointed down the street behind her, which they traversed until they came upon the old slate-roofed church.

"There," Alex indicated. "That little cafe across the street with the awnings is where Briggie and I first met Etienne."

Looking at the gray stone church, she forced herself to remember that scarcely more than a week ago, Etienne had come out of that church with Genevieve on his arm, looking dashing and virile—like Cary Grant, Briggie had said. Now he was in a morgue in London. And Charles was in jail for his murder.

"I wonder if they'll bury him here," Briggie mused, looking at the churchyard.

"I hope so," Alex said sadly, pausing next to the iron gate of the churchyard and looking at the little patch of soil that covered the most recent Guison casket. "His grandfather's grave is still fresh."

"Food, ladies," Richard urged heartlessly.

After their snack, during which Alex merely picked at an excellent *omelette aux champignons,* she used the telephone in the cafe to call Genevieve Guison. The lady was polite, but her joie de vivre was obviously missing.

"She'll see us," she announced. "But she's not happy."

"I didn't expect her to be," Briggie replied.

"How do we find her house?" Richard wanted to know.

"It isn't far from here."

The widow's home was in a tall, narrow building with

window boxes, wedged between a pharmacy and a book shop. Built of the same gray stone as the church, it looked ancient compared to everything around it. As she rang the bell, Alex felt her stomach knot. What could she say to the poor woman?

Genevieve Guison answered the door dressed in mourning. There was not a jet black hair out of place, but her face was haggard, with bigger hollows in her cheeks and beneath her eyes. Nevertheless, she made an effort to be gracious.

"*Bon jour.* You will follow me, please?" She led them through a dark hall to a room at the back of the house. There, unexpectedly, large windows looked out on a small walled garden. The room itself was furnished in scrubbed pine, which Alex had no difficulty in recognizing as the real article—the country French antique that was so popular in the U. S. The furniture had probably been in the family for generations. Upholstered and draped in a small red and white print, the room was graced with vivid touches that revealed Genevieve's personality. On the coffee table sat a copper bowl of pomegranates, in the corner a begonia bloomed atop a tall white pedestal, and the walls were hung with bright watercolors of flowers.

"A gift from Etienne," she told Alex curtly as she saw her looking at the paintings.

"I'm so sorry," Alex told her, tears suddenly stinging her eyes. "If I hadn't met you that day, this would never have happened."

The woman looked at her, steady and dry-eyed. "You did not do this to Etienne. He should have left it alone."

Left what alone? Sensing anger in Genevieve's rigid posture, Alex was afraid to ask. "Let me introduce you. Briggie, you remember." Genevieve gave a short nod. "This is Richard Grinnell, the lawyer who is handling the Borden estate I told you about. Richard, this is Madame Genevieve Guison."

After they had all shaken hands, Madame Guison seated herself on the edge of a chair, her back straight, her heavily ringed hands clenched on her lap.

Richard asked her to recount what she had told Alex about the soldier named Joseph who had lived with her family.

When she had finished her story in halting English, he said, "I know this is a terribly sad time for your family, but you are a vital part of this probate procedure." He broke off, looking at Alex, who translated the words Genevieve might not understand. "I would like to take a formal deposition. You can speak in French if you like, and someone can translate."

"When would you do this?"

"It needs to be a sworn statement, so I propose to find a magistrate. Is there one here in town?"

Alex translated, and Genevieve replied, "At the Hotel de Ville. But tomorrow is Sunday. You will have to find him at his home."

"Do you think he will meet with us on Sunday?"

"Monsieur Lenoir is an old friend. I will talk to him. You telephone to me later. I will tell you what he says."

Richard agreed, presenting his business card. "Just write your telephone number for me."

Alex, who had been shifting uneasily in her chair, felt the eyes of the old lady return to her face when she handed back the lawyer's card.

"My Etienne . . . the English police, they tell us so little . . . "

"We think he witnessed the murder of Philippa Cuendet." Alex related the story of Philippa's murder. "Someone in England knew I was going there and knew about the inheritance. That person told Philippa. She was on her way to meet me when she was killed. Etienne was standing next to her on the pavement when she was pushed under a bus."

Genevieve nodded slowly.

"Can you remember if you told anyone about my going to England to find the Cuendet family?"

The woman closed her eyes. For a moment, it appeared as though she had gone to sleep. Alex realized she was gritting her teeth waiting for the answer.

"*Non,*" she said finally. "I discuss this only with Etienne. No one else is interested in the past. They become . . . tired of it."

There was such a melancholy look in the old lady's eye that Alex suddenly lost her nerve. How could she possibly ask this grief-stricken old woman whether her husband or Joe Cuendet was the father of her son?

"Young people can get very bored by the past," Briggie agreed. "But Etienne wasn't, was he?"

"He was. Then you come with this story about the inheritance, and suddenly, *voilà!* He is interested."

"*Pour quoi?*" Alex asked.

The old lady drew herself up and focused with some confusion on her questioner. "I do not know. But if Etienne was interested, he must have thought there was the money someplace." She laughed a dry, mirthless laugh. "I told him 'leave it alone. This is not for you.'" She threw up her hands and suddenly tears spilled over onto her carefully rouged and powdered cheeks. "He would not listen to an old woman."

Wetting her lips, Briggie said, "Etienne was very curious about the American you loved during the war."

Genevieve straightened her spine once more, and for the first time that afternoon the expression on her face became the formidable one Alex remembered. "Etienne was a Guison. The American, he is nothing to do with him."

"But did Etienne believe that?" Richard asked peremptorily. "Isn't there a chance he might have believed Joe Cuendet was his great-grandfather?"

"*Pardon?*"

Alex repeated the question in French, grateful that Richard at least was demonstrating some nerve. Madame Guison's nostrils flared in anger. "How am I to know what he thought? He had the head like the pig—like his father. Always he had his own ideas. For this, he is killed."

Glaring from one of them to the other, Genevieve seemed to challenge the company.

They were going to get nothing more from her, Alex decided. "When is Etienne's funeral to be?" she asked.

"They will send the body today. On Monday we have the funeral mass."

Nodding, Alex repeated, "I am so sorry and so sad about this, Madame. We will leave you now. Until tomorrow."

"*A demain,*" she agreed as she shut her stout wooden door against them.

"Whew!" Briggie said. "I hope I never have to cross her!"

"She's something," Alex agreed. "Thank you, Richard, for being courageous."

"I've handled a feisty widow or two in my day," he said, looking pointedly at Briggie, who wrinkled her nose at him. "Now, it seems to me the next order of business is to find a place to sleep. Where did the two of you stay?"

"There is an inn just outside town," Briggie told him. "It's pretty old, but it's clean. I think they even allow lawyers to stay there."

Retracing their footsteps through the town, they came at last to their car and drove back through the narrow streets into the open countryside. Briggie pointed out the little inn that looked as though it had been standing for centuries. With half-timbers and white plaster on the outside, it also had tiny windows and window boxes planted with still-blooming geraniums.

"I imagine this is one of those charming places without a square corner in the whole structure," remarked Richard.

"That's about right," Alex agreed. "But the people are nice."

A stout woman with iron gray hair and a jutting lower jaw recognized Briggie and Alex. "Ah!" she exclaimed speaking to Briggie. "You like Bar-le-Duc! You bring your husband!"

Looking at Richard, who grinned, Briggie said quickly, "No, he's just a good friend. Do you have two rooms? Madame Campbell and I can share."

"*Mais oui,*" the stout woman said with a twinkle in her eye as she looked them over.

Briggie and Alex had the same room they had occupied before. Whitewashed and carpeted with an ancient patterned rug in royal blue and red, it contained a brass bed, a utilitarian washbasin with a single glass shelf and mirror above it, and an old walnut wardrobe with exactly two hangers.

"Poor Richard is going to hate it," Alex said.

"Well, he'll just have to lump it, won't he?" Briggie answered cheerfully. "Do him good to see how the other half lives."

When they met again and ventured back outdoors, the sun had just set. A north wind had begun to blow, and Briggie said she smelled frost in the air. Alex asked Richard if he would like to visit the American cemetery before dinner. He agreed.

Pulling up to the cemetery, the threesome got out and stood for a moment in silence. Though this was Alex's second visit, the sight took her breath away and brought instant tears to her eyes.

The acres of white marble crosses looked dark and sober silhouetted against the fading pink and purple of the sky.

"I wonder if they even understood what they were fighting for," Alex whispered with a shiver.

To her surprise, Richard put an arm around her shoulders and squeezed her. "The British and French never acknowledge it, of course, but it was the Americans who turned the tide. I think both sides would have fought until there wasn't a single man left." He paused. "You know, looking back, I don't believe either France or England really recovered from this war until the seventies."

Briggie nodded. "World War II was just the second act. Did you fight, Richard?"

"I was with Patton," he said. "Battle of the Bulge. Not far from here."

Alex began to walk between the markers, reading the names. Milton Hayes, Clarence Barber, Ronald Morgan . . . so many, many men. So many, many lives. It seemed such an awful waste for them to have died so young. Her own problems were dwarfed by comparison. It was impossible to comprehend the tragedy wrought by the death of two people multiplied by hundreds of thousands. How did Heavenly Father stand it?

Death is not the ultimate tragedy. The still, small voice sounded in her mind. *Nineteen-eighteen was not the end of the line for these men.* Moving through the lines of markers, she held on to the words of the Spirit as though they were tangible. Thank heaven she had found a way to help make sense of this vale of tears.

It was of the utmost importance to be brave. This was no time to battle her tendency to despair, to languish over things she couldn't change. There was too much to be done. There was a murderer to find.

She had left a note with Antonia to take to Charles, and she remembered it now with a smile.

Dear Charles—
I hope you don't mind being rescued by a woman, because that's what I intend to do. We're off to France.
Love,
Alex

Rejoining Briggie and Richard, who were conversing quietly on a marble bench, Alex suggested Etienne's uncle's restaurant for dinner.

They found the little biscuit-colored eatery lit cozily by candlelight. There were white linen tablecloths and bouquets of hothouse flowers on the tables. Alex marveled at the effortlessness with which the French could endow the simplest of surroundings with their unmistakable ambience.

Monsieur Guison remembered her and came to their table, dabbing at his perspiring forehead with a linen napkin.

"*A ma petite!* How sad this business is. Genevieve tells me you have been to see her."

"Yes," Alex told him. "I'm so sorry, Monsieur Guison."

"But you must call me François."

"François. I am so sorry about Etienne. I feel it is my fault."

"But of course not, *ma petite*. Etienne, he made the decision to go to England himself. My nephew, he must concern himself in other people's affairs. It has always been the same."

"He talked to you about it?"

"Yes. He had the . . . what do you call it? The *idée fixe* . . . "

"Obsession?" Alex suggested.

"Yes, the obsession. He is convinced this man, your Joseph, is our ancestor, as well."

"Was he really?" Alex said.

TWENTY

But I detain you!" apologized François. "You come to my restaurant to eat, not to hear me talk."

"We will eat soon," Alex told him. "You must finish telling us about Etienne. This is very important to the murder investigation."

"Ah, you investigate the murder? I think that is a job for the police."

"They are investigating, too. But we came to France to find out if Etienne talked to anyone about going to England. Did he know any of the Cuendet family at Oxford?"

"No. He only knows that you go there to meet them."

"We think he was killed because he knew who the murderer was." Pausing, Alex bit her bottom lip. "I don't suppose you telephoned to anyone in England?"

"I? I know the Cuendet family at the chateau, but not in England. Who do I call?"

"I don't know," she said. "It's just that someone told them that I was coming."

The chef pushed out his lower lip. "No, I discuss it with Etienne, with my wife, with my son. None of us think Etienne knows what he is talking about."

"You don't think Joe Cuendet is your ancestor?"

François rolled his eyes. "Me, I do not like to upset my grandmother. I do not suggest such a thing to her. She is very angry with Etienne."

"Even though he is dead?"

The little chef nodded. "But now," he said, "we talk

enough. You want to order the *caneton roti*. It is the speciality of the house tonight."

Briggie looked to Alex questioningly.

"Roast duckling," she translated.

They all ordered the roast duckling.

"So," Richard said, tearing off a piece of baguette, "Charles was right. Etienne was up to something. He thought he merited a share of the loot."

Alex was almost giddy with relief. "Yes. It seems more likely that there was an Oxford/Bar-le-Duc connection, too. We'll have to talk to the whole family."

Richard agreed. "Whatever his uncle says, he could have gotten someone pretty excited over all this. Would you care to hear the American law about illegitimate issue?"

"By all means," Briggie replied.

"In cases of intestacy," Richard pronounced in his ponderous legal voice, "illegitimate children have a claim on the estate."

"I guess we'd better hit the parish register tomorrow, Alex. We'll soon see if there's any foundation for Etienne's little idea."

"How would the parish register tell you?" the lawyer asked.

"Honestly, Richard, work it out!" Briggie teased. "It's a matter of the elapsed time between Genevieve's marriage to Guison and the birth of her first child. If it looks like there's anything to the theory, we need to trace all the descendants, too."

"I don't relish asking the old lady about it," Richard said ruefully. "She's so stubborn that she'd probably rather deny her heirs their inheritance than admit to any hanky-panky."

"Provincial Frenchwomen have a strong conventional streak," Alex observed. "It's her good name we're talking about. No wonder she was accusing Etienne of going after the money. Who knows? Joe Cuendet might not even have known if the child was his. Maybe when he started courting Marcelle, Genevieve had too much pride to tell him."

"That sounds like her," Briggie agreed.

Richard grinned. "Do you often find this kind of thing in your research?"

"You'd be surprised," Briggie told him. "You never know what you're going to find. About the only consistent rule is that what you find isn't what you expect."

Sunday morning, the party slept in, knowing there was no sense in their beginning inquiries until after mass. The appointment with the magistrate had been set for ten o'clock.

After croissants and chocolate in the tiny breakfast room of their inn, Richard dropped Alex and Briggie at the old stone church on his way to Genevieve's. She had assured him the magistrate was perfectly capable of translating for them.

"I don't exactly know how we're going to go about this," Briggie admitted.

"Well, for starters, I suggest we go in," Alex said.

Mass was apparently over for the morning. The inside of the church was cold, and there was a pervasive feeling of damp. Windows high above and covered with decades of dirt let in only a minimum of light.

"The stained glass must have been broken in the war," Alex remarked. "They only have plain glass now. What a shame."

As she spoke, a figure in a black priest's robe detached itself from the dark surroundings near the altar and moved towards them.

"*Puis-je vous aider?*"

Briggie and Alex walked down the short nave of the church to meet the priest, a tall angular man whose harsh features lightened as he smiled.

"*Avez-vous les registres paroissiaux?*"

"*Oui,* why do you wish to see them?"

"We are genealogists."

The priest appeared to consider their request. "*Avez-vous la famille en Bar-le-Duc?*"

Alex decided that their current suspicions of the Guison

situation justified her saying, "*Oui, effectivement les Guisons sont mes cousins.*"

"You have talked to Madame Guison?"

"*Oui.*"

"*Bon.* Follow me, please."

Having been prepared for difficulties, Alex marveled at his willingness to give them access to the parish registers. Perhaps Genevieve's partiality towards Americans was well known. At any rate, she wasn't about to question their luck.

Leading them out of the church, the priest walked next door to a stone house of moderate size, which she took to be his residence. Once inside, she saw that it was nearly as dim as the church, sparsely furnished in heavy oaken furniture that might well date back hundreds of years. The priest led them into a little room, which apparently functioned as a study. A small fire burned in the grate, and there was a large black desk with enormous clawed feet and an untidy litter of letters, books, and papers scattered across its surface. He indicated a row of black, leatherbound volumes on a shelf behind the glass door of his bookcase.

"*Quelle année?*"

Alex thought. For their supposition to be correct, Genevieve's son would have been born after the end of the war, but not too long after the Americans had departed. "1919," she said.

The priest consulted the gold imprints on the backs of the books and then, carefully sliding the right one from its place, handed it to her. He indicated that she should sit at his desk. He remained standing beside her while she consulted the register.

The first section was devoted to births. Surnames were listed in a column to the extreme left. The next columns contained, in order, the name of the child, the father, the mother, the date of baptism, and the names of the godparents. Beginning with January, Alex checked for the surname of Guison. The handwriting was full, round, and thick—a true Roman hand, for which she was grateful.

Finally, in the month of June, she saw the entry she was looking for: *Guison/Gaspard/Guilliam Guison/Genevieve Moreau/2 Juin/Paul et Sophie Moreau.* Signalling to Briggie to write it down, she realized her hands were trembling. They wouldn't know for sure until they checked the marriages, but Genevieve's child was born only seven months after the end of the war.

Turning to the marriages, Alex quickly went down the columns under January. No Guison marriage. Gambling that Genevieve would have married before her figure began to swell, Alex closed the volume, handed it to the priest, and asked for the year 1918. He replaced it carefully, handing her the one she had requested. His steady regard was unnerving. Did he intend to stand there and keep watch the entire time?

Turning to the marriages, Alex found it almost immediately. *Guilliam Guison/Genevieve Moreau/14 Decembre.* Her heart leapt. Gaspard Guison was born six and a half months after Genevieve's marriage. More than likely, her American lover had been his father.

When Briggie had finished making a note of the entry, Alex handed the book back to the priest. Now it had become a possible probate matter. They needed to find the son Gaspard's marriage and his children.

As she was trying to figure out how to frame this request, Briggie said, "We need to see these." She pointed to the whole row of books between 1940 and 1950.

Bowing slightly, the priest pulled out the first volume. "I will give them one at a time, *s'il vous plaît.*"

It seemed he had no more important work than to stand over them and observe all they were doing. At first it was bothersome, but soon they were so engrossed in their task that they hardly noticed him at all.

At the end of an hour they had found Gaspard's marriage to Françoise Collette in 1940 and the births of their sons, Albert and François.

Alex began a descendancy chart before things could get jumbled in her head:

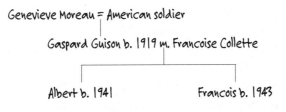

Genevieve Moreau = American soldier
|
Gaspard Guison b. 1919 m. Francoise Collette

Albert b. 1941   Francois b. 1943

She explained to the priest that they now needed the books for 1960 through 1970. Patiently extracting the requested volumes, the priest handed them to her one by one.

Albert had been married to Estelle Primavere in 1962. Later that year Etienne was born. It seemed he was an only child.

Uncle François, the chef, had married much later. In 1970, he had apparently succumbed to the charms of Marie Thielbault, and almost immediately they had become the parents of Gaston. It appeared there were no other children.

Since it looked as though their job was done, Alex sketched a final chart of the descendants of Genevieve and the unknown American:

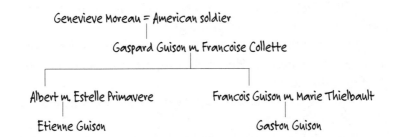

Genevieve Moreau = American soldier
|
Gaspard Guison m. Francoise Collette

Albert m. Estelle Primavere   Francois Guison m. Marie Thielbault
| |
Etienne Guison   Gaston Guison

With her nicest smile, Alex thanked the priest for his time and help. Then she asked, "Monsieur Etienne Guison, did he ask to see these?" she indicated the books.

"*Mais oui.* Last week. The same books as you."

"*Merci beaucoups,*" Alex replied, rising from behind the ancient desk.

The priest bowed graciously and escorted them to the door.

"Wow!" Briggie said once they were in the street. "Do you suppose he thought we would steal them?"

"I only hope he doesn't mention the matter to Genevieve. She might not like it."

"It doesn't matter if she likes it or not. This is a murder investigation. It looks as though Etienne was on to her."

"Yes. Charles will be pleased as punch. And now we know for sure why Etienne followed me to Oxford. It makes me feel a little less guilty, somehow. He wasn't trying to help me—he was trying to help himself."

"Right. I guess we ought to look for this Gaston Guison now."

"And Etienne's father, Albert."

It was nearly two o'clock. Alex suggested they return to Etienne's uncle's restaurant to kill several birds with one stone.

To their surprise, Richard was already seated in the dining room, munching a baguette as he waited for his food. Alex and Briggie joined him.

"Did everything go all right?" Alex asked.

"Yes," Richard said. "For a fee, the magistrate was most obliging. How did your morning go?"

"The plot thickens. Genevieve was married almost exactly a month after armistice. Her child, Gaspard, was born six and a half months later."

"Aha!" Richard exclaimed. "We may have a whole new passel of heirs, then."

"We still have to find out who the American was, remember," Briggie cautioned. "It might not have been Joseph."

"I elect Richard for the job," Alex said.

"Why me? I don't know French."

"You have the official demeanor and standing. I don't think she will claw your eyes out, and her English is perfectly adequate for nontechnical conversation."

"I hope not. Assuming her lover was Joseph Borden/Joe Cuendet, how many more heirs are we talking about?"

"Well," Alex began to enumerate them on her fingers, "Gaspard just died, so you can count him out. François, the chef here, and Etienne's father, Albert, are the other two heirs. François has a son, apparently. Briggie and I need to find him and speak to Etienne's father also. They may have called England."

After they had eaten their lunch, Alex asked François for his brother's telephone number. The little chef obliged, suggesting that she place the call from his office.

"Etienne's father Albert is an architect in Nancy," Alex told the others when she returned. "I called him from François's office. I'm afraid it's bad news. Albert Guison didn't even know about the inheritance. Etienne never told him."

"What was he like?"

Alex shivered. "'Cold' is the word, I think. He obviously held Etienne responsible for his own murder. I wouldn't like him as a father, I'll tell you that."

"It sounds like he takes after his grandmother."

"I don't know how the French got their reputation for being a romantic people. I've always found them hard as nails," Richard ruminated. "By the way, François's son, Gaston, works at the local garage." He held out a scrap of paper with scribbled directions. "I asked François while you were on the phone. They're open Sundays."

"Thanks," Alex said. "Are you going to go back to talk to Genevieve about the American?"

"Yes. We'll meet at the church at four o'clock," Richard declared as Alex and Briggie alighted from the car at the unpromising establishment that was Gaston Guison's place of employment. "*Bon chance!*"

"You, too," Briggie called over her shoulder.

A tall, scrawny youth with grease smudged over most of his body informed them that Gaston was under a Peugeot at the moment.

Walking in the general direction he indicated, they saw a pair of legs sticking out from under the car specified. The garage evidently did not run to car lifts.

"Monsieur Guison?" Alex asked.

A boy slid out from under the car and squinted at her. He,

too, had grease over much of his body, but they could see that he had blond hair and the heavy nose and lips of his father.

"*Oui.*"

"*Je pourrais etre votre cousin.*"

The boy looked her up and down rather insolently.

"You're Alex," he said.

"Yes. Did Etienne tell you about me?"

Grinning, he said, "But of course." Then, apparently remembering what had happened to Etienne, he let the grin fade. "What do you want?"

"Your English is very good."

"Etienne tutored me. He wanted me to go into his firm, but I like cars."

"You must have been close," Alex said sadly.

"*Oui.* Yes, we were. What do you want?"

Alex explained that they needed to know if he had contacted anyone in England about her intended visit.

"England? I don't know anyone in England. Who would I tell?"

"We just needed to be sure," Alex told him.

As they left the garage on foot, walking towards the church, Briggie sighed. "Well, things don't look too good for Charles. No one here seems to have telephoned England but Maurice Cuendet."

"They could be lying," Alex said. "In fact, Etienne could have been in touch with someone, too. *He* could have been lying. We've certainly proved that he wasn't above deceit. What if he'd met Philippa?"

"How are we going to find out who's lying?"

"Maybe we'll have to tackle it the other way around."

"What do you mean?"

"From the Oxford end."

Briggie sighed. "You just say that because we're in France. Once we're back in England, you will be convinced the answers lie in France."

Alex and Briggie found Richard awaiting them at the

church. "Did you ask her?" Alex demanded through the open window of the car.

The lawyer pretended to mop his brow. "I asked her. She became quite the grande dame, but as soon as she found out you'd been at the parish register, she began to swear furiously. She put us under an oath of silence."

"But did she tell you anything?"

TWENTY-ONE

Whoever her lover was, it wasn't Joseph Cuendet, I'm afraid. She swore to it."

"Oh." Getting into the car, Alex processed this unexpected thought and tried to rearrange her ideas. "How tragic!" she said finally, balling her hands into fists. "If she had told Etienne that, he never would have gone to Oxford, never would have gotten murdered."

"Yes. I think she realizes that. Her anger is just so much bravado," Richard said sadly. "Inside, she knows her refusal to tell him the truth led to his death."

Briggie fastened her seat belt. "It's sad, all right. If only people could see that secrets in families always end up making trouble."

Alex grimaced. No one knew this truth better than she. "Poor Genevieve. What a burden to live with."

"Don't you go taking the blame for this one, Alex," Briggie warned her. "Everyone has his own choice of how to play it. You couldn't make any of them choose any differently."

The trip back to Oxford was accomplished with a minimum of fuss the following day. On reaching the Randolph at four-thirty in the afternoon, the first action Alex took was to put a call through to Antonia.

"Alex! You're back. Perhaps that will cheer Charles up a bit."

"Is he out on bail?" she asked hopefully.

"No. I'm afraid not. Murder suspects can't be admitted to bail. Philip explained it all to me." Her voice broke. "I still can't take it in properly. As though Charles could commit a murder! It's a ghastly mistake."

Hoping to buoy the woman's spirits, Alex told her, "We may have found something that will help. Hannah was right. Etienne definitely thought he was descended from Joe Cuendet. We're certain that's why he came to Oxford. We haven't made a connection yet between him and anyone over here, but he told some of his family about the Joseph Borden estate. He was sure he was going to be an heir. He had just as much reason to kill Philippa as anyone."

"Alex, I know you and Charles didn't believe me, but I honestly didn't tell another soul about Maurice's call to me. So Etienne *must* be the connection. He has to be. Until we find out what the connection was, Charles is likely to stay in custody." Her voice was rising, becoming hysterical.

"We're working on it," Alex assured Antonia solemnly. "If there's a connection, I promise you we'll find it."

Hanging up, she slumped in an armchair. It was a good thing Charles's mother didn't know how utterly helpless she felt. Thinking of Charles in jail was almost more than she could bear. *Who was the murderer?*

Briggie entered from her room.

"Is Charles still in jail?"

"I'm afraid so. No miracles yet."

Briggie pulled out her notebook. "There's got to be *something* we can do. Let's make a list of suspects."

Standing, Alex went over to the window. For once she was completely unmoved by the view. She didn't even see it. Briggie's pen was scratching on the paper.

"The most obvious is John, of course," her friend said. "He'd met Etienne, and he doesn't have an alibi for Philippa's murder. So he had opportunity. Motive, well . . . " she shrugged, "It's pretty obvious. That kiss. We don't really know how much money Dr. Brown can raise compared to Olivia's income. I'd still say there's a chance there. If he wants a divorce from Olivia, he'd want a secure income."

"You're right," Alex agreed. "I think he cares more about his research than either woman."

Sighing, Briggie went on. "Then there's Frederick. His mother could have told him you were coming. He has no convincing alibi for Philippa's murder, and he needs money. Therefore, he has motive and opportunity."

"If Antonia had told Frederick I was coming, she would have told the police by now. She's frantic. She's certainly not likely to let one son be convicted in order to save the other. Use your head, Briggie."

Undaunted, her friend chewed the eraser of her pencil. "Well, on to Mr. Rochester. He has motive, and no alibi for Philippa's death, but how would he have known about the fortune and your coming?"

"Philippa could have told him. But we still haven't figured out how she knew."

"It keeps coming back to that, doesn't it?"

Alex took handfuls of hair and yanked, as though she would pull it out by the roots. "It's just got to have something to do with Etienne. I keep feeling that there is something we found in France that rings a bell. I just can't think what it is."

"I suppose we shouldn't ignore Hannah and Olivia," Briggie went on doggedly. "They'd profit through their husbands, although both of them have money of their own. Did Hannah have an alibi?"

"No. But Olivia did. Her housekeeper. C'mon, Briggie! Can you really picture either of them caring enough about this money to commit murder over it?" Closing her eyes, she leaned back in the chair. "No. It's got to be one of the men. And the facts stack up the most convincingly against John."

"Richard and I thought we'd go see Chief Inspector Hubbard about what we gathered about Etienne. We'll try to find out if there's anything new that's come up while we've been gone."

"Okay. Find out if we can visit Charles, too. Do you have

that stuff we copied down from the parish registers? I just want to look it over again."

Briggie handed her the notebook she'd been writing in. "Here it is. We'll meet you back here for dinner at about seven. Okay?"

"Fine," Alex said absently, looking over the descendancy chart they had drawn. She didn't even hear Briggie leave.

But at length she had to admit there was nothing particularly helpful about the descendancy chart. Sighing, Alex turned the page to the transcriptions of the actual parish entries themselves. She started reading them in order, beginning with Genevieve's marriage.

Moments later, she stared fixedly at the page. That was it. *That had to be it.* It explained some things, but there was still a lot that made no sense. Grabbing her peacoat, she pulled it on and left.

———————

Olivia's housekeeper answered the door and led her to a small sitting room decorated beautifully with low tables and chairs and what looked like oriental treasures.

"It will be a few moments before Madame can see you," the servant told her. She had protruding teeth, a head of wiry red curls and walked with a slight limp.

"When is Dr. Cuendet expected home?" Alex asked, looking at her watch. It was five-thirty.

"He should be here in about a quarter of an hour. Now, if you'll excuse me, I'll tell Madame you're here."

Left alone in the room, Alex began to feel foolish. Why had she dashed over here so impulsively? She should have called the clinic and simply talked to John on the phone.

Looking around her, she tried to calm herself. The surroundings were obviously meant to foster tranquillity. The simple flower arrangements were skillfully done with an obvious oriental touch. Did Olivia do her own flowers? Or did her housekeeper? Alex stood and went to look at the scroll on the wall. It must have cost the earth. It was bordered in gold leaf and appeared to be ancient. Who would have thought Olivia would have a taste for the East, with all of Europe at her feet?

Nearly ten minutes later, the actress made her entrance.

"I'm sorry to be so long, Alex. I'm afraid I was on the telephone with my manager. How was your trip?"

"Tragic, in a way. Hannah was partly right, it turns out. Etienne *did* think he was descended from Joe Cuendet. He wasn't, but the important thing is that he thought he was."

Olivia's forehead creased. "I'm afraid I don't see . . ."

"That's why he came to Oxford. And it gives him a motive for Philippa's death. He would have wanted Joe Cuendet to be Joseph Borden, too."

The actress nodded. "I see. But why was *he* murdered?"

Alex stood abruptly and wandered over to a sparse arrangement of pussywillows. "I've no idea, unfortunately. An accomplice, maybe? The sad thing is, it need never have happened. It wasn't really any of his concern at all."

"Did you want to see John? Is that why you're here?"

"It was just . . . do you think I could have another look at his genealogy chart? He wouldn't mind, would he?"

Shrugging, the woman said, "I don't see how that's going to help. John didn't know anything about his grandfather."

"Just humor me," Alex asked, smiling.

At that moment, they heard the front door open. "There he is. You can ask him yourself," she said.

John entered the room, looking exhausted. There were dark rings under his eyes and he moved slowly, all the animation drained from him. Seeing Alex, however, he immediately stood up straighter.

"Well, hello, Alex. Tell me you've brought good news. I've had a beastly day."

Olivia was all concern. "What is it, darling?"

"Terrance has been hospitalized. Pneumonia. I don't think he's going to last the night."

"Maybe I should come back another time," Alex said, rising.

"No. No." John motioned with his hand for her to be seated. "You're just what the doctor ordered."

"I only wanted to have another look at your genealogy," she said. "We can do it another time."

John sank wearily into a chair. "Livy will get it, won't you darling?"

His wife smiled lovingly. "Of course."

Both of them watched as she walked out of the room.

"So. Did you find out anything in France?" he inquired.

Alex reported the facts she had told Olivia. John rubbed his forehead. "What a pity. The man needn't have been involved at all."

Olivia reentered with the wall chart and handed it to Alex.

She studied it eagerly, her heart immediately slamming into high gear. *She had been right.*

"Have you twisted an ankle, darling?" John was asking his wife with concern.

"It's nothing," she told him. "Just a little cramp in my foot."

Thankful for the byplay that gave her a moment to compose herself, Alex wondered what on earth she should do.

"What is it, Alex?" John asked, as though sensing her excitement.

Suddenly, she chickened out. She couldn't possibly confront them. Not like this. She needed more information.

"Nothing," she sighed, trying to sketch disappointment. "I must be losing it. I remembered my facts wrong."

Rising, she handed the chart back to John. "Thanks for humoring me."

"I'll be so glad when this beastly investigation is over," Olivia said with a shiver. "Though I must say, I can't believe Charles did it."

"I'm certain he didn't," Alex said firmly.

"But haven't you heard?" the actress queried. "A witness has come forward. She recognized Charles. He was standing there on the pavement when Philippa was pushed."

Alex's legs folded under her, and she collapsed back into the chair. "When was this?"

"Yesterday."

"But why hasn't she said anything until now?"

"It was Charles's picture in the paper, you see," John said gently.

Alex looked at the two of them. Olivia was perched on the arm of John's chair, her arm across the back. Both wore expressions of concern.

Suddenly, she was very angry. But she mustn't do anything stupid. The thing to do was to tell Chief Inspector Hubbard and let him handle it—if there was anything to handle.

"I've got to go," she said briskly. "I'm meeting Briggie and Richard for dinner."

John heaved himself out of his chair and walked with her to the door. "I'm sorry, Alex. You're fond of Charles, aren't you?"

"Yes," she said, walking out into the night.

When she reached the Randolph twenty minutes later, Alex put in a call to Chief Inspector Hubbard. He had gone home for the night, but they would ask him to get in touch with her. Going to Briggie's door, she knocked. There was no answer. She entered the room and found evidence that her friend had dressed in a hurry. There were garments flung all over the room. Searching the closet, she found her partner's cranberry dress missing. She had dressed for dinner and gone.

Puzzled, she dialed the front desk. "Did Mrs. Poulson leave a message for me? I'm Alex Campbell."

"No, Mrs. Campbell."

"Did you see her leave?"

The desk clerk pondered. "She would be the lady with white hair and the American lawyer?"

"Yes, right."

"They left about a quarter of an hour ago."

"Did you call a taxi for them?"

"Yes. As a matter of fact, Mr. Grinnell did order a taxi."

"Have you any idea where they were going?"

"No. I'm sorry."

Hanging up the telephone, Alex felt peeved. They could

have at least left her a message. They were probably off on one of their hare-brained chases.

But it was time to think.

What exactly was happening? Grabbing Briggie's notebook from the table at her elbow, Alex tried to structure her thoughts, but she found she was trembling. A wave of nausea overcame her and she belatedly noted the signs of low blood sugar. Her last meal had been a sandwich on the plane. With a call to room service, she ordered soup and a sandwich and then returned to Briggie's notes.

Etienne's uncle François, the chef, was married to Marie Thielbault. Tonight she had confirmed that Olivia's maiden name was Thielbault. Du Bois was just a stage name.

And of all the people they had questioned in Bar-le-Duc, they had not questioned Etienne's Aunt Marie! His father, yes. His uncle, yes. His cousin, yes. But not his aunt.

What if Olivia was a relative? What would have happened when Marie Thielbault Guison had heard Etienne's story of a fabulous fortune, his theory about being descended from Joe Cuendet/Borden and Alex's mission to Oxford? Surely, she would have telephoned Olivia. The coincidence would have been amusing, if nothing else.

But why, when they were searching for a connection, had nobody mentioned that Olivia was from Bar-le-Duc? Perhaps she wasn't. Maybe her branch of the family lived somewhere else.

Alex put her hands to her temples. Her head throbbed. So. What did all this mean? Did Etienne know of the relationship? Did he know Olivia? Once he found out she was married to a Cuendet . . . what? What did Olivia have to fear?

That they would suspect John, of course. She must have told John about the fortune and Joseph Borden. He would have called Philippa immediately. And Philippa would have told him her news about Harold Simpson. He would have arranged to go with her to see Alex and then, wham! He pushes her under a bus.

The telephone rang shrilly. Alex jumped, staring at it as though it were alive. Finally, heart hammering, she answered.

"Alex?" It was her mother.

Taking a slow, deliberate breath, Alex replied with relief, "Mother, what a wonderful surprise! How are you?"

"Fine, dear. But I've been worrying. Are *you* all right?"

"Yes. I'm doing just fine."

"Have they caught the murderer yet?"

"No. Not yet. But I think we're a little closer."

"Don't do anything foolish, dear. I keep remembering . . . "

"Nothing like that's going to happen this time. I'm taking good care of myself. How're you feeling?"

"Oh, all right. My legs are giving me a little trouble again, so I haven't been able to get around like I want to. The doctor's given me a walker."

Alex felt dread like a physical weight. The doctor had told her this day might be coming. Soon it would be a wheelchair. And then, finally, her mother would be confined to bed.

Trying with an effort to speak cheerfully, Alex told her about the trip to France. Then, as though her brain had been busy behind the scenes, it suddenly clicked. Legs. Hands. Multiple sclerosis. Her mind raced, constructing a scenario she'd never considered. "Mother, can I call you back?" she managed to say.

"Of course, dear. What is it?"

"Something I've just thought of. I'll tell you later."

Hanging up the telephone, Alex dialed the police station one more time. "It's vital that I speak to the chief inspector," she told the sergeant on duty. "I have some important evidence in the murder of Philippa Cuendet."

"I'll give him your message, Mrs. Campbell."

She began to pace the room. The dropped glasses. That was something her mother might have done. Her hands had just stopped working when she was knitting. And, tonight, John had asked his wife if she'd turned an ankle. She'd been dragging one foot slightly. That's what happened to her mother when her legs started to go. *Did Olivia have MS?*

What a disastrous thing for a world-class actress! Did John know? Did he suspect? How would it affect his clinic if he knew Olivia wasn't going to be able to bring home the bacon? He'd be desperate for money, of course.

Flinging herself across the bed, Alex considered the evidence one more time. Then she rolled over on her back and stared at the ceiling. There was a flaw. Darn. Dr. Brown. Maybe she was his ace in the hole. Maybe he'd already faced the issue and provided for it. Also, Olivia had thought John was in Norway. She didn't know he was in London with Dr. Brown, so she couldn't have telephoned him with the news about the Joseph Borden fortune.

A knock sounded at the door. "Room service."

Absently, Alex got off the bed and walked to the door. Opening it, she looked at the food and then at the woman holding the tray. It was Olivia's housekeeper.

TWENTY-TWO

Briggie peered at the little building. "Are you sure this is it?" she asked the taxi driver.

"It's the restaurant, Ma'am."

Richard had his wallet out, preparing to pay the driver.

"But it looks closed! It must be closed on Mondays."

"I wouldn't know," the cab driver told her. "So are you going to stay, or is it back to Oxford then?"

Briggie stared at the slip of paper in her hand. "The Lilacs." That was the name Hannah had given her, all right.

"I don't like this, Richard," she said suddenly.

The lawyer looked at her and then back at the restaurant. "You're right, Brighamina. It begins to look like we've been gotten out of the way."

"We need to call the chief inspector," she said, suddenly desperate. "They're going to try to get Alex."

Richard spoke to their driver. "This is an emergency. Can you get through to the Oxford police on your car radio?"

———

What was Olivia's housekeeper doing here? Alex could only stare. Using the tray, the woman pushed her back into the room. Catching her heel on the bunched up edge of the rug, Alex fell. The intruder dropped the tray with a crash and, stooping, seized the knife that lay upon it.

It was a large butcher knife. Alex screamed.

———————

"Olivia?" John knocked on his wife's door. "Darling, let me in."

There was no answer. Turning the knob, the doctor entered his wife's bedroom. She wasn't there. The dress she had been wearing was thrown across a chair. Her shoes had been tossed off next to her vanity bench. "Olivia?" he called, thinking she might be in the connecting bathroom. She wasn't there.

Puzzled, he walked down the hall. "Olivia, where are you darling?"

———————

Before the woman could raise the knife, Alex grabbed at the housekeeper's calves. Her assailant went down, cursing. It was Olivia's voice.

"Olivia?" Alex said, astounded.

"So you hadn't figured it out?" The actress frowned disbelievingly. And then she went after Alex once again with the knife.

Rolling away, Alex seized a loose pillow from the chair and thrust it in front of her for a shield as she stood up. Like someone crazed, Olivia stabbed it over and over, the knife slashing the purple velvet and scattering feathers.

Alex tried to think. She must get Olivia off balance.

The next time the actress lunged and stabbed, Alex dropped the pillow, and Olivia stumbled forward on to her knees. Alex sprinted for the bathroom, slammed the door and locked it. Going to the window, she threw up the sash and started to scream for help. Olivia was ramming the door. It sounded like she was using the furniture.

"You've got to understand, Alex! We need that money!" She was sobbing. "I can't let him leave me!"

The woman's strength was positively manic. The door was pretty solid, but how long could it hold out under this treatment? Five minutes? Ten?

"You've just got to go faster," Briggie told the cab driver.

"Try to relax, Brighamina," Richard told her, patting her knee. "The police are on their way. If something's wrong, they'll take care of it."

The car was gone. John stood staring at the empty garage as though he couldn't believe it. She had said she had a headache. That she was going to lie down. Where had she gone?

He was uneasy. She had been so mercurial lately. First, in a fit of pique totally unlike her, she had fired the housekeeper who had been with them for years. Then she had taken to spending long periods of time alone in her room. She had turned down three scripts and a movie. What was wrong?

The door was splintering. It wouldn't be long now. Her screams had yielded nothing. Looking frantically around the bathroom, Alex tried to find something that would save her. On the shelf above the sink were toothpaste, toothbrushes, soap, a safety razor, Briggie's Listerine . . . that would have to do. Opening the bottle, she poured the mouthwash into a glass.

She heard the sound of sirens. Had someone heard her after all? Reaching the window, she screamed again. "Help me!"

The street light fell on four uniformed men, running into the hotel. Just then, the ramming noises ceased. Alex whirled around to face the door. Olivia's hand was snaking through the splintered opening and unlocking it.

"The police are here," Alex told her as the door opened. "You can't get away with it."

"Liar!" Olivia cried, tears blotching her face and her red wig askew as she lunged for Alex with the knife. "I've got to have that money. You aren't going to stop me!"

Alex threw the Listerine in Olivia's face, aiming for her eyes. Screaming obscenities, Olivia dropped the knife to shield her face.

Alex seized the weapon from the floor and stood over her attacker. When the police entered a moment later, Olivia was sobbing into her apron like a child. "He'll leave me, now. He'll leave me. Just like Victoria . . . I can't bear to be left again . . . you don't understand . . . "

TWENTY-THREE

"I don't understand," John was saying dully an hour later as he sat in Alex's room. He was like an automaton. Briggie and Richard couldn't seem to get through to him. "Why did she come after you, Alex? Why did she pretend to be the housekeeper? And most of all, why did she kill Philippa?"

"I could be wrong," Alex said, hugging herself as she shivered in belated horror. Her pity for Olivia couldn't quite overcome the stark fear she had felt at being face to face with a lethally minded madwoman. "But I think she has multiple sclerosis."

John stared at her, and then she could see his mind finally start to work, as he considered the possibility. "Of course! I can't believe I didn't see it! And I'm a doctor!"

"My mother was just stricken," Alex explained gently, "or I never would have picked up on it. Obviously, she was worried about the clinic and how it would be financed once she couldn't act any more." She didn't tell him her suspicions about Olivia's fears regarding Dr. Sandra Brown. He was dealing with enough guilt as it was.

Thank heaven it is all over. Alex looked at Briggie and Richard, still hovering close by. *Thank heaven for friends who loved her.*

"She played the part of the housekeeper to give herself an alibi," Briggie explained. "She must have sat in that house every day dressed up like the housekeeper in case the police or anyone came."

John gave a half-smile. "She's an incredible mimic and very good with make-up. She would have enjoyed that."

"She must have called us, mimicking Hannah's voice," Richard said. "She asked us to meet her at a restaurant about twenty minutes away."

"If it hadn't been closed, we might still be waiting there," Briggie said.

"Fortunately, Brighamina is of a suspicious turn of mind," Richard remarked, patting her heartily on the shoulder.

"I suspect she was the new 'witness' who came forward to accuse Charles, too," Alex added.

John shook his head as though to clear it. "But you still haven't explained why she came after you tonight. She seemed perfectly normal when you were there."

"I found out when I was in France that Etienne had an aunt by marriage who was a Thielbault. I thought I remembered Olivia's maiden name from your genealogy chart. Did she come from Bar-le-Duc?"

"No, but she's from another little town not too far away. I never thought of her having relatives in Bar-le-Duc. I don't think I ever knew it. But Thielbault isn't that common a name."

"She must have realized what I was up to when I asked to see the genealogy," Alex went on. "Particularly when I didn't ask her about it straight out. That was pretty dumb on my part. She probably knew I'd figured out that Marie Thielbault Guison would have called her and told her about my coming. Philippa probably called John to tell him about her letter from the American researcher. But when John wasn't there, she left the message with Olivia. Olivia would have told her about me then, and the rest . . . well, I suppose you can imagine it. She was probably in make-up of some sort when she pushed Philippa. Otherwise she would have been recognized."

The doctor put his head in his hands. "But it's all my fault. She knew I would be desolated without the money. She of all people knew how much I've counted on finding a cure for this bloody disease. Victoria . . . "

He looked up. "You never knew my little girl. If ever there

was an innocent life, it was hers. She trusted me. She thought because I was a doctor that I could make her better. She believed it until the very last . . . " Closing his eyes against his tears, John got up and began pacing the room like a caged beast. "I should be sharing Olivia's cell. She did this for me, for Victoria . . . *My* obsession is what killed Philippa and Etienne. I drove my wife to murder . . . "

Alex got up and went to John's side, laying a hand on his shoulder. He was as unyielding as steel. "She loved you and she loved Victoria, but it's possible to love and not be a murderer. Olivia's sick, John. The things she did weren't the acts of a rational woman. Wasn't she hospitalized after Victoria's death?"

Flinging himself in a chair, John nodded, "They were afraid she might be a borderline schizophrenic, but I discounted it. Olivia was an actress." Running a hand through his hair, he sighed. "Can't you see how it could have happened? At first it was just another role to play. Once she took off the makeup, she would see herself absolved of all guilt. She was no longer the murderer." For a moment he just stared. "I never saw it until now," he said heavily, "but obsessions can be the very devil."

John's pain filled the room. Alex knew that her words hadn't registered. Slumped and grim, he was oblivious to all of them now that he knew the story. He was going to blame himself for a long time to come.

––––––––––––

The morning after Olivia's arrest, Alex, Briggie, Richard, and Charles took a bus to London. From Victoria Station they took a cab to a small church wedged between two skyscrapers in the City. How it had escaped the Blitz was a mystery, but like St. Paul's Cathedral, it still stood, modest and dwarfed by its surroundings.

Entering, they thought at first that the church was empty. Then an elderly clergyman made his way slowly down the nave toward them.

"Is there something I can do for you?"

"Yes," Charles said. "My grandparents were married in this

church in 1919. I was hoping to see the entry in the parish register."

Silently, the man led them into the little vestry next to the chapel. Taking a key from his pocket, he unlocked a large cupboard and took from it a dusty, black book, one of several which apparently resided there.

Alex watched as Charles leafed through the record until he found the exact date. "There we are," he said triumphantly. "Joe Cuendet and Marcelle Cuendet. What do you think?"

Alex took two photocopies out of her briefcase. One was of a will Joseph Borden had made in 1917. The other was of his enlistment papers the same year. Scarcely daring to breathe, she looked from the signature in the register to the signatures on the photocopies. Fortunately, Joseph Borden had had a distinctive, ornate hand.

"Well, Richard?" she asked the lawyer. "Do you think that's going to do it?"

"We'll need an expert to make certain, of course. But it looks pretty good to me. Brighamina, take a photograph of it, please."

Alex's partner looked at the clergyman. "This is a probate matter, sir. Would it be all right if I took a photograph?"

For some reason, the clergyman sighed and then gave his consent. Alex looked at Charles. He was standing a little apart from them now, hands in his pockets, staring into the nave of the church.

Going over to him, she felt she knew what he was thinking. "Philippa should be here," she said quietly.

Charles seemed to come out of some sort of trance. "Do you know," he smiled a little, "I think, somehow, she is."

Alex felt her eyes fill with tears. Charles put both arms around her and held her tight.

———————————

Briggie and Richard decided quite suddenly to remain in London. "I want to see *Phantom of the Opera*," Briggie explained. "I might never get another chance."

Alex laughed. "And we're not invited?"

Briggie looked from Charles to Alex and said, "Something tells me you have important business elsewhere."

————————

Charles was clearly an expert punter. Placing the pole carefully in the water until it met bottom, he walked his hands along it, pushing their boat so that it moved gently down the Cherwell.

Here on the river where thousands of Oxonians had punted over countless years, it was almost possible to feel that nothing really terrible could happen. At this place, the English earth seemed particularly old, as though the Cherwell had worn its path eons ago and had been continuously traveled by those who loved it. Along its banks, trees and shrubs were twisted and black with age, and every bend revealed a small, magical scene. Alex half expected to see an elf or dwarf whisk out from behind the greenery.

"I almost expect to see a hobbit," Alex remarked.

Charles laughed, a robust, happy laugh. "Freedom!" He saluted the sky, holding the punting pole in both hands. "I'll never take it for granted again."

"That sounds remarkably enthusiastic for a jaded theater critic."

He pulled a face. "There's nothing like having your life in jeopardy to put things in perspective."

"But there's no death penalty in Britain, Charles."

"Spending the rest of my life in prison would have been like ending it, all the same."

"So." She studied his face intently. The lines she had seen before were no longer etched as heavily. There was a new animation in his eyes. "What kinds of things did you think about in jail?"

"Justice. God. Life. Oh, I had a lot of time for metaphysics."

"And what conclusions did you come to?"

Setting the pole solidly on the river bottom, he looked down at her with a smile. "You talked about a hunger once. A need to understand. Maybe that's what it was. All I know is that when I really got down to it, I found I didn't know much of anything about anything that mattered." Maintaining his grip on the pole, he sat down across from her in the punt, his countenance thoughtful. "At one time, I guess I would have thought there wasn't anything to know. But I kept thinking about the things you said about there being order in the universe, and I found myself hoping mightily that it was true. I even prayed on my knees, if you can imagine it." He looked out across the river, grinning now. "And I resolved that if you were able to rescue me that I'd be willing to listen to you for as long as you cared to talk."

"You made a bargain with the Lord."

"Well, maybe it was. Don't they say there are no atheists in foxholes?" Standing, he resumed punting in silence for a few moments. "You're a strange woman, Alex. You've had an odd effect on me."

His face, so perfectly molded, was in profile as he squinted across the meadow that lay along the river. She couldn't read the expression there.

"Strange-intriguing or strange-weird?" she demanded. Suddenly it seemed imperative to lighten the atmosphere.

"Fishing, are we?" He grinned again.

"I was simply requesting clarification."

"I haven't quite made up my mind about your order of strangeness. Perhaps it's merely that you're an American."

"We're kin, you know."

"Yes," he said softly. "Third cousins, isn't it?"

She nodded. "You're one-quarter American, Charles. That should make for a fairly good-sized unconventional streak. Room for you to maneuver."

"To get out of my intellectual rut, you mean?"

"To explore an alternate universe."

Once again he sat across from her and, pulling the pole out of the water, laid it alongside him. Leaning forward, he smiled into her eyes and took both her hands in his. "That would be a turn-up for the books, wouldn't it? Charles Lamb takes a serious look at life?"

Meeting his glance, Alex found she had no resistance left. She was warmed clear through, as though the sun were shining directly into her soul. It had been years since she'd felt this kind of warmth. Thudding disgracefully, it seemed her heart was working properly at last.